Amber,

THE SUICIDE TREE

Always
say yes to
adventure!

Shayla Raquel

First Edition, October 2018
Curiouser Editing LLC
Yukon, Oklahoma
ShaylaRaquel.com

Content Editing: Sarah Grace Liu, ThreeFatesEditing.com
Proofreading: Andrea & Ashley Hultman, ThePolishedOpal.com
Cover Design: Monica Haynes, TheThatchery.com
Interior Formatting: Melinda Martin, MelindaMartin.me

ISBN: 978-1-7291593-1-6

THE SUICIDE TREE

SHAYLA RAQUEL

To Joshua, Justin, and Jessalyn:

I hope your love for reading will be fueled by the flames of your imagination, curiosity, and wanderlust. May you always be smitten by the written word as I have been.

CONTENTS

Pensacola News Journal,
"3-Year Anniversary Since
NovaVita Cure Catastrophe, Two Killed"

Mindy Brewer, Senior Editor

While most anniversaries are a time of celebration, this three-year anniversary serves as a painful reminder of what could have been.

Doctors Benjamin and Athena Kevel, Nobel Peace Prize winners, were killed in an explosion on May 21, 2023, leaving behind their only son, Knox.

The Kevels were hired in March 2023 to develop a cure for the Raven Virus outbreak. Two months later, the Kevels made worldwide headlines when they successfully created a cure called NovaVita but then refused to release it to the federal government, prompting protests across the country. Both doctors hid in their laboratory in downtown Pensacola during the protests. An explosion occurred and killed Benjamin and Athena Kevel.

"No one was ever charged in their deaths," said Sheriff Tipton. "The case is still open, but we believe it to be foul play."

Sheriff Tipton asks anyone with any information to please contact the Pensacola Police Department.

"It was just weird," Dallas Wyatt, a resident of downtown Pensacola recalls. "Weird that we could have had a cure for one of the deadliest diseases in history, and then it's just gone in an explosion? I don't think so. Someone killed those doctors."

CHAPTER 1

Anniversary

My life changed the day a grocery deliveryman rang my doorbell.

I wiped the sleep from my eyes as I ambled to the front door. I squinted through the peephole, and my voice cracked when I said, "What?"

"Knox Kevel?"

"Yeah?"

"Here's your groceries!" The man handed two overflowing grocery bags to me, and I wondered what it would be like to strangle him in my doorway for waking me up this early.

"Thanks," I mumbled, remembering my late-night online order. "Didn't I say seven-thirty *p.m.* for delivery on the phone yesterday?"

The stupid little man checked some stupid little note on the receipt. "Nope. Says a.m." His cheesy grin enraged me. "Oh, and this was left for you on the ground, I believe." He held up a small envelope. Probably another "you're late on your payments again and we're going to shut off the water" kind of letter. But those were usually in my mailbox downstairs.

I growled at him, then took the envelope and slammed the door shut, rattling the condo's paper-thin walls.

"Hey," the deliveryman shouted through the door, "thanks for the tip, moron!"

I made a mental note to write a scathing Yelp review for this guy. But then again, it was the only online delivery service on the island, so I shrugged it off.

Eyeing the lack of countertop space for my groceries, I dropped the bags on the dirty carpet, pushed the stacks of crusty dishes and greasy pizza boxes farther away, and tossed the envelope in the mail basket. I moved the bags to the countertop, opened a bag of jalapeño chips, and munched on them as I walked to the living room.

I shielded my eyes from the blinding Florida sun—the same sun that rose over the emerald-green Gulf Coast each morning. I grimaced and wiped my hands off on my boxers and went to shut the balcony screen door and close the aging curtains. The same cheery sun taunted me daily, beckoning me to come outside and do something, anything.

I lived on the thirteenth floor of Tristan Towers in Pensacola Beach, Florida. I lived every twentysomething's dream: living on the beach, hardly any responsibilities, and plenty of sun and sand. Only, I didn't get out much. Not that I wanted to.

I plopped down on the rickety couch and grabbed the remote, turning on the TV. I dug my hands into the bag of chips, stuffing them into my face as little bits of crumbs fell onto my shirt, the same shirt I'd been wearing since Monday. A robust weatherman pointed to the forecast, and I turned up the volume. "Hello, Pensacola! It's a sunny day on this Thursday morning, May twenty-first. Perfect weather for—"

I immediately shut off the TV.

The anniversary, I thought. *It's today.*

My breaths quickened, and invisible hands squeezed my chest. I grabbed my inhaler from the coffee table. I shoved it into my mouth and took a deep breath of the medicine.

After a few minutes, the pressure released and my wheezing dulled.

I had no excuse for forgetting. It'd only been three years, so I should've remembered. But I guess with everything else recently, I just blocked this day out.

I left the room, leaving my chips behind. Walking down the hallway, I passed piles of filthy laundry in need of washing. I found my bed and fell on top of it, exhausted, my legs hovering above the floor.

My phone rang—it was Aunt Jane's ringtone.

"Ugh." My face still planted in the sheets, I reached for my phone on the end table and hit the button on the side to silence her. I knew I could expect at least seventeen million more calls. She could be incessant. I rolled over and put the phone on silent.

A text message popped up. "Just calling to check on you, sweetie." And then another: "Think positive thoughts on this day." Then, a praying hands emoji.

Super.

I tossed my phone behind me, where it landed somewhere underneath my chair.

I smashed a pillow into my face. "I hate this day."

———————

My watch beeped. It was noon, and I still had several more hours to get through the day and avoid hearing or reading about my parents, the horrible, no-good, rotten scientists who ruined everything for everyone. And, as much as I hated to say it, for me too. After they died, everyone—and I mean, everyone—rallied against me. I could deal with people cursing at me and writing stupid blog posts about me. But once obsession and conspiracies kicked in, it got weird.

Fear shook America when the Raven Virus struck, but it was unbridled pandemonium that took over everything when the cure was kept from them.

People wrote books, published articles, and recorded videos about my parents. Hatred flowed from their tongues and never seemed to stop. The media couldn't get enough of the two scientists who withheld our nation's most important cure. And right when I thought things were calming down, these conspiracy theorists included in their repertoire how Knox Kevel, the scientists' only son, must have the cure somewhere, apparently hiding it from the world in this very condo.

Not that I had a thing to do with the Raven Virus cure or its elimination, but sure, let's blame everything on the son, who is, in fact, *not* a scientist.

I tried to think of a way to pass the time in radio silence. I could've attempted to clean my condo, but that would've taken days. I'd played all of my video games a thousand times over. I didn't have a computer . . . anymore . . . so nothing to do there.

I finally thought of something to take my mind off my parents.

Coffee.

———

"Ya late," Adam said, pulling down on the espresso machine's lever. I loved the *tssss* sound it made.

"Late for what?" I pulled up a barstool and swung my elbows around to rest on the bar.

Adam scratched his scruffy beard. Puffy bags hung beneath his eyes. "Said ya'd be here fifteen minutes ago."

"That's hardly late," I retorted. "You getting enough sleep?"

Adam owned the Drowsy Poet, the only coffee shop on the island. I was secretly jealous of his full beard, but I'd never admit it to his face. "I'm managing," he said. "Where's ya cah?" The way he said *car* reminded me that Adam might've left Boston for Florida, but his accent didn't stay there. "Noticed ya didn't park it—"

"Or drive it," I interrupted. "Got repossessed. So I rode my bike."

With a sniff, he said, "That explains the smell."

I winced. I could feel the sweat under my armpits. "You're hilarious." I gestured to a sandwich on the grill. "What are you cooking, Adam?"

"New creation. Once these two meats meld into one, it's gonna be one heckuva sandwich." After leaving the grill for a quick minute, he served me an iced coffee concoction from the secret menu. He called it the Jimi Hendrix, and it tasted stronger than ever. I refocused my gaze outside the window, where catamarans lined the dock, red snapper flapped up and down in barrels, and tourists pointed their iPhones high.

"Try," Adam said, placing the sandwich in front of me. I raised my eyebrows, and he urged me to dig in. One bite of his salami-and-ham sandwich, and I was in heaven.

"Dude," I said, my mouth full, "you gotta add this to the menu."

"Ya think?" He grabbed the sandwich and sunk his teeth into it. Chewing on his creation, he said, "Yep. Ya right 'bout that."

I wiped my mouth with my sleeve and noted the dark circles under Adam's eyes. "Seriously, man. Why aren't you sleeping? What's going on?"

Adam worked here from sunup to sundown. He had three kids and a supportive wife, but still. Owning a business takes a toll, and I should know.

He scratched the back of his neck. "Don't worry about me, Knox. I'm all right. Just need to hire someone to take over for me during the day to lighten the load."

"And?" I prodded.

"And . . . we're losing money. I'm not sleepin' 'cause I need this place to make more money. Okay?"

I nodded, understanding that like me, he didn't want to talk about things he had no way of fixing. "All right. I get you. Just . . . tell me if I can help in any way." *Not that I could possibly offer any money to do so*, I thought.

"Oh yeah? All right, well, can you wipe down those tables?" Adam threw me a wet rag.

I caught it and threw it back. Squeezing my temples, I said, "Adam, you know I don't work here."

"Come on!" he whined. "Ya haven't been out of your little dungeon in a decade. Ya need some activity. Besides, you've done it before. And you did just say if I needed anything—"

"Yeah, but if I were in the mood to clean today, I'd be cleaning my . . . uh . . . dungeon."

"Good point." He headed to the tables, wiping them off one by one, his sandwich in the other hand.

After downing my secret menu drink, I added my coffee cup to the stack of dishes. I left a few bucks on the counter and checked my phone for the time. I waved goodbye to Adam and headed for the door.

"Leavin' so soon?" he called back. "Ya just got here."

Adam's problems reminded me of my own. It was time to face what I was avoiding.

"Yeah, I know. I just got something to do, that's all. Sandwich was great."

"Hey, buddy," he called. I stood stock-still, knowing what he was going to say. The same thing he said last year and the year before that. "I know this isn't an anniversary you wanna remember, but don't forget that I'm here if ya need me." He gave me a sympathetic smile as I walked out.

———

Fully caffeinated, I hopped onto my bike and headed over the bridge toward Gulf Breeze. A quaint suburb with just a few thousand people. And my parents. Well, their graves, anyway.

At the entrance to the cemetery, I pulled my bike over and looked over my shoulder. No one was around, so I swiped a few daisies from the flower bed in front of the entrance sign. Hopping back on my bike, I went farther into the eerily silent cemetery. The rocky road only reminded me how ticked I was at not having a car. I turned down a narrow path and rode toward the big cedar tree.

My parents never planned for their funeral. And why should they? They were young enough that it hadn't seemed like something worth planning for. All of their time was devoted to their work—the future of their creations. So the burden fell on Aunt Jane. Three years ago, we walked into the Duncan Funeral Home together, where a pale man who looked like death himself helped us plan their funeral. We picked out a verse from the book of Psalms for the memorial pamphlet and left the funeral home in a heap of tears.

Finally, I came to the towering cedar tree, its allergens already suffocating me. As I wiped a tear from my eyes—from my allergies, I wanted to believe—I knelt down beside my parents who shared a tombstone. The tip of my fingers met the inscription.

FLIGHTS OF ANGELS SING THEE TO THY REST

Where were the flights of angels when my parents were burning alive? I thought. *Where were they when the lab exploded and the heat engulfed them?*

I shook my head, pushing away the morbid thoughts. I checked behind me and all around. There was no one there. So I talked to my parents as I planted stolen daisies next to their tombstone.

"Mom. Dad. I am so angry. I know it's not the day to be angry, but I am. I'm mad that you were taken away from me. I'm mad that I'm completely alone. I'm mad that I have nothing worthwhile in my life. You guys were my everything, and I don't know my purpose anymore. You probably know—"

I halted and checked once more to be sure no one was listening.

"You probably know that I'm in trouble," I said, quieter. "I'm so sorry. It's just that it's the only thing I know to do, and I needed money. I have nothing and I had bills to pay. I had no idea it would blow up this bad. I don't want you guys to be ashamed of me. I want to make you proud, but I'm so tired of life and everything it keeps throwing at me. I wish you guys could tell me what to do."

Patting the soil around the daisies, I sighed and wiped the dirt onto my jeans. "I love you, Mom, Dad. I miss you."

I trudged my weary legs out of the elevator and up to my door, walking my bicycle toward my unit.

When I entered my condo, I saw the basket of mail on the counter. Remembering that envelope from this morning, I grabbed it out of the pile and opened it. It was an actual letter, not a bill, after all. It was the year 2026, and somehow, people *still* wrote letters.

As I read, I reached for my inhaler.

Dear Mr. Kevel:

I'd like to invite you to dinner tomorrow night at McGuire's in Pensacola. Order anything you like—it's on me.

I've been keeping my eye on you for a while now and would like to employ you. Think of it as a summer job, if you will. The pay is quite decent, and I think we both know that your bank account could use some attention. Your savings from previous . . . projects . . . will keep you fed and clothed for only so long.

The job is different from hacking, but it does require your expertise. I'll tell you more about it tomorrow—say six o'clock? The hostess will take you to my table.

Oh, one last thing: I know you don't wish to be called the Suicide Tree anymore. Your secret's safe with me.

All the best,

Arlo Jenson

CHAPTER 2

Job

It was my science teacher who taught me about the suicide tree. "It may have a chilling name, but it looks harmless," she'd said, a warning tone in her voice. She showed the class pictures of the tree itself, which looked like a magnolia tree to my naïve eyes. Deep-green buds with white blossoms overwhelmed the tree. Its fruit looked like a cross between a walnut and a coconut. "The seeds stop your heart when ingested. Before you know it, you're dead. Gone," my teacher said. "As an added bonus, it goes undetected in autopsies."

Every ninth grader *oohed* and *aahed* at this information, but all I heard was, "the perfect murder weapon."

When I joined the hacker world, I realized I needed an online handle like MafiaBoy or c0mrade. I needed a handle that was cool (er, as cool as a nerd can get) and that showcased my individual . . . talents.

To me, a computer was more than just a brain—it was alive with a real-to-me heart: the motherboard. To stop the motherboard without a single trace of ever being there, a hacker needed the skills to poison it *just* right.

So that's what I did. I infected computers to get what I wanted without being detected. Get in and get out. I was the Suicide Tree.

At least, that's how it began. As time went on, anonymous users of the dark web would hire me to keep their very illegal yet very lucrative sites protected from the FBI. From websites that offered fake driver's licenses and passports to ones with knockoff designer clothes and watches. Perhaps my highest paying gig to date was setting up a gigantic firewall and triple-failsafe security for the drug marketplace called the Bermuda Triangle. The anonymous owner, Miss Disappear, still runs it to this day, as far as I know.

The FBI and every nosey goody-two-shoes called me a cybercriminal. And cybercriminals like me spend time in prison. Except, I was a first-time offender, and it was *hardly* criminal activity, thank you, so I got off easy with community service.

But the second offense was no slap on the wrist.

On June 1, I'm going to trial for cybercrime, and there is no way I'm avoiding prison this time. My lawyer said I'm looking at ten years. In fact, the FBI has so much evidence against me that she said I might as well prepare my family for prison time.

Probably a good thing the FBI caught me for hacking and not while I was working on my side project. I never really had a name for it. And maybe I never will. I was developing a computer program that could hypnotize an individual and prompt them to truthfully answer whatever question someone asked. I had made serious progress, but then I got the cyberpunk medal of shame, so I never got to complete it.

Imagine if the feds found out about *that*. I'd easily be looking at twenty with no parole.

Instead, they caught me working for a sleazy politician who had hired me to stiff the competition. Thanks to it being my second offense, I'll be spending quality time with guys who see me as raw meat.

So when I received a letter from this Arlo Jenson guy, my immediate suspicion was the feds were testing me, trying to see if I'd take the bait.

I paced the condo all night long wondering if I should meet him the next night. Which was good, I guess, because it made me forget about my stupid dead parents and their stupid death anniversary and my aunt's stupid "be strong" text messages.

She was so optimistic. It really dragged me down.

———

Several hours had passed since I first read Arlo's letter, and all I'd managed to do was eat mac and cheese and turn my phone into a hologram projector. All you need is a sharp knife, pen, ruler, graph paper, tape, and a CD case. Bam. Instant hologram projector and hours of useless entertainment.

I had always been into tech and tinkering and building. When I was ten, my dad—genius scientist Benjamin Kevel—couldn't figure out what was wrong with his laptop—white screen of death—so I, being ten, managed to fix it in just a few minutes. I think he thought he had a child prodigy, and maybe he did, but I think he was expecting another scientist, not a hacker.

It wasn't until 2:00 p.m. the next day that I decided I would at least meet Arlo Jenson. I was rummaging through my entertainment center drawer to find another DVD I had watched countless times since my banishment from the internet. Upon finding some lame rom-com that was clearly Aunt Jane's, I tossed it behind me to throw away later. However, it flew right into a picture frame, which clattered to the floor. I heaved a sigh and picked it up, wincing as I held it in my hands. Turning it over, I saw my mother, father, and me on Pensacola Beach. It was the spring before they died. Mom's hair was pulled back into a wet, messy bun, her arm around my shoulder. I was already towering over her by then. Dad wore a T-shirt to cover his gut, and his hand rested firmly on my other shoulder. My jet-black hair was slicked back, sandy from a day at the beach. My crooked smile made me roll my eyes—a trait my mom said girls would love, but I had yet to find one who did. I threw the glass and broken frame into the trash can and left the family photo on the counter.

There was really no point in even meeting this guy. I knew I was headed to prison after this trial. They were going to throw the book at me. But it was a free meal, so it would just be rude not to accept. Not to mention, I was broke. And not the ha-ha, "you're not totally broke, you have savings" broke. The real-deal, "I'm about to be on the streets" broke.

Which, again, didn't really matter that much seeing as how my prison time was about to commence.

But then the truth hit me. I wasn't going to see this guy for a free meal or a paycheck. I wanted to know how he knew about the Suicide Tree.

————————

Irish music blared from a green and beige building adorned with gold sham-rocks and the words FEASTING, IMBIBERY, AND DEBAUCHERY across the top of the walls. At McGuire's, pictures of famous people lined the walls inside, and dollar bills with names scribbled in Sharpie hung from the ceiling, ac-cumulating to a staggering one million dollars. The waitresses wore white button-ups and long green skirts, while the men wore tuxedos.

Inside the dimly lit restaurant, on the wall hung a photo of a sickly man consuming their famous Garbage Burger—"it's disgusting," the menu blunt-ly proclaimed. I thought it was tolerable. The key was to ask them to hold the peanut butter.

"Dining for one?" the hostess asked.

I hovered over the host stand, looking for the list of names. "Actually, I'm waiting for someone else."

She pulled the list closer to her. "Name?"

I whispered, "Knox Kevel."

She lifted her eyes to mine, accompanied by a suspicious smile, and in a hushed tone replied, "Your party is waiting for you in the Politician's Club. Please follow me."

I did as I was told. Past the gift shop, past the booths, and right before the wine cellar was the Grand Hall—reserved for wakes and weddings and other gatherings. Before we reached the event room, the waitress opened a door with a sign that read POLITICIAN'S CLUB. INVITATION ONLY.

Opening the wooden door, the hostess led me to a matching wooden booth in the back, where a man in a suit sat waiting for me.

"Mr. Jenson? Your party has arrived."

A shamrock-decorated menu covered my potential employer's face, but his hand gestured for me to sit.

Cautious, I sat down in the booth, accepting the menu from the hostess without opening it. I faced Arlo Jenson, I assumed, the strange man who had sent me a letter with an even stranger job offer. He dropped the menu to the table, revealing his face. An older man, his leathered skin greeted me with a sincere smile. His eyebrows matched the color of his hair: stark white. I guessed him to be in his sixties. "Mr. Knox Kevel," he said a little too loudly, "it is a pleasure to meet you, my boy. Hungry?"

"S-starving." I cleared my throat, looking this way and that, hoping to see some celebrities in this club. "Thanks for the invitation."

He bent forward and grabbed his glass, jostling iced tea back and forth. "You're probably overflowing over the brim with questions, hm?"

I crossed my arms. "I wouldn't say overflowing, exactly. Curious, maybe."

"What can I get you to drink?" the waitress asked, her hair in a tight bun, pulling her eyes back to her ears.

"Coke, please," I answered.

"And can I start you all off with an appetizer? Some Irish boxties?"

"Sounds good," Arlo said, nodding. "We'd like that."

We'd like that. I was a *we* already.

She scampered off, leaving us alone. I kind of wished she had stayed.

He downed the rest of his drink and then smacked his hands together. "Let's get down to it then. I'd like to hire you to help me with an overseas project."

I chuckled, and I could feel my boyish dimples giving away my age. "You're out of luck. I can't travel right now."

For a very long time, I thought.

He returned the laugh, pointing a bony index finger my way. "Oh, I think you can make an exception." I didn't trust that sly smile that accompanied his optimism.

I glanced to my left, making certain no one could overhear. "I don't know how much you know about me—"

"Plenty."

"But . . . I'm honestly not allowed to leave this state at the moment. I'm sorry."

He interlocked his hands, resting his elbows on the table. "Got a trial coming up, hm?"

My body stiffened and the hairs stood up on my arms. *How does he know about that?* I didn't reply but simply stared at him, waiting for him to finish his train of thought.

"What if I told you that you won't have to worry about it and that there's half a million bucks in it for you if you accept my offer?"

My mouth fell open, and a flush of adrenaline coursed through my body. I tightened my grip on the menu. "What did you just say?"

"Here you go, honey." The waitress set down my fizzing Coke and a plate of Irish boxties—round, deep-fried mashed potatoes with cheese and chives inside.

"Are you ready to order?" she asked, pen in hand, annoying smile at large.

Arlo handed her the menus. "We'll both have the grand burger, darlin'."

The grand burger was a one-hundred-dollar hamburger served with caviar and champagne. Not exactly the type of thing normal people ordered at an interview. Then again, I'd never really been on an interview before. *Was* it normal?

"I don't want a grand burger," I said dryly, feeling disoriented.

They both stared at me.

"Everybody wants a grand burger, my boy. Add some hot sauce to mine, will you, my dear? And give the bottle of champagne to someone who could use a drink."

"Yes, sir." And off she went, her green skirt flowing behind her.

I furrowed my brow. "Are you kidding?"

"No, I'm not." He grinned this toothy grin, exposing silver fillings in the back. "The grand burger is delicious. You'll love it. Unless—are you one of those vegans or vegetarians or hipsters or whatever the devil they call themselves these days?"

"Those are all three different things, and no, I meant, the *payment.* Well, and the no trial or prison thing."

Arlo reached for a boxty, saturated it in ranch dressing, and popped it into his mouth. Crumbs scattered across the table, and he brushed them off. "Oh, that. Yes, I'm serious. You want the job or not?"

I drew a deep breath, slowly releasing it before answering. "Let's pretend for one second that I believe you and that I think you're somehow capable of overriding the federal government . . . I don't even know what the job entails, Mr. Jenson."

"Arlo's fine. Just call me Arlo."

I reached for a boxty and bit into the deep-fried delicacy. Was there anything better than potatoes, cheese, and fat?

"Here's the job, boy: find someone for me, and you get paid five hundred Gs. Easy peasy."

The boxty stopped in the middle of my throat, and I reached for my Coke, chugging it all the way down until that traitor appetizer stopped choking me.

"You all right?"

"Yes." I wiped the drink from my lips. "You've got the wrong person for that. I'm a ha—a computer guy, not a PI. Er, I used to be. Not anymore. I'm nothing now. There is literally no way I can be of any help to you."

"I don't need a private investigator. They're not worth squat because they can't do what you can do. I need an ambitious, intelligent young man who can . . . open virtual doors, so to speak."

I clenched my jaw. "I'm not opening any doors because in the next few days, I'll be walking into court because of those 'doors.'"

He smirked. "I told you. I can fix that problem." He put two fingers up. "Scout's honor."

"How can you make that kind of promise? And something tells me you weren't a Boy Scout."

He laughed at that. "That's a good one. I like that."

"Tell me how it's possible for you to get me out of this trial—how can you get my felony charges dropped? If I'm to accept this job, then I need to know how you're going to do it."

He rubbed his chin and thought for a moment, as if he were for the first time plotting out his answer. "Let's just say that the DA over the trial owes me the world's biggest favor."

"What kind of favor warrants a get-out-of-prison-free card?"

"Not that you need to know, but since you're so inquisitive, the DA and I go way back. I once got him out of a *very* sticky situation with his finances. He was quite the gambling man at one time."

"Casinos?" I asked.

"Dog fights, actually."

I winced. "That's kind of messed up."

"Yes, and when I got him a large sum of money within a day to pay for an . . . incident . . . with his dog, he's owed me ever since." He reached into his back pocket, pulling out a small slip of folded paper. He set it on the table and pushed it to the center. "Now, last chance. Do you want the job or not?" Leaning back, he dared me to pick it up.

And I did.

When I unfolded the check, my full name was scribbled in the middle with $250,000 written on the right side. I fumbled around in my back pocket, trying to pull out my inhaler. Quickly, unashamedly, I sucked in that precious air and stowed the inhaler back into my pocket.

"You're serious." It wasn't a question. I was just trying to say it out loud for my own benefit.

"Call it a down payment," he said, dipping the last boxty into the ranch dressing before shoving it down his throat. "You'll get the rest when the job is done."

The waitress set down a tray with our food. "Here we are, boys. Two grand burgers, one with hot sauce, one without. Your caviar is on the side."

My dad once taught me that bad decisions were best made quickly. So I was quick.

I grinned. "So tell me about my new job."

CHAPTER 3

Assignment

Arlo moved the caviar back and forth with a mother-of-pearl spoon. "Before you begin your project, there's something you must know about me."

I narrowed my eyes. "What might that be?"

"Well, I have what you'd call a mental disorder."

"Excuse me?" I said, setting my gigantic, overpriced burger down on the plate. "What do you mean?"

"A personality disorder, to be exact," he clarified. "I am prone to becoming a number of different persons at any given time."

I racked my brain for a moment, remembering something about this from a movie. "Like schizophrenia?"

He rolled his eyes at my naïveté. "No, my boy. Schizophrenic people hear voices. I have more than one person within me. It's simple to understand, really."

I just signed on to work with potentially several people trapped in one body.

"So are you, like, *you* now—or someone else?" I asked, genuinely curious.

"All of my selves are myself, I suppose you could say. But you need to understand that my disorder is different from what you might have heard."

I haven't heard much. "How so?" I asked.

"One prominent difference is that my disorder isn't a remnant from a childhood trauma, like mental or sexual abuse. Generally, when you look at people who escape into another persona, it's because they can't handle the reality of what they went through. But that isn't what happened with me."

He set the spoon down and reached for his grand burger, only to stop and push it away, seeming to have lost his appetite.

"Then what happened? And what does this have to do with the job?"

With a heavy sigh, he replied, "Someone cut open my skull and pushed a needle into my brain. Whatever came out of that needle prompted what are known as alters."

I couldn't help myself—I laughed. A nervous laugh. "You are joking. You can't *inject* anyone with a *disorder*. That's impossible."

He frowned. "Oh? Kind of like how you can't cure the Raven Virus, yes?"

All right, I thought. *He's done his homework. But then again, everyone knew my parents.*

"But that's a *disease*, not a mental disorder. You can't just give someone a mental disorder. It's not chicken pox." I suddenly noticed how squeaky my voice had become and tried to lower it.

"But someone *did*, Knox, and your job is to find the person responsible."

I sat up straighter. "How? Tell me how."

"That's why I'm hiring you. I need to know how it happened."

"You're telling me the truth? This is real?"

He wiped off his mouth with a napkin. "You keep asking me if what I say is true. Would you like for me to take a lie detector test?"

"N-no, of course not. But what can I do, though? Like I said, I'm not a private investigator. What can I *really* do to help you find the person who did this to you?"

This whole thing had gone from weird to weirder to flat-out ridiculous.

He replied in a hushed tone. "You can unlock virtual doors, get into computers, find information, do things I could only dream of doing. You're the Suicide Tree."

It was the first time someone had actually said my handle out loud, and it was uncomfortable. An uneasy feeling. Like I shouldn't have heard it.

"And I know what you're capable of," he finished.

But what *was* I capable of in Arlo's eyes? How much did he really know about me?

I had finished off my caviar already, having discovered it was the single most delicious thing that had ever graced my taste buds. "Assuming I believe you—which, I haven't decided on that yet—what makes you think someone tampered with your brain like that?"

"Flashes of memories. It's peculiar. The older I get, the more I remember. Sometimes I remember someone hurting my head. Other times I remember my parents sobbing as they realized what happened to me. But it wasn't ever really a secret to begin with. My family knew what happened to me."

"Your family knew? Then why can't you just ask them? Wouldn't your parents know who did this to you?"

His glassy eyes met mine. "I'm not sure. I tried to ask them, but they wouldn't let me talk about it. I was never, ever allowed to ask about it, no matter how hard I persisted. In my twenties, when the disorder began, I was sent to America."

"Sent here? Where were you from originally?" I asked.

He looked away from me as shame swept across his face. "A town called Sorrento, in southern Italy. I guess they thought it would be best for me—to get better psychiatric care here that's not available in my hometown. I just saw it as them getting rid of a problem, personally."

"Well, you're older now. Ask your parents what happened. Maybe they'll be honest." Wow, I was really working hard to get out of a high-paying job.

"Oh, dear boy." He stared at his hands and replied in a flat, monotone voice, "My parents passed mere days ago."

I caught my breath. "Both of them?"

He nodded. "Yes, of old age, apparently. Kind of a sweet story, you might say. My father died just moments after my mother slipped into eternity. Probably from a broken heart."

"I'm really sorry. That's . . ." I wanted to say that I knew what it felt like, that I knew how painful it was to lose the two people you love the most. "Awful," I finally said.

He moved his caviar to the side of his plate and reached for his glass, bringing it to his lips.

I eyed his untouched caviar, considering snatching it up and gorging myself on it. But I thought better. "Why now?"

"What do you mean?"

I looked at his half-eaten exorbitant burger. "Why do you want to do this now? You had all your life to figure out how you . . . got the disorder, to figure out who did this to you. Why go through all of this now?"

It didn't take a genius to realize that Arlo was old. Wealthy or not, an old guy like him probably didn't need to be trekking across Italy to uncover the solution.

He eyed the check still sitting on the table. "Because I didn't have the capabilities of paying anyone until now, of tracking down someone like you to help me. And, my boy, I just have to know. I don't want to die knowing what happened to me . . . could happen to someone else. We need to stop her."

"*Her?*" I tilted my head to the side. "A *woman* did this to you?"

He nodded. "Yes, it appears women are capable of breaking more than just your heart. I know she's out there still. And I have to stop her from doing this to other people."

"I see." I swallowed the last of my drink, still feeling parched. I wondered how exactly he was able to afford this little adventure now *and* how he knew this information about his persecutor, but maybe some questions were better left unanswered.

"I'll help you find who did this to you and . . . stop her from doing it to anyone else."

He met me with a sincere smile, as if I had already found the person responsible, his gratitude evident in the small lines that met his lips.

I returned the smile and reached for his caviar. "As my first assignment, I'll be finishing that caviar for you."

"Ha!" He slapped his knee. "Showing initiative, my boy. I like it!"

I spooned out a heaping mound of blue fish eggs and spread them on bread. "Can I ask you one last question?"

He bowed his head, urging me to ask.

I took a big bite of my new favorite treat, asking with a mouthful, "How did you find me? It's not like I'm super easy to track down, so there must have been something I left unprotected."

"I had my guesses, my hints from locals around here." He pointed a bony finger at me. "But you should be less greedy with your grocery money."

Heat slapped my cheeks, and a vague flash of the angry deliveryman lit up my consciousness—the man yelling at me and calling me a jerk. Moron? "But . . . that guy wasn't you."

He raised a thick white eyebrow. "You think you're the only person I've ever hired to accomplish a job?"

"All right. All right. I'll tip better. So what kind of—"

"One last thing," Arlo said, reaching for the bill the waitress had left behind. He leaned over the table once more. "Our flight for Italy leaves this Monday."

I woke up to a phone call and drool on my pillow.

"Why are you not answering your phone?" Aunt Jane asked, her voice far too loud at this hour.

"I'm good. How are you?" I asked, wiping the sleep from my eyes. I pulled on my pants while she droned on and on about how irresponsible I was and how I needed to get my life together.

"It's about time you start being more responsible when—"

Heh. Isn't that the pot calling the kettle black? She was off gallivanting around on some God-forsaken island with some surfer dude who's my age, and she wanted to call me irresponsible?

"Anyway," she said, "I'm calling to let you know our flight gets in tomorrow morning at eight, so I'm sorry I won't be there in time today."

Fumbling, I grabbed my phone before it dropped. "In time for what?"

Aunt Jane laughed in my ear. "Okay, right, hilarious."

My eye twitched at the thought of my aunt being here, of her getting in my way, of listening to her yammering. "What are you talking about?" I asked.

"This is your own fault for not answering your phone or your texts!" she yelled. I could almost see her hands on her hips, that disapproving scowl to match. And maybe I'd care more to answer my texts if it weren't on a dinosaur-era phone with no internet. "Are you not ready for them? Is the condo a disaster or something?"

"Who?" I bellowed.

"The news! They're coming out for the interview. Remember?"

I shut my eyes and panic set in. The last interview I had was when I was seventeen, right after my parents' deaths. It didn't go so well. Kind of freaked out, ran out of the room. Might've knocked over a news crew guy.

I smacked my forehead with my fist. "The freaking interview! I forgot."

"Well, if only someone had called to remind you. And apparently, you've forgotten several times. They wanted this interview done before the anniversary and certainly before the trial, but couldn't get ahold of you. They reached me and set it up. I've told you about this—"

I gripped the phone in both hands and swung it back and forth, silently strangling it. Bringing it back to my ear and taking a deep breath, I calmly stated, "Gee, thank you for the reminder. As you know, I've been a little caught up with other things. What do they want to know, anyway?"

"I have no idea." I heard a long sigh at the other end. "You can't just hide from everyone, you know. I'll be there tomorrow, and so will Dax."

"Dax is coming?" I could feel the tension between my eyes—pounding, pounding. The guy had the IQ of a walnut. He was her brand-new husband, complete with surfer lingo and cargo shorts. Basically, my worst nightmare.

"Yep. Okay, you better go—they should be there soon, right?"

"What time did you say the news crew would be here?" I asked, turning my alarm clock to face me.

"I think two in the afternoon."

The clock read 10:15 a.m.

"We're renting a car, so no need to pick us up. But I—"

"Yeah, okay, great. Can't wait. Gotta go."

I hung up and slid my phone in my pocket and looked around at the disaster area that was my condo. There might as well have been caution tape around the rooms. I opened the closet to see if I actually owned cleaning supplies, and it appeared I did. As I scrubbed and sprayed and mopped, I thought about my new job, which, consequently, would start not too long after Aunt Jane and Dax got to Pensacola.

Thank God.

I showered and put on my nicest outfit. Well, my cleanest outfit, anyway. I even shaved, which I immediately regretted because it made me look young. I stared in the mirror, trying to rehearse my answers to the interviewer's questions.

"Yes, I miss my parents very much. No, I don't know if someone attempted to murder them. No, I don't know where the cure for the Raven Virus is. Yes, I hate you all very much."

CHAPTER 4

Interview

"**R**ight there's fine, yes." A woman named Sofia pointed to different locations of my condo, directing the videographers. "We're going to need more lighting. Heath, pull open those curtains."

The news crew was right on time to talk to me about the anniversary of my parents' death—to dig up old memories of the two most hated people in the world—and to remind me of my trial for cybercrime.

I heard a ringing sound, and Sofia tapped the Bluetooth device on her ear. "Go." As she talked, I noticed how young she looked. Not a wrinkle in sight, curvy in all the right places, and were those freckles? "That won't work. Reschedule it. Two's fine. Bye." She tapped her ear again and approached me.

"Why don't you sit down right here?" She motioned to my living-room chair, which had hardened macaroni on it. *How did I miss that?*

"Are you gonna go over this before we start? Like, what questions you're gonna ask?" I nonchalantly swept off the pasta and placed my butt on the chair.

"Quick rundown: We're going to ask you about your life, how you're feeling about the anniversary, how you dealt with it, the latest with the trial. Easy stuff." She leaned into my face and straightened my tie, leaving me slightly mesmerized by her cotton-candy perfume. Girls shouldn't smell like things you eat. That's not good for any man's brain.

"Are we ready? Heath? Heath!" Heath skidded around the corner, and I became even more uneasy at having these people in my home. It was like I was being invaded. Sadly, not by aliens, which would've been super cool.

Unfortunately, it was just plain old annoying humans. "All right. I'm going to ask you questions back here, and you answer. Ready? Set? Go."

I straightened up, suddenly aware of how dorky I looked, and when I smiled, my lips trembled, an inconvenient twitch of mine. I remember walking down the aisle at Adam's wedding. I was told to smile big, which I did. Only problem was that I looked like one of those chatter teeth toys.

And now, sitting there during the interview, I once again found my lips quivering.

"What's wrong with you?" Sofia asked, standing up from her chair.

"No, no. I'm fine," I said, stretching my jaw. "Just start with the questions, and it'll go away."

She sat back down, giving Heath the "start it back up" gesture. "Are you in college?" Sofia asked.

"No."

Who needed college when you weren't even allowed to breathe near a computer? I mean, how would I have written my essays—by hand? Deliver them to my professor via carrier pigeon?

"Why not?" she asked.

I shrugged. "I wouldn't be challenged enough, I guess." My charisma was top-notch.

Sofia clenched her jaw, and I suddenly felt less attracted to her, more so terrified. "What do you do with your spare time? Do you *work*?"

And there it was: the nausea that gripped me when people asked me what I did for a living. What was I supposed to say? *No, strange woman, I don't currently work. I've just been dipping into my savings from my former hacker life to sustain me until I bleed it dry—you know how it is.* "I . . . *was* a web developer," I replied. "Then, as you know, I got in trouble for hacking, and now I am unemployed, I guess." There. I said it.

"You'll be heading to your trial on June first for cybercrime. What exactly did you do? What makes someone a cybercriminal?"

I clenched my jaw. "I'm not really supposed to talk about it. Basically, I was paid to hack into some accounts that had confidential information, but it wasn't what I thought it was. It was a setup, and now I'm going to trial and prison, probably."

Except . . . if Arlo wasn't kidding, if he truly gets me out of this trial, then I won't wind up in prison after all.

"That's awfully vague," Sofia said.

"Well, I don't know how much I'm supposed to say." I sighed, then relented. "I changed some election results and got caught."

"Are you scared that you'll be physically abused while in prison—if your sentence includes prison time?" Sofia asked.

I grimaced. "Um. I . . . well, now that you mention it, I guess I am a little concerned about that." Was I sweating? Yep. Great. "Look, I know I did something wrong, and I'm paying for that crime. Can we move on now?"

Sofia nodded, but I didn't like the smile on her face. "How are you handling the third anniversary of your parents' passing?"

My chest tightened, and my knee-jerk instinct of reaching for my inhaler kicked in. But I didn't want to tick her off by fumbling around in my pants pocket to find it in the middle of the interview. "I . . . uh . . ."

I uh . . . uh . . . don't remember too much because I was too busy accepting a shady job from an even shadier man? Yeah, that about summed it up.

"I'm handling it, I guess."

She stared at me and waited. Typical journalist tactic. Silence got more answers than interrogation. She crossed her legs and bobbed one ankle up and down, indicating that her patience was wearing thin.

And it *felt* thin in here—like the oxygen was thin. And all I wanted was to suck in the precious drug that came from my inhaler.

"Um, actually, it's . . . hard. I miss them. I wish they were here. I turned on the news the other day without even realizing it was the anniversary. When I heard them announce the day's date, I . . ."

Sofia nodded at me, urging me to continue. Apparently, this was good stuff.

"I turned off the TV. I didn't want to hear about it, I guess. It's just hard being reminded of . . . of them. And everything that happened that day. I went to their graves to see them. Planted some daisies, actually."

"Do you think someone murdered them, or do you think it was an accident?" Sofia asked, leaning forward.

I looked down at my shoes, then remembered to face Sofia—*face the pretty lady, not your shoes, not the camera.* "I like to think that it was just an accident." That was the truth. Plus, I'd spent nearly three years trying to find the person responsible. I was always afraid it was a victim of my hacking, some no-good, piece-of-trash exec who wanted revenge, but no leads ever showed up.

Her ankle had stopped bobbing up and down, and she listened intently to my responses—for a moment, it seemed like Sofia actually cared about my plight. "Do you know where NovaVita, the cure for the Raven Virus, is located? Does it still exist?"

Or not. Like herpes, that question never stopped rearing its ugly head, popping up at all the wrong times in all the wrong places. "No," I said through gritted teeth. "Like I've said a hundred times to every news outlet, my parents never showed NovaVita to me, never told me where it was, never explained how it worked. If they had, I would have turned it over." I took as deep a breath as I could manage, hoping they could edit out my wheezing. "Not to mention, it was completely destroyed in the explosion. As you know. As everyone in this *stupid* town knows."

And I thought of everything else that was destroyed that night. Their lab. Their formulas. Their research. Their years and years of research.

And them.

Sometimes late at night when I'm too antsy to sleep, I wonder how long they burned in that lab. Were they killed instantly without having to suffer? Or were they trying to get out? What were their last words before the explosion? Did they hold each other tight and enter into eternity together like they do in my dreams?

"Have there been any new developments in the investigation of your parents' deaths? Anything you'd like to share with us?"

"No." *That was too curt.* "No, nothing new," I whispered.

She asked me a few more annoying questions, but I hated the last one the most. "If they were alive today, what would you want to tell them?"

I squeezed my eyes shut, trying to remember a world not so far away where my parents were alive. A world where they cooked me macaroni and cheese—much better than that cardboard crap I eat. A world where they took me deep-sea fishing on a boat named *Lucille*. A world where their bodies weren't charred to dust.

"I would tell them to stay home with me and not go to their lab that day."

––––––––––

Hacking came naturally to me, which was odd since nothing else ever did. I couldn't cook and I couldn't throw a football and I couldn't paint the color white, but for some reason, I could create codes.

It all started innocently, as most things do. The black hat didn't grace my head until later in the game. I encrypted my dad's computer to make it ten times more secure, which meant brownie points since he had so many highly classified projects on his laptop.

"And no one can get into it?" my dad had asked me one day.

"Nope. At least, I don't see how. They'd have to be better than me to get to those files."

He grinned, and that made me intensely happy. "And does such a person exist?" he asked with an arched eyebrow.

I smiled. "Not in this world."

We had a great relationship, even when my white hat got a little dirty. He didn't approve of my career, but I don't think he had time to spite me for it, what with his own career choice.

I knew I had crossed into murky waters at age fifteen when I got my first paying gig.

A nameless man contacted my handle one day and asked me to create a ransomware code for a company he had a grudge against. They had supposedly wronged him, fired him, I don't know. I was fifteen, and it paid five hundred dollars. That felt like a million bucks to a teenager. I took the job, and it went a little something like this.

The CEO of MDM Enterprises turned on his computer and was greeted by an intrusive pop-up I created. It said:

"Your files are encrypted. To get the key to decrypt the files, you must pay $5,000 USD."

I had suggested lowering it to something reasonable, like five hundred or a thousand dollars, but my client had said: "Don't worry. Not only does this backstabbing jerk have the money, but he'll also be throwing it at us to get those files."

"Maybe so," I had countered. "But really, he can just get another guy like me and have him shut it down—if he's good enough to do so."

"Oh, he won't be doing that. He doesn't want a single soul to know what's in those files, but I know what's in them. He'll pay it after he sweats a bit."

So we let him sweat. If Mr. CEO failed to pay within a week, the price would go up to ten thousand dollars. After that, the decryption key would be destroyed and any chance of accessing his thousands of files on his PC would be lost forever.

But something told me my client didn't want them to be lost forever, so I was hoping the sweating-him-out phase would work.

And it worked like a charm. He didn't even hit the seven-day mark before paying in full, to which my system kindly thanked him for his deposit and sent over his files.

I was instantly addicted to the rush. This kind of hacking felt completely different from the white hat kind I had been accustomed to. This was exhilarating, intoxicating. I knew it'd take something catastrophic to pull me away from it.

And that's exactly what happened.

CHAPTER 5

Todd

"Welcome home," I said, opening the door for Aunt Jane and Dax. I refused to call him Uncle Dax. I would rather tell the whole world my online handle was the Suicide Tree than call him Uncle Dax.

Aunt Jane wrapped her thin arms around me and squeezed me way too tight.

"Asthma," I breathed.

"Oh! Sorry! I just missed you." She planted a wet one on my cheek and tossed her suitcase on the couch. I stretched my arms above my head and yawned, still trying to wake up.

"How'd the interview go yesterday?" She sniffed the air and winced. "What's that weird smell?"

"Uh, just guy smell, I guess." I took her suitcase from off the couch and to the guest room, Dax following behind me.

"No, it's, like, bleachy?" she said.

"Oh. I . . . uh . . . cleaned before the interview," I replied.

She arched her eyebrow. "Hm. Interesting."

Aunt Jane's skin was bronze, no doubt from her time on the beach. It had even lightened her hair, which was always dirty blonde, but now looked golden. Concealer didn't cover the bags under her eyes, though, and I wondered if she had them every day like I did. From the nights without sleep.

"Yo, man. What's up, bro?" Dax nodded while he said this. He wore cargo shorts, puka shells, and a wife beater.

"Nothin', man." I scooted past him and headed to the kitchen, where I offered Aunt Jane a drink.

"Diet Coke's fine," she said, plopping her feet on the coffee table. She was wearing shiny heels, and I couldn't imagine why a woman would wear those on an airplane. Her fingers were covered in gaudy rings to match her extravagant personality. I'd be scared crapless if she ever raised that metal-covered hand to slap me. I used to call them her brass knuckles. "The airline didn't have any, so I'm dying of thirst. Anyway, so when does it run?"

"Huh?" I poured the Diet Coke into a cup.

"The interview!" she said, slapping her hands onto her too-tan legs. "When can I see it?"

"Oh, right." I walked into the living room and handed her the cup. "I guess it comes out in a few days." Actually, I had no idea. I just figured if I said "I don't know" to all her questions, I might risk the brass knuckles.

"Well, that doesn't work for me, Knox." She took a sip of her drink. "I need to know the exact date."

I rolled my eyes. "Monday."

"That's . . . tomorrow, not a few days."

I sighed the most exaggerated sigh I could muster. "Aunt Jane, I'm not even awake yet. Gimme a break."

"All right, all right. So what kind of questions did they ask?"

"Just questions about Mom and Dad and the trial."

And then the sniffles came. "Oh, Knox. I've been trying so hard not to think about it." Suddenly, she put her arms out, awaiting another embrace.

"W-we already hugged."

"Well, I need another one!" Her arms wrapped around me as she swayed from side to side. "It's going to be so hard if you have to go to . . . that awful place. I can't even think about it."

"Yeah, I feel bad for you," I mumbled into her neck.

She tussled my hair, and I remembered being younger and her playing video games with me. Sometimes I let her win. "When the interview comes out, we can all eat popcorn and watch it. We'll make fun of the reporter or something."

"Yeah, about that . . ."

She eyed me suspiciously, and I opened my mouth to explain the new situation with my job and the whole not-having-to-go-to-prison thing.

Until, that is, a knock came at the door.

"Dax," I yelled. "It's open. Is he still bringing in stuff?" I asked Aunt Jane, but she shook her head.

"Bro, I'm right here, man." I looked up, and lo and behold, there was Dax in all his ethereal glory.

"Who's at the door then?" I asked as I got up. I looked through the peep-hole and jumped back, ramming my elbow into the countertop. "Agh! Why, *why*?" I yelled, rubbing the throbbing pain in my funny bone.

"What's wrong with you?" Aunt Jane asked, setting down her drink. "You're acting weird."

"It's uh . . . my . . . boss?" I peered through the peephole once more.

Her eyebrows squished together. "Wait, you have a boss? Since when?"

"It's—it's complicated!" I hissed. For some reason, I became frantic. I hadn't had a chance to explain to Aunt Jane that I'm leaving. Let alone, that I'm leaving *the next morning*. Plus, this job had shady written all over it, so the last thing I needed was Aunt Jane interrogating me.

I opened the door, and there he was.

"H-hey there, Knox." This wasn't exactly the straitlaced, secret-club-going man I had met at McGuire's the night before. He smelled sour, and his hair was greasy and in disarray. He looked like he hadn't slept.

"What are you doing here?" I asked, feeling my aunt's eyes hovering behind me.

He leaned forward, inspecting my condo. Although his body leaned past the doorway, his feet stayed planted to the ground. "C-can I come in?"

I scratched the back of my neck. I don't remember Arlo greeting me like this in the Politician's Club the other night. I stepped aside and gestured for him to come in.

"So what are you doing here?" I asked in a hushed whisper.

He fiddled with a folder he held in his hands. "Oh, yes, yes. Well, I uh . . . could we talk somewhere more private, please?"

"Sure. We can go to the balcony," I said, guiding him to the balcony door.

"You're a bit early—like a *day* early." I bulged out my eyes, trying to key him in, trying to give him the hint not to drop the bomb about my new job just yet.

He glanced at Aunt Jane behind me and offered a shy wave in her direction. "I j-just need to explain a few things before our fli—uh . . . before tomorrow."

Leaving her fizzing Diet Coke behind, Aunt Jane timidly approached Arlo. "Aren't you going to introduce us?"

I cleared my throat. "Arlo, this is my aunt Jane and my . . . Dax."

Aunt Jane shook Arlo's hand, but not before Arlo wiped his hands off on his slacks. Dax waved rather than extending his hand, which Arlo seemed to be grateful for.

"Guys," I gestured to my weird family, "this is Arlo Jenson. He's my . . . friend."

Arlo laughed way too loudly, and for no reason. I shot him a weird look, but he spoke up. "Knox, m-my name isn't Arlo," he whispered in my ear.

"What did he say?" Aunt Jane asked.

"He wants to see the ocean!" I said, once again shoving Arlo toward the balcony doors. "We'll be back." I slid open the screen door and gestured toward a lawn chair that had seen better days. "Just pull up a chair. I'll be right back."

He nodded and sat down, his hands clasped together on his lap. Although I didn't sit on the balcony as much as I should've, the view was breathtaking. Hopefully, it would be enough to distract him while I dealt with Aunt Jane.

"Aunt Jane, I'm so—"

"Who *is* that guy?"

"I told you. He's my friend."

"No, he's not. You don't have friends."

"Gee, thanks." I rolled my eyes.

She sighed. "I didn't mean it like that. I'm just saying that you don't get out much, and you're trying to tell me that guy is your friend? The dude who's as old as Grandpa?" She crossed her arms over her chest, and I think I actually saw her tapping her toes. "And I'm pretty sure I heard you call him your *boss*, not your friend."

I led her back to the kitchen so Arlo couldn't hear us. "Well, in a manner of speaking, you're right. He's not my friend. He's my boss. I wanted to tell you tonight, but he just showed up. What else was I supposed to do?"

She raised her eyebrows. "You've got the trial coming up. I think you should focus on that. Besides, why would anyone hire you right now with what's going on? No offense."

"None taken. And it's temporary. I'll uh . . . be done with it before the trial." That wasn't the whole truth, but I'd get to it soon enough.

"Can you do that?"

"Yeah, yeah. Of course."

"Well, I want to hear more about the job, but get that guy out of here. I'm exhausted from the flight and don't want some *creepy* old man here."

"He's not—never mind. I'll explain it later. Just go . . . take a shower, and he'll be gone before you're back. Just need to discuss some business matters, okay?"

She threw her hands in the air, defeated. "All right. Come on, Dax."

I opened the balcony door and stepped outside, the bright morning sun warming my skin instantly. "Hey."

"H-hi, Knox." He fluttered his eyes and wiped the sweat from off his puckered brow.

"Listen, you could've called me before coming over, Arlo. My aunt just got here, and I haven't had time to explain our situation. Like, at all."

He blinked at me, clearly trying to process what I had just said. "Well, I . . . I don't have a phone." I remembered the letter under my door and thought back to the restaurant. I don't ever recall him having a cell phone. "And I hope you don't take this as rude, b-but my name is Todd. Todd Williams. N-not Arlo."

I plopped down into the lawn chair, my head spinning. "So . . . you're . . ."

"Yes?"

"You're so different from Arlo."

He looked down, twiddling his thumbs. "Y-yeah, well, we're all different."

My hands slid down my face. I'd never been around anyone who had a mental disorder, so this was all new to me. Arlo was bold and boisterous, but Todd . . . he was just so quiet and nervous.

"So when you say, 'we're all different,' you're talking about . . . ? Personas?"

"We call them alters, but yes."

We. What *we* call them.

"I don't know if I can do this." I stood up, shoving my hands into my pockets. "It leaves room for error, and I can't have any screw-ups. I'll go to prison if I'm caught, and you know it."

Todd stayed seated and hid his hands under his butt. He began to rock back and forth in his chair. "Oh, please don't say that. We need you. You're the only one who can help us."

"Why me?" I asked.

He finally looked me in the eye. "Because Arlo said you're the only one who can help, and I believe him."

With a heavy sigh, I sat back down. "All right. Okay. I can make it work. I can do this."

He smiled, and I returned the favor. "I'm r-really glad to hear that, Knox."

"Yeah. So what do you got for me, Todd?" I asked, motioning to the folder.

He grabbed the folder off the small plastic table. "Our flight leaves at precisely 6:00 a.m. tomorrow. You'll want to go to b-bed early. Second, you'll want to bring your laptop and any other items that'll help us when the time comes. F-finally, we'll be staying at Arlo's sister's condo in Sorrento."

"That's it? You came all the way over here to tell me *that*?"

He vehemently shook his head. "No, no! I c-came over here to give you some p-papers. They say something about you no longer being going to trial—I'm not quite sure I understood it. But Arlo wanted you to have them now rather than later."

I reached out and took the papers in my hands. Sifting through them, I saw at the top, NOTICE OF DISMISSAL WITH PREJUDICE. *They dropped the charges,* I thought. *Arlo actually pulled it off.*

"Are these . . . real?" I asked.

He nodded, a beaming smile overtaking his face. "Yes, th-that's what I was told. I'm glad you don't have to go to trial . . . or prison. Sounds scary."

The judge had signed off on it and everything.

"Yeah, tell me about it," I mumbled, looking through the file. "Well, thanks, Todd. I appreciate you bringing this to me."

He stood up and wiped the sweat from his forehead once more. "Y-you're welcome." Then he walked past me, back into the condo, heading for my front door. He rested his hand on the doorknob and with his back to me, he said, "Oh, one o-other thing, Knox. Arlo said you'll be meeting his niece too."

CHAPTER 6

Explosion

Pensacola News Channel 5, May 21, 2023

Quinn: If you're just now joining us, our very own Jeremy Staton is live at the scene in downtown Pensacola. He's across the street from the Kevel lab, where husband-and-wife duo, Benjamin and Athena, are situated. The protests have become violent, and more and more citizens are gathering around the building. Jeremy, can you tell me what's going on with the protests?

Jeremy: Good morning, Quinn. Yes, a very tense situation here that's quickly getting out of hand. Police are asking people to make way so they can get through to try to calm the situation. The Kevels have barricaded themselves in, but that isn't stopping civilians from trying to get through for NovaVita, the cure to the Raven Virus.

Quinn: Have there been any injuries?

Jeremy: Two that I know of. One woman has been taken by ambulance for a head injury, and a man has sustained small injuries to his leg.

Quinn: Can you tell us about their teenage son, Knox Kevel? Is he in the lab?

Jeremy: Knox is not in the lab, according to my source. The police are working swiftly to calm the protestors.

Quinn: Can you confirm that the Kevels have the cure in—Jeremy? Did we lose you? Jeremy? Can someone check to see—

Jeremy: —plosion!

Reporter: Jeremy! Can you hear us? Are you there?

Jeremy: There's been an explosion! They need help—someone! The building's . . . fire. Are you . . . this?

Quinn: We've lost video feed. What's happening out there?

Jeremy: Someone has either bombed the building or there's been an explosion—I'm not . . . people are running. We need to move out. Get down, get down!

Quinn: Jeremy, can you tell us what's happening now? Jeremy? Jeremy? Jeremy!

"You aren't going anywhere with him, you doofus." My aunt's hair was still dripping wet from the shower, and Dax stood behind her, nodding his head up and down like a bobblehead doll.

After staring at the $250,000 in my bank account for about ten minutes, I made my decision. There was no way I could back out. Could I just go get a job as a pizza delivery guy? Sure. Would that cover rent for this condo? No. And . . . I don't know. That just didn't seem reasonable.

Although, my current choices weren't so reasonable, either.

"First of all," I said, unplugging my crappy TracFone from its charger, "I don't need your permission, *Aunt* Jane. Second, I think you and I both know I'm not a doofus." I grinned my cheesiest, most sarcastic smile, and she smacked me on the arm. "Hey!"

"He came over here unannounced and acted like a total weirdo. What kind of a boss just shows up like that?"

"Yeah," Dax said, narrowing his eyes at me.

She dried her hair with my yellow towel. "You can't just run off to Europe with some old man. It's like you're not even using your head."

"Yes, actually, I can." I placed my donut pillow in my carry-on. "And he's not bad, Aunt Jane."

She tilted her head to the side, pursing her lips. "Oh, really? Then what's his deal? Why did he stutter and act so suspicious?"

Trying to explain to my aunt that my new employer suffered from a mental disorder meant more yammering, more interrogation. "It's complicated," I said.

Complicated: the worst word in the English language, right next to *whatever*. "It's complicated" was what tween boys and girls use for their Facebook relationship status. And yet, I couldn't think of a better way to describe it.

"Knox!" Aunt Jane countered. "How is it complicated? Talk to me." Her eyes pleaded, and I just wanted her to stop yapping.

"It's . . . it's not. Okay, here's the deal. He is rich. He is paying me a huge sum of money to help him find someone. He is not a weirdo—he has a personality disorder, which makes him turn into different people. What you saw back there—the stuttering and awkwardness—was just . . . one of his alters."

She blinked before finally asking, "He has more than one personality?"

I nodded. "That's right."

She seemed to have a hard time digesting this news, but I tried to remain patient. "Well, what about the trial? You can't go anywhere right now."

"Oh, he got me off the hook with the DA. Surprise." I walked away, searching in my drawer for my spare inhalers.

"I don't want you to leave." Aunt Jane stood before me, her hot-pink toes firmly planted into my stained carpet. A disappointed Aunt Jane would eventually go away. But bankruptcy kind of hangs around for a long time. And so do memories of prison.

I sat down on my bed, where hours ago I had been ignoring her calls and texts. Soon afterward, I "celebrated" my parents' death anniversary by accepting a job from a stranger with alter personalities.

"I have to," I calmly replied.

"No, you don't." She sat down next to me, grabbing my hand in hers. For the first time, I noticed the wrinkles spreading down her fingers. "We just got here. You have to do this trial."

"I already told you: he got me covered. I don't have to go." I forced a smile. "I already cashed the check, the flight leaves tomorrow morning, and I need this job." I squeezed her hand. "I'll call you and let you know I'm safe."

"What about . . ." She looked away, glancing down the hall for an eavesdropping Dax. "What kind of job is this exactly?"

"A complicated one."

There it is again. That word.

"*How* complicated?" she asked.

"He's going to use my . . . skills . . . somehow, but he swears he'll keep me safe. I have to find someone for him. That's all."

She held the yellow towel in her hand, now damp. "How do you know you can trust him?" she asked.

"I don't." And I didn't know, because truth be told, I trusted hardly anyone these days. But I didn't have much of a choice. Not to mention, I missed my laptop, Josie, so much. I wanted to get back into the hacker world.

Aunt Jane stood up from the bed. "When does your flight leave?"

"At six in the morning. Why don't we all go out for an early dinner tonight, okay? My treat."

She nodded as I kissed her cheek, and I headed to my bathroom to pack up what little things I had.

"I know you're anxious," my aunt said, gently putting her hand on mine, "but can we please have a device-free dinner before you go gallivanting across another country?"

I slid my phone into my back pocket. "Sorry." I scanned the menu and for some reason wanted only pasta. I had heard many things about Italy, but not enough about Sorrento itself. I wondered what they were famous for, what their stories were.

"I think I'm gonna eat the bo-log-na."

I stared at Dax in bewilderment, wondering if he actually *heard* himself talk or if he just drifted in and out. "Dax, it's pronounced *baloney*. It's just spelled b-o-l-o-g-n-a."

A crooked, idiotic smile crept up his face. "Oh."

"I'm going with a light salad and some soup." My aunt sipped her Diet Coke, suppressing a burp.

"It's, like, ninety-five degrees outside." I felt that nervous tick—the itch you just have to scratch when you haven't checked your phone for over a minute.

"I know, but it sounds good. Are you ready for your . . . trip?" Her eyebrows shot up when she said *trip*. To say my aunt was indignant was an understatement.

I crossed my arms over my chest, leaning back in my chair. "Don't hate me forever. You always said I needed to get out more. So I'm getting out. I'm experiencing life."

She stirred her Diet Coke with a straw, and I could tell she was starting to warm up to the idea of my being out of the house—especially since they'd be living there now. Plenty of time for her and Dax to canoodle and do whatever those two do. I doubted it'd be talking about science and politics.

It wasn't like my aunt couldn't get any guy she wanted, so I never understood why she settled for Dax. After my parents died, I lived with her for a while until I could move out on my own. She had every guy from the Florida panhandle to Key West calling her, asking her out, whisking her away on candlelit dinners.

And these weren't halfwits.

They were intelligent, well-to-do men with charisma and 401(k)s. And yet, here she was, with Dax the dunce.

"Hey, bro, you got any girlfriends or what?" A piece of romaine lettuce was stuck to Dax's extra-white teeth, and I didn't have the heart to tell him it was there.

"No, I don't." I twirled my fork into my pasta.

"Why not?"

I swallowed down a bite of the fettuccine. "Because I don't need that in my life. As soon as she realizes who I am, she's going to drive me nuts with questions about the conspiracy and my parents and NovaVita. They. Are. All. The. Same."

"Knox!" Aunt Jane didn't like it when I generalized. "You shouldn't group them all together like that. Not every girl acts that way." Gesturing with her spoon, she continued, "You don't like it when people stereotype you—when people judge you before they get to know you."

"Fair enough," I mumbled. "I'm just saying that right now, there are no women I'm interested in around here."

"I'm sure you'll meet someone when the time is right," Aunt Jane said. "Someone who is fun and outgoing and makes you laugh."

My mom had the most ridiculous laugh. Her tight curls, as black as my straight hair, stuck up all around her slender face. And when she danced, which was often, her hair would shake with her every movement. Everything about my mother was full of life. Her hair, her smile, her laugh.

Especially her laugh.

In the dead of the night, when I was young, I once awoke to the sound of a familiar, rambunctious laugh rattling the walls until my feet left the bed and I peered out of my bedroom door, only to hear my mother, my beautiful mother, laughing at my father's jokes.

"Knox!" she had said, happy tears streaming down her face as she held her stomach. "Baby, did I wake you?" She still couldn't contain her giggles.

I nodded, rubbing my weary eyes.

She held out her arms as I fell into them. She nuzzled me the way only a mother can do, and that's the first time I remember staying up all night, listening to my parents cackle into the early morning. It was a rare moment that they weren't working into the wee hours—they were simply living and laughing.

And it was then, at the small restaurant surrounded by familiar faces, that I realized how deeply I missed my parents.

How deeply I missed seeing them each day. How deeply I missed what my life was like when they were still alive. When they laughed into the night.

Even though Aunt Jane enjoyed sowing her wild oats, she took good care of me after Mom and Dad died. Since I was seventeen, I had the right to choose where to live and with whom, so of course I chose family. Aunt Jane was alone then, but after a year of denying herself any men, she began dating here and there. She made me her priority that first year, and I always felt guilty for that. No one should have to be alone.

But we had each other then. She worked as a deck hand for a marina that did deep-sea fishing and dolphin cruises. Then every other weekend, she was a lifeguard for Fort Pickens Beach. She was cool like that.

When I turned nineteen, she left me here and moved to Cozumel and met Dax. I was happy for her at first. I wanted her to find someone, to get away from the ghosts of this town, but the longer I stayed here, the more I resented her. She was able to get past my parents' deaths and find love and a new home, while I stayed here—as stagnant as swamp water.

I wanted to go back to the times when we'd meet at Flounder's late at night to indulge in their heaping pile of nachos after a long day of lifeguarding. One night in particular, she had broached the topic of Mom and Dad.

"Do you miss them? Like, every day?" she had asked.

I nodded while swallowing down my chips. "Every day, yeah. It's weird to go about life knowing they're not here anymore. It feels like a dream most of the time." I tried to laugh, but it was too forced.

"I know the feeling. Sometimes, I'll go to text your mom to tell her something that happened at work and I remember . . ."

I wiped off my hands and finished her sentence. "That she's not there anymore. I know. She loved the photos from your dolphin cruises, though. She loved *you*."

That brought a big smile to Aunt Jane's face, but it didn't stop the tears from rolling down her freckled cheeks. "Yeah, she would geek out anytime I showed her a picture of marine life. I think that's the main reason why they stayed here."

But we both knew that wasn't true. That's not why my parents stayed here.

My parents stayed here to be closer to the research facility funding them so they could continue their work on NovaVita and cure the world of the Raven Virus. Except, as soon as they did, something changed their minds and they didn't want anyone to have it. My parents, who were pure geniuses, created a tiny pink pill that could stop people from choking on their own blood, but they chose not to let a single soul have it.

I may never know why Mom and Dad didn't want anyone to have that cure, but I know they didn't deserve to die the way they did.

CHAPTER 7

Leaving

The Drowsy Poet stayed open later during the summer, so after dinner, I swung by to pick up something for my trip.

"Twice in one week?" Adam said, pulling his attention away from the dishes. "To what do I owe this great honor, huh?"

I rolled my eyes. "Just missed you, Adam."

He brought down the espresso machine lever to make my favorite drink: the Poe, a signature coffee drink with dark chocolate and raspberry—just the way Edgar would've wanted it. He handed me the beverage, and I dipped my finger into the whipped cream.

The door's bell rang, and some tourists shifted in, scanning the place. I ducked in my seat and lowered my hat over my brow, hoping to hide from the world just a little while longer.

"I finally found a coffee shop," a lady said, throwing her hands in the air. You would've thought she had found the Holy Grail. "I've looked all over this beach for one. You know, where I'm from, we have them on every corner." It sounded like she was scolding Adam for not fixing this problem sooner.

Adam nodded, clenching his jaw. "What can I get ya ladies?"

I turned to watch the sunset from the bay window above the couch. Speckled across the white sand were rainbow umbrellas, happy children, and striped beach towels. My mom loved the beach, but my dad always fried like a lobster. And yet, my mom dragged him with us anyway, every single Saturday. She'd scold me to watch out for jellyfish too. "The water is good for your soul," she would say.

She was right. It did us good to drink in the sun and the sand and the ocean. It did us good to be a family.

Awakened from my daydream, I heard the door shut. The ladies had moseyed out of the coffee shop, uninterested in Adam's delicious sandwiches and signature drinks.

"You know those broads had to be from Seattle." He shook his head in disgust, wiping down the counter.

I replied, "You say that about every customer who can't find a coffee shop around here."

"I'm just sayin'. It's always the people from Seattle. They got a Stahbucks every ten feet and think—"

"All right, all right. You win. They were definitely from Seattle. Now, I hate to turn this joyful conversation into business, but I need to retrieve something from the back."

Adam's eyes swiftly met mine. "What exactly do you need to *retrieve*?"

I smirked. "You know exactly what I need to get."

Adam walked to the front door and switched the OPEN sign to CLOSED. "I thought you were done with that life."

"I am. I was. It's for a new job."

He shook his head. "I don't like this. You want to add more time to your sentence or something?"

"I don't . . . uh . . . have to go to trial anymore." His eyes met mine. "My new boss made it clear that wasn't going to happen. So you don't have to worry."

"Now I'm more worried than I was before. What boss can get someone out of a trial for cybercrime?"

I shrugged. "Mine can, apparently."

"How do you know?"

"He gave me the paperwork. It's legit."

"So you're already off the hook? You're not going to get sentenced? Like, no trial? No nothing?"

I shook my head. "My case has been dismissed."

Adam charged toward me like a bear and wrapped his huge arms around me. My feet left the ground as he swung me from side to side. He finally set me down and put his hands on my shoulders. "I can't believe it! I'm so happy! You're not going away!"

"Er . . . well, I'm still going away, just not to prison."

Adam's shoulders fell. "Where to?"

"Italy."

His eyes bulged. "I don't know what job this is, but I hope you bring me back some of their food."

I laughed. "Can I get Josie now?"

Reluctantly, he nodded. "You know where she is."

I pushed open the back door and made my way to the third shelf on the right, where Adam kept all the jams and other condiments. I pulled the shelf away from the wall and smiled. Duct taped very securely to its back was Josie.

"Hey, Josie," I whispered. Her charger was still neatly wrapped beside her, sticking quite well to the back of the shelf. I carefully took off the tape, and when I wiped off the dust, my heart slammed into my chest. Josie was a 15-inch, first-generation Pinnacle Slim, purchased with my first big check from some sleazy corporation. I splurged and got the touch bar, optimal 4K display, and discreet-class Radeon graphics. I got Josie a year before her kind hit the market, thanks to being a beta tester for the company who made her.

"Easy now," I whispered.

It had been a while since I last used her. Hacking was the only rush I ever cared for, and it had been too long since I'd had my last hit.

And believe me, it was a rush. That risk of being caught for doing what other people could only dream of being able to do.

Stuffing Josie under my hoodie and shoving the charger into my jeans pocket, I waved goodbye to Adam and headed back to my condo, where my bed was calling for me.

———

My phone's alarm sounded at 4:00 a.m., and the dread of trekking over

Europe with Arlo had been replaced by excitement. I was deliriously tired for some reason, but my eagerness pushed away my exhaustion, and I headed for the shower. I figured I had time, since we'd be stuck on a fourteen-hour flight and deodorant doesn't always cover it.

It wasn't but a few minutes later that my phone rang.

"Hello?"

"Are you going to let me in?"

I thought Arlo didn't have a phone, I thought.

"Depends. Which one is this?" I wrapped the towel around my waist as I heard a click on the other end, and headed for the door. I opened it and he stood there with two cups of coffee. God bless this man.

"Arlo, my boy!" he said.

It was him.

He handed me the coffee and a passport. He winked as he walked inside.

I opened the passport, revealing a photo of a man who looked *almost* just like me. "You gave me the name Julian Taylor?" I asked. "I like it."

"Good. You don't have to use that name while we're at my sister's, but do answer to it when the authorities check your passport in the airports."

I sipped my coffee. "Wait, if my charges were dropped, then why do I need a different passport?"

"Good question, my boy. Just to keep us on the safe side, that's all. Oh, and the fact that the DA said he doesn't want you leaving the country for at least six months. But we don't have time for that."

"Makes sense, I guess. So I know how *I* would get a passport like this, but how did *you* get a passport? You don't seem like you'd be on the dark web purchasing one."

Arlo smirked. "You'd be right. Remember the delivery boy who brought your groceries to you? The one you didn't tip?"

I sighed. "Yeah, I remember."

"He makes passports too." Arlo winked before walking into the kitchen.

I shoved the passport into my back pocket. "What a guy," I mumbled.

Arlo raided our fridge before plopping down on the chair, free of macaroni this time.

"Wait," I said. "What are you doing with a phone? I thought you didn't use them?"

Arlo reached into his pocket. "Oh, this isn't mine. It's your new one. You won't be using your current one anymore."

"Oh." I grabbed it and shoved it into my pocket. "Thanks. So what's your sister's name again—the one we're staying with? When was the last time you saw her?"

"Her name's Norah. And many, many years ago." He had a bowl of purple grapes and was popping one after another into his mouth.

"So, have you not been back to Italy since . . . everything?" I grabbed an empty laundry basket from the living room, carrying it into the hallway.

"No, I haven't. I don't even know if I'll recognize my sister. She was a teen when I left."

"You didn't see her at your parents' funeral?" I shouted as I pulled clean laundry from the dryer, rolling up each shirt to fit into my duffel bag. Then I remembered: Aunt Jane and Dax were here, trying to sleep. I tried to lower my voice.

"I didn't attend their funeral."

"Why's that?" I whispered.

"Because I do not much care for them," he whispered back.

I zipped up my bag and brought it back to the living room. "Oh. Sorry to hear that."

He popped the last grape into his mouth. "Besides, I didn't know about their deaths until a few days after the fact."

I thought about my own parents and their horrible deaths. The last time I saw them was a few hours before the explosion. They had dropped me off at my aunt's condo (the one I'm in now) and had gifted me with the coolest present I had ever received: my first Linux USB flash drive—a favorite gadget of hackers. You simply insert it into a computer and get instant access to someone's hard drive. I kept it all this time on the top of my shelf, but this morning, I grabbed it and tossed it into my duffel bag.

I figured it was my mom's idea to buy me that. Couldn't have been my dad's. He always tried to steer my genius toward physics rather than hacking.

"You shouldn't encourage him, Athena," he'd say. "He can get in big trouble for that stuff."

Well, he wasn't wrong.

I left my room and quietly slid into Aunt Jane's, tiptoeing all the way to her end table. Thankfully, Dax's snores drowned out any other noises I would've made. I picked up Aunt Jane's phone, checking to make sure it was on silent, and pulled up Google. I wasn't allowed to have the internet, so this was my opportunity to see how factual Arlo was being.

I went to the Florida public court dockets and typed in my name. It took way too long to load, and my hands turned clammy.

Finally, I saw it: no results.

Nothing. Nada. Zilch.

Arlo really did it. My record was clean. I guess Arlo wasn't joking about helping out that DA. I was a free man before I was even a prisoner. I put up Aunt Jane's phone and sneaked out, carefully shutting the door.

"Hey, Arlo," I said. "How exactly did you help that DA quit the dog tracks?"

He smirked. "Simple, really. I found a different hobby for him."

I snorted. "That's it? A different hobby? And he owes you that big for just . . . finding him a hobby?"

"Right."

"Well, what was the hobby?"

"Something that paid him better than the dog tracks, kept his interest, and kept his wife happy: dog *breeding*."

"No way."

"Yes, it's true. On the side, he and his wife run a very successful business selling beautiful trained Samoyeds. They get up to ten grand for one puppy."

I shook my head. "That's . . . that's amazing and crazy at the same time. So the DA owes you a favor because you got him into dog breeding?"

He laughed. "No, he owes me because I saved his marriage. And broke his addiction and made him tons of money. Perspective, Knox. Perspective."

I smiled. "All right. You win. That's pretty good. Hey, how many siblings do you have?" I asked.

"Just my sister."

Unlike many an only child, I never wanted other siblings to play with. I was too afraid they'd mess up something I was tinkering with or building. And thankfully, my parents didn't want any more children.

Heck, they didn't even want me. I was a big fat surprise. Children would've caused disruption to their mad scientist plans, so it was never something they pursued.

Well, they pursued it, I guess—accidentally.

Our flight left in two hours, and we would need to be there an hour and a half early. I left Arlo to his own devices while I pulled on some jeans and my favorite T-shirt. It said, I WANTED TO CHANGE THE WORLD, BUT THEY WOULDN'T GIVE ME THE SOURCE CODE.

I tidied up my bathroom and patted the back of my butt to ensure my inhaler was in my jeans. I shut my bedroom door, wondering when I'd see it again next.

"You ready?" I asked, jingling the car keys.

Arlo stood in front of the balcony doors, his hands behind his back. It was dark, and there was something about the black ocean and its dark mysteries that allowed the soul to escape—to forget there were other people in this world. To forget I had problems without solutions.

"You know," he began, his focus still on the waters, "this is going to be quite the adventure." He turned to face me, a hint of a smile lurking at the corners of his mouth.

"What if I can't find who did this to you?" I asked. Not that I really cared. I already had half the money promised to me. Although a small part of me wondered if he'd be sorely disappointed and take back the money if I didn't find the woman responsible. Would I waste all that time and be right back where I was before? Poor and alone? Worse off?

"My boy," he said, resting those bear-claw hands on my narrow shoulders once more. "What if you can?"

I swallowed hard.

He patted my shoulders twice, thin lines forming around his eyes. And for the first time, I could really *see* Arlo. This man was full to the brim of hope. Full of faith—in me. In someone he didn't even know.

"That's the spirit!" His hands left my shoulders and he picked up my duffel bag. "Just like your parents."

I stopped dead in my tracks, the echo of his words still blaring in my ears. "What did you just say?"

He stopped, and everything fell silent. The gentle hum of the refrigerator, the crashing waves, the sound of my beating heart. It was silent for a fleeting moment until three words escaped his lips.

"I . . . can't remember."

CHAPTER 8

Eli

We both had the middle aisle on the plane, which kind of sucked for the fourteen-hour flight to our first layover in Paris, but hey, at least I heard they were going to serve us French food.

We got comfortable, and Arlo looked genuinely pleased with himself, as if we had already found the person responsible for his demise and had won the world. I, on the other hand, had much to deliberate—like figuring out what this whole "just like your parents" thing meant.

After I had asked Arlo about twelve times what he meant by that, he finally replied with, "Your job right now is to focus on my instructions. My instructions are to drive to the airport, and when I can *remember* how I know your parents, I'll discuss it. But right now, I truly can't recall, my boy. My brain is void of the answer. I'm so terribly sorry."

In all fairness, everyone knew my parents. The whole world knew of Athena and Benjamin Kevel and NovaVita. But Arlo knew I was *just like them*. How could he possibly know that? Before we left the condo, I threatened to stay, to give back the money and quit if he didn't tell me how he knew them. But the old man wasn't lying: he really couldn't remember. Arlo said it had to do with his disorder. Sometimes parts of him remembered things and other parts didn't.

Lucky me.

Reluctant but perturbed, I obeyed his wishes. I had a fourteen-hour flight with Josie stored above me. I didn't feel ready yet to tinker with her, so I left her there. Instead, I pulled out the new phone Arlo got me and turned it on airplane mode. I started typing questions to ask Arlo and Norah. Which, to be honest, felt dumb. I didn't know enough about this situation to ask good questions. So I started with the basic ones:

Do you remember anything about the person who injected Arlo with a mental disorder?

What's her name?

Is there any way you can explain how this is possible?

Who else knows about this?

Is this person even still alive?

"Have you noticed anything extraordinary?" Arlo asked, bouncing from foot to foot.

Listening to Arlo was kind of like listening to a cartoon character. I set down my phone. "Uh, I'm on a plane with someone I just met headed to a country I've never visited to complete a job with almost no details? Did I win the game?"

"I could do without your sass." He smacked me on my knee with his book—a fantasy novel called *The Five Warriors*. Leaning in so only I could hear him, Arlo said, "There are no children sitting near us."

I chuckled and high-fived him. No screaming, kicking children on our flight would be fine with me.

The first couple of hours weren't too exciting. I learned more about Sorrento thanks to a little travel guide and confirmed we would have to visit Pompeii while we were there. I had read about it in fifth grade and obsessed over it for months. I asked Arlo if he had ever been there, but he had fallen asleep. I took the hint and snuggled into my donut pillow as best as I could without disturbing my neighbor.

When I woke up an hour later, Arlo was gone.

Eli had replaced him. And Eli was a first-class jerkface.

Growing up, my favorite show to watch was *Transformers*. I loved that one Transformer could be two things at once: a sleek muscle car and a giant robot all in one. Arlo was a lot like my Transformers, only bigger and more unpredictable. At least I knew what I was getting when I played with Optimus Prime.

When I woke up and realized Arlo wasn't *quite* Arlo anymore, I asked if I was sitting by Todd. According to the two middle fingers and a curt "I'm Eli, jackwagon," I was, in fact, not sitting by Todd.

"Can I bring you a drink, sir?" the flight attendant asked. I had read once that the longer one's career as a flight attendant, the shorter her skirt could be. She must've had tenure.

"Baby, I'd love that," Eli said, pursing his lips. "Why don't you make me one of those fruity girly drinks?"

She nodded uneasily, wondering what had happened to the polite old man who sat there moments ago.

He gently grabbed her wrist. "Just one other thing." He kissed the top of her hand. "You are just too beautiful for words." He released her palm, and I couldn't be sure, but I could've sworn she blushed, when she should've cold-cocked him. I had no girlfriend, yet the dirty old geezer with split personalities made the ladies swoon.

"What's the WiFi password?" Eli asked, not bothering to make eye contact.

I shrugged. "I don't know."

"You *did* buy WiFi, right?"

"No," I replied tersely. I was still mesmerized by the magical juju within that allowed him to become these different people.

"Of *course* you didn't." He stood up, opened the overhead, and yanked Josie out of her cubby.

I panicked and took her from his hands. Eli stared at me, squinting his eyes. "What's your problem, punk?"

"N-nothing," I said. "I just . . . need to put the password in for you. That's all. Why don't you get the flight attendant so you can pay for WiFi?"

He let me have Josie and summoned the flight attendant back, and I sat down, trying not to make a scene. My hands covered the top of Josie and my fingers made their way to the slit. I opened it up, carefully. My heart raced. I felt like the feds were behind me, watching me, their hot breaths on my neck. But all I had to do was type in my password. I overheard Eli paying for WiFi, so after I typed in my password, I put everything in safe mode, allowing Eli to access only the internet, and handed it over.

Eli set to work, checking this and that with some site for stocks. It hadn't occurred to me that perhaps that's exactly how Arlo paid for everything he did, including caviar burgers.

I threw my hands up. "So, okay, I'll be the one to say it."

Eli stole a glance at me, looking annoyed that I would interrupt him during work time.

"I mean, where's Arlo? Why are you here and not Todd?"

"Not that it's any of your friggin' business, but Arlo had to go be old somewhere else, and Todd had to go tremble at his own thoughts." He studied his stocks carefully, taking notes on my laptop. "Shut up, though. I'm working."

Maybe a kicking, screaming child would've been better after all.

"Boom!" he shouted, startling the couple on my right as he threw his hands up in touchdown mode. "Look at that! That's ten thou' right there. Money in da bank, baby." He did a little jig in his seat, and I looked for a dark crevice to crawl into and die. "Daddy's back!" he finished. You'd think Josie had literally spewed out cash like an old-school slot machine.

I watched him the way a new mother watches her firstborn child: completely in awe and totally petrified. I wondered, *How long will he be like this? Did Eli actually know what we were doing? He knows who I am, so Arlo's subconscious must have told him that. What else did it tell him? Does he know about the alleged individual who created him, so to speak?*

The stewardess handed Eli his ruby-red drink, and he gulped it down. "That hits the spot. You know what else sounds good? A cheeseburger."

"You ate a couple hours ago," I said. The French cuisine was delicious.

"No, *Arlo* ate an hour ago," he corrected. "I'm hungry."

"So you know who I am," I noted, almost talking to myself. "Does that mean you know what we're doing?"

"Yes, we're heading to Sorrento to find out who made us. Yada yada." Like an encyclopedia, this one.

"How will *you* be able to help us?" I was always taught to plan for the unexpected, yet I didn't consider the consequences of working with a completely different person. I don't know why I had it in my head that I'd have Arlo for the research side of things.

He shrugged. "Who said I'm going to help you?"

Getting more ticked off by the minute, I asked, "What do you mean? I need your help. This was all *your* idea!"

He shifted his index finger back and forth. "Uh-uh. Arlo's idea, specifically. I haven't had a vacation in years, and this is just what I need to catch up on—"

I snatched Josie from off his lap, setting her in mine. I wrenched his shirt in my hand and brought my nose to his face. "Listen, you arrogant piece of crap. I need Arlo's help, but he's not here. So I'm stuck with you, and you clearly suck. And if I need your help, you're going to give it to me. Or else I will open up this laptop and transfer every last penny into the next Enron. Test me—I dare you."

He furiously nodded, begging me with those eyes not to do it—not to take away his precious money. "All right, all right. Jeez. Calm down, man."

I released Eli from my death grip, put my headphones on, and thought about May 21.

Pensacola News Channel 5

Quinn: If you're just tuning in, there's been an explosion in the Kevel lab in Pensacola. The world is on the edge of its seat as we await confirmation that the

Raven Virus cure—known as NovaVita—has been saved. No bodies have been confirmed yet, but sources tell us Athena and Benjamin Kevel were hiding out in their lab. Their son, Knox, is confirmed to be safe with a family member. News Channel 5 is on the scene. Jeremy, what are you seeing right now?

Jeremy: Two bodies have been recovered, believed to be Benjamin and Athena Kevel, but confirmed identification is not yet possible, as the bodies are too badly burned. Behind me are the last of the firefighters and exhausted volunteers who have worked tirelessly to calm the flames.

Quinn: Can you tell us about the cure? Has it been saved?

Jeremy: I'm not sure, Quinn. We're all wondering the same thing.

Quinn: And the explosion?

Jeremy: Police have neither confirmed nor denied that this explosion was foul play.

Quinn: Does the FBI have any leads?

Jeremy: I've asked, but the chief said, "No comment."

———————

After fourteen hours, I was ready to stretch my legs and get off this plane.

Eli sat with his legs crossed and had managed to slick back his hair and roll up his sleeves. I rubbed my weary eyes as the plane came to a jolting stop in Paris, France—our layover.

Ah, Paris—the city of love. What could be better than landing in Paris and getting a glimpse of the Eiffel Tower?

CHAPTER 9

Ciao, Bella

Paris was more like the city of "kill me now."

In all fairness, I wasn't roaming about their streets. I was stuck in their airport. Maybe it was the stress; maybe it was the sweat dripping from my forehead to my nose. But when Eli and I deplaned and walked into the Charles de Gaulle Airport, I just wanted to quit the whole job and go back home. Never mind the money—this wasn't worth it.

Walking into that airport made me feel like a tiny mouse trapped in a maze. We had no idea where we were supposed to go, and heaven forbid one of Arlo's alters spoke French. Feeling flustered at the French signs, I approached a man in a suit and asked him where our gate might be, pointing to my ticket. His lip curled in disgust and he muttered something in French before he turned away.

"Great. Now what?" Eli asked.

Finally, I found an American woman who pointed us in the right direction, but then we were met with new complications: the checkpoints. Rather than having just one checkpoint to go through the security screening, we had several.

After our fifth or sixth checkpoint, we finally made it to the final screening, where a misshapen line of sweaty, agitated people packed together like sardines. An employee grabbed my arm and pulled me away from Eli, saying I had to go to a different checkpoint.

"No! No, I'm with him," I shouted, frantic. Travelers stared at me.

"Different checkpoint!" the employee said, wrinkling his nose.

"No, I am with that man right there." I pointed to Eli who pretended like he didn't know me.

"Together?" he asked, nodding at Eli.

"Yes!" I was out of breath. "Well, I mean, not in *that* way. He's my boss. Well, *he's* not actually my—"

With a curt nod, he pulled the rope over my head so I could stay with Eli. It was at this point I wished I had let that man take me with him.

There's something about me, I suppose, that screams, "Terrorist! Search him!" in airports. After I walked through the security-scanner-bleeping thing, it went off and signaled the morbidly obese and hairy female agent on the other side to search me.

Remembering my very fake passport, I tried to remain as calm as possible.

The only problem was that I was used to being patted down in an *American* airport, not a French one. Apparently, they do things differently.

"Arms out," the woman barked. I was lost for a moment, staring at the massive wart that sat on her nose. Transfixed, in fact. "Arms out!" she shouted once more. I shot my arms up in surrender, still focused on the protuberance that stared me down.

Eli waited past the checkpoint, rolling his head. "Try not to take forever, punk. We got places to be." I grimaced at him.

The obese lady's hands started at my armpits and ran down my stomach. Her search became more aggressive as she ran down my legs and up my thighs. I winced as her hand crept too closely to Little Knox. Until it didn't creep anymore and cupped him in front of God and everybody.

"Hey!" I yelled. "What do you think you're doing?"

She threw a smug laugh my way and called out, "Clean."

I muttered something vulgar and grabbed my duffel bag and walked-ran to Eli.

"That was funny," he said, smirking. "Shoulda got that on camera."

"Funny?" I snapped. "Let me know how 'funny' it is when someone you don't know fondles your junk like that in a public place."

"Did she find anything?" He burst out laughing and slapped me on the back. "Come on. Let's get out of this hellhole and find our plane."

And so I followed, keeping Josie safe by my side. As we walked what felt like miles, I was still steaming over that lady until I realized: she hadn't questioned me about my passport. *Phew.* Trying to take my mind off it, I asked Eli, "Did you know my parents? Athena and Benjamin Kevel?"

"Know 'em?"

"Like, do you, Eli, not Arlo, have any memories of them? Arlo said he remembered them, but he doesn't know how."

"Yeah, I didn't know them. That's before my time."

I nodded and let it go at that.

After all of those checkpoints, our final location was our gate. We wandered around trying to find it, sweating and huffing and puffing. We finally showed a man our ticket, and he pointed us in the right direction, which was upstairs—even though we were told to be downstairs. They had been boarding the plane for thirty minutes already.

We finally saw our gate number and ran to it. Miraculously, and only to the great power of the Almighty Jehovah, we made it. Well, we made it only after being taken to our plane on the runway via stinky, sticky shuttle.

I don't totally remember the plane ride to Naples, probably because I blocked it out or snoozed through its entirety while Eli did God knows what. With a great big bump, we skirted our way into Naples, Italy.

───────────

I was relieved to see our bags rolling along the conveyor belt. As a paranoid person, I imagined our luggage would be long gone, sailing away in a sea of other lost baggage, never to be seen or heard from again. Kind of like socks.

We headed to the restroom to wash our faces and clean up, only to find that the restroom in the Naples airport was a lot like a sewer: uninviting, smelly, and dark, with the possibility of an alligator nearby. We hurried up and walked outside, the cool breeze waking up my senses. It was about 4:30 a.m. now, and we still had to make the trek to Sorrento.

We found a man holding a white board with our names on it and greeted him.

"*Ciao!*" he said, shaking our hands and picking up our suitcases. "Let me get that for you."

"*Grazie,*" I replied. I loved the way the Italian language sounded. Both Italian and romance were foreign languages to me, but if I could find a way to speak Italian, I figured the romance would follow.

He grabbed our bags and I tipped him with a euro—Arlo had given me about fifty bucks' worth back at the condo. The bus was surprisingly cozy, and the forty-five-minute trip to Sorrento was more peaceful than I thought it would be. I actually felt kind of . . . good . . . being there. The gentle lull was enough to make me fall asleep. Except for one thing.

"Man, I can't believe I'm back in this craphole again." Eli sat with his feet propped on the chair in front of us, leaning back with his ugly sunglasses on. "Food's great, though. I'll say that."

"How can you not like Italy?" I studied the map of Sorrento, following the line to Norah's villa with my finger.

"I never said I didn't like it. I'm just saying that Naples is like the armpit a' Italy, that's all. There's better places to be."

I gazed out the window, where clotheslines connected apartments, zigzagging their way down as shirts, pants, and skirts hung low. Mountains came into view, and I wondered what the view would be like at Norah's home.

"Well, we're heading to a different place. Sorrento. So maybe it won't be so armpit-ish."

"I'll keep that in mind." Eli reached into his back pocket and pulled out a pack of Marlboro Reds. Resting a cigarette in his mouth, he tapped an older gentleman in front of us and asked, "You got a light?" The man nodded and handed him his lighter. Eli lit the cigarette and took a long drag.

"What on earth are you doing?" I asked, appalled.

He narrowed his eyes at me before he breathed a puff of smoke into my face. "Are you stupid or something? I'm smoking."

"I see that, you idiot," I hissed, covering my mouth with my hand. "I meant that you can't smoke on a bus or near me. I have asthma."

He chuckled. "First, we're in Europe now, so better get used to the smoke. You can smoke anywhere—like, *anywhere*. Second, ain't my problem that you got the wheezies. Get over it." He pulled an even longer drag this time, leaning back as the smoke took over his lungs. I reached into my bag and pulled out my inhaler, took a quick puff, and silently cursed him.

"When you're done being a major jerk, can you answer something for me?" I asked, irritated.

He waved a cloud of smoke away. "Maybe."

"Tell me about Norah."

He smiled and held the cigarette in his hand. "Norah, Norah. She's . . . different."

"In what way?" I asked, stifling a cough and plotting Eli's slow and painful death.

Placing the cigarette back in his mouth, he rolled up his sleeves and said, "Did you ever watch *The Addams Family*?"

Finally, for one blissful moment, I had something in common with Eli. "Yeah, totally. Classic all the way around. I named my hamster Wednesday."

"Get out." He pulled up his sunglasses, revealing young eyes surrounded by sage wrinkles. "You still got the hamster?"

I looked back at the map, trying to feign apathy. "Tragic balcony accident I'd rather not talk about."

He covered his eyes again with his shades. "Poor Wednesday." He took a final drag and then snuffed out his cigarette on the ground before flicking it out the window. "Anyway," Eli began, resting his folded hands behind his head, "Norah is basically Morticia."

My eyebrows shot up. While guys my age slobbered all over blonde-haired, blue-eyed valley girls, I had my eyes set on the queen of macabre: Morticia Addams. I don't know what it was about her—maybe that vine-like, creeping dress or those dark eyes, but she had always entranced me.

"To be honest, she actually sounds really cool," I said.

"It's cool for about ten minutes." He pulled his sunglasses off his face again. "Think long and hard about the character Morticia, and then tell me if *you'd* want to live with that."

Contemptuous, fierce, witty, dark—yep, I could live with that. "So does that mean her daughter is like Wednesday?"

"I dunno," he said. "I never met her, remember?"

"Oh, right." I wondered what the daughter would be like. If she could help us. I even wondered what Norah could do to help, except maybe tell me what she knew about Arlo's disorder.

At this rate, I'd rather know how Arlo knew my parents, but one freaky mystery at a time.

Sorrento was full of hills and greenery and charming Italians waving hello. Purple and hot-pink flowers lined the windows, and bicycles and mopeds scooted across the stone streets. The Tyrrhenian Sea wrapped around the southern town, and it was hard to compare it to anything I had ever seen. I was used to emerald-green waves, but this was a deep, dark blue I had never seen before, beckoning me to dive right in.

But for the next several days, I'd be living in a villa affectionately called *Ibisco*. As if Italy weren't charming enough, they named their homes. Our bus abruptly stopped in a narrow street, and we walked uphill for a couple of blocks, our suitcases bumping along the rutted road. There wasn't a soul in sight as the sun rose over the hilltops.

Over the hill, both of us sweating and out of breath, a stone villa with yellow shutters and a bright-green door greeted us. This was it—*Ibisco*.

We came to the front door, where a mat on the porch read BENVENU-TO. Wiping my shoes on the mat, I leaned forward and rang the doorbell. Cobwebs filled corners and crevices, while buzzing bees zoomed around blossoming hibiscus.

Oh. Ibisco. Hibiscus. I get it.

"What if the broad ain't home?" Eli asked, hands in his pockets.

"The broad?" I rolled my eyes. "She's your sister, moron. And of course she's home."

"Yeah, then how come she ain't answering the door, Einstein?"

He had a point.

I rang the doorbell once more, leaning in to hear it ring. But I didn't hear anything. *Arlo did contact her, right? Norah knows we're coming, doesn't she?*

"I can't believe I'm saying this, but I think you're right, Eli."

"*Be*lieve it," he said, pushing me out of the way to turn the doorknob and let himself in.

With the door wide open, a spiral staircase ascending into the second story welcomed us, where a gothic chandelier hung above, illuminating the living room. A deep-purple clawfoot couch sat in the middle of the room, and the overpowering scent of incense tickled my nose. Natural light shone through the antique windows. A kitchen sat to the left of the staircase, and my stomach rumbled at the sight.

We left our luggage at the door, and Eli took a few steps forward before calling out, "Norah? You here?" His voice echoed, and I suddenly feared we were in the wrong house—breaking in.

"In here, gentlemen," we heard Norah call. Eli led the way into a room on the right, apparently some type of study where rows and rows of dusty books lined the shelves. A wooden desk that must've been a century old sat underneath a bay window, overlooking the town square.

And there, right in front of us, was Norah Delgado, palms to the carpet, one slender leg in the air. Incense and melodic music permeated the room.

"Welcome to my home," she said, staring at us upside down. Her alabaster skin struck me as beautiful, as alluring.

"What'd I tell ya?" Eli whispered with a nudge. "She's a weirdo, huh?"

I didn't have enough sense in me to shush him. Instead, I was overtaken by this woman hanging around like a bat in a home creepier than a cave.

"H-hi," I said. "I'm Knox. Knox Kevel, Arlo's—"

"*Ciao*, Knox. I'm happy to finally meet my brother's accomplice."

"Well, Norah," Eli began, walking toward her with his hands in his pockets, "you look as weird as ever. I mean, jeez, what are you doing? Is that yoga or something?"

Norah's feet gently met the carpet, her midnight-black hair covering her glistening face. As she straightened her silky locks, she muttered, "Oh my."

"Oh, yes." Eli wrapped his arms around his sister and held her tight. "Sorry to disappoint you."

I know Arlo couldn't exactly control when different alters decided to surface, but I wished someone had left me a how-to guide for handling *this* alter.

"Hello, Eli," she said, her words muffled in Eli's chest.

"Nice place ya got here. Too bad Arlo has to miss it, huh?" He patted her on the back and left me alone with Norah as he headed out of the study—snooping around, no doubt.

"You'll be in the guest room at the top, last door on your right," she called out, watching him leave for a moment. "You're sharing a room with Knox, so be good." Then she turned to me, her palms together and her eyebrows arched, intense.

"He turned into Eli on the plane," I said. "I don't know why." I gave her an apologetic look, as if to say, *If I could've beaten Eli out of him, I would've.*

"No matter," she said, her face serious. "Eli is a difficult alter, but not the worst. Come, come. Let's take a tour."

"What do you mean not the worst?" Before I could be answered, I bumped into a girl who had to be close to my age, maybe older. She had light-brown hair pulled taut with a ponytail holder. Her olive skin, covered in freckles, drew me in like thick honey. But then I looked into her eyes: they were violet. This girl had purplish-blue eyes that took my breath away.

"Meet my daughter, Jessa," Norah said.

I close my gaping mouth and stuck out my hand. "Hi, I'm—"

"I know who you are," she answered. "Nice to meet you in person, Knox Kevel."

CHAPTER 10

Sorrento

"*Zucchero?*"

I came out of my daze. "Huh?"

"Sugar. If you're going to be here for a while, you should learn as much of the language as you can. So! Would you like sugar in your coffee?"

"Sure, sure." I took the warm mug in my hand and smelled it. The flight had drained me, but a new surge of energy would have to get me through our first day in Sorrento. After we got in, Eli and I were so exhausted from our trip that we napped until about nine in the morning.

I wondered how Jessa knew me. I guess I shouldn't be surprised. Everyone knows the Kevel name.

"Get used to that, and I'll treat you to an espresso." A long mermaid-style dress hugged Norah's tall frame, and it was blacker than the night. Parted perfectly in the middle of her forehead, her hair flowed down her back, and ruby-red lips called out, "Eli? Eli?" She peered into the living room and then back into the kitchen. "Where is he?"

I swallowed my coffee, along with my admiration. "Oh, he was taking a shower. He should be down soon."

She nodded before downing her shot of espresso. "How do you like my little town?"

"It's incredible. Unlike anything I've ever seen. I can see why you never left."

With a mischievous smile, she said, "Who said I never left, darling?"

I wasn't typically one to marvel at women twice my age, but Norah had a way of making a man turn bashful.

"Where's Jessa?" My voice cracked at the end of her name, and I pretended like I hadn't just hit puberty. "Work? College?"

Norah reached for an apple on the table. "I believe she's getting ready for her morning run. Then she'll go to work."

"What does she do for a living?" I asked.

"My daughter works as a tour guide, all over, really. She takes tourists out and tells them the history of each place. She goes to Pompeii, villages in Ravello, here in Sorrento, and sometimes goes all the way to Rome and Florence if they're short on guides."

"Wow. That's an awesome job. What about you?"

"I took over my parents' business. They owned a little grocery store for as long as I can remember, mainly selling fresh produce."

"Oh, that's cool. Why aren't you there now?"

"Perks of being the owner, *mi amore*. I hired employees and they took over. I drop in a few times during the week to check on everything, though." She gave me a warm smile before refilling my coffee.

"Thanks." I pulled the coffee back to my lips, blowing the steam away. "When I met Jessa, she said she knew who I was. I take it you know who I am too—beside Arlo's . . . helper?"

She looked at me from under her long lashes. "Of course. The news of your parents and their debacle didn't stay in America." She crunched into her apple.

I frowned. "Well, yeah, that's my parents. They weren't exactly the best. I mean, they were to me. Just . . . not to society."

"We all have our sins, *mi amore*." She swallowed down her bite of apple. "But to be perfectly honest, Jessa had no idea who you were until I explained it to her. She doesn't keep up with current events."

Thank God.

Norah looked up to the stairs as Eli walked down.

Eli graced us with his presence and poured himself a cup of coffee. He pulled up a chair and made himself at home. "Honestly, Norah, I know quaint is in when it comes to homes, but that shower is itty-bitty. I might have to stay at a hotel."

"That'd be a shame," I mumbled.

"A hotel?" Norah asked, eyebrows raised. "What? And miss out on your brilliant personality?"

Eli shot her a dirty look. "Whatever. You missed me and you know it."

With her hands calmly placed on her lap, she eloquently replied, "As much as I missed a root canal, Eli."

To my surprise, Eli let out a hearty laugh. The guy sure could dish it out, but at least he could take it. I wondered how long Norah had been around Eli. So many questions with so few answers.

"Did you catch up on your sleep?" she asked.

"Not really." Eli stirred sugar into his coffee. "That bed is as hard as a rock." He grabbed an apple from the basket, rubbing it on his shirt to clean it off. "I think," Eli said, "that I'm in the mood for some pasta today. What do you think, Norah?"

"Sounds delicious. We can all get better acquainted."

"Sure, sure," he said. "Then tomorrow, if I'm feeling like it, I'll help you with this whole thing, Knox."

"Eli," I began, feeling jittery from the coffee, "you *have* to help me. You brought me here to find the person who did this to you."

"That was Arlo, kid," he said with a wink. "But I'll try to clear out some space in my schedule."

"What schedule?" I screeched. "What do you have to do here?" I threw my hands up in annoyance.

"It's Italy, baby! Food, beach, chicks."

Norah calmed us down, shushing us before the bickering took over breakfast. "All right, boys. Lunch later today. Then we start working on Arlo's . . . quest. No sense in wasting too much time, I suppose. Might as well get down to it. And, Eli, you *will* help Knox in any way you can, or I'll cast a spell on you."

Eli gulped and offered a nervous laugh. "Right, right."

"Sorry to miss lunch today." Jessa waltzed into the kitchen, opened the fridge door, and searched for something. Her hair was pulled back as it had been when I first arrived. Her eyes, like plums, stupefied me. "Hope you all have fun."

"Tour today, Jessa?" Norah asked.

"Yep, but not until later. Right now, I've got a date with the open road." She grabbed a bottle of water and headed out of the kitchen. I listened to her shoes hit the stony road outside and wondered why my heart beat so fast.

————

My first Italian cuisine was a toastie—like America's ham and cheese sandwich but more delicious somehow. We ordered a bottle of *aqua minerale* for the table, and the sparkling water became my new favorite beverage. The waiters anticipated our every need, filling our basket with fresh bread and whizzing by every ten seconds to check on us. I had read that working as a waiter in Italy was the exact opposite of working as one in America; it wasn't some low-end job to make ends meet—it was an admirable job the Italians took seriously. They didn't want to disappoint anyone and worked their best to serve us. Not to mention, they didn't accept tips.

"*Burro, senor?*" the waiter asked, his right arm at his side, with a white towel over it.

"*Si.*" I spread the sweet cream butter on warm bread. I dipped it in balsamic vinegar and decided to never leave this restaurant. I would just stay here and drown in balsamic vinegar and butter forever. "So, Norah, tell me more about yourself. How did you all end up here in Sorrento?"

Norah sat straight as an arrow and took small bites of her salad. I noticed there was no thick dressing but an oily sauce that coated the leaves. She set her fork down and replied, "My father was in the military. He was an American who came here on duty many years ago. He fell in love with this charming town and a very charming woman, my mother. She had grown up here and met him at her little shop, where she sold produce and other groceries. After his tour ended, he decided to stay here. They got married and had us."

I smiled, thinking about my own parents and how they met. Mom always said she had to tell the story, because Dad left out all the juicy details. They were in college at the time, completely unaware of each other's existence, until my mom fell into my dad's lap—literally. During an assembly for the fraternities and sororities, all the students had crowded into the auditorium, taking their seats and awaiting the opening ceremony. My father was sitting in the back with a vacant seat next to his left. My mother, never one to be punctual, raced into the auditorium, looking everywhere for a seat as the president approached the stage. Spotting the vacant seat, my mom raced to it—but she forgot about one thing: her always-reliable clumsiness. She tripped three times in a row, "as graceful as a rooster wearing socks," as she told it, and landed right into my dad's lap. They couldn't stop laughing, and the president had to shush them from the podium.

"So what about you?" I asked Norah.

"And what about me?"

"Well, were you ever married?"

She took a sip of her water before answering. "Briefly—while young and stupid. I wish I could say he was charming and brilliant and romantic, and all of these other things. But the truth is, he wasn't anything special. He was just very persuasive. He left me after I had Jessa, and I haven't seen him since."

"So Jessa has never met her father?"

Norah shook her head. "Doesn't want to."

"Oh."

"Good riddance," Eli said. "Sounds like a total jerk to me."

Well, if that isn't the pot calling the kettle black.

"Yes, I suppose so." Norah went back to eating her salad, but her mood clearly changed.

I tried to steer the conversation on a lighter tack. "So how did you get into contact with Arlo again? I mean, has he even been here since . . .?"

"Since my parents sent him away? No. We wrote letters back and forth in the beginning when I was young—I probably still have them somewhere—but then we lost touch. It's difficult living so far away from one another. Then, after our parents passed recently, I tracked down Arlo to let him know.

I felt he needed to know. And then, he decided he'd come to see me and meet Jessa."

And also hunt down some lunatic who injected him with a mental disorder, which I'm still unclear on. Let's not forget that part.

"So now I'd like to know," Norah asked, clasping her hands in front of her. "What all do you know about this person who . . . *caused* all of this for Arlo?"

I shrugged. "I would say as much as you do. Maybe less, actually. He hasn't told me anything yet. Not even a name. Just that it's my job to track down this person." I glanced at Eli. "I think Arlo believes it'll be easier to figure it out if we're here where it all started."

"What makes him think she's here in Italy or that she's even still alive?"

"I don't know that she's alive. Maybe he thinks she would still be here after all this time. To be honest, he has given me hardly any information at all, and once Eli came around on the plane, I've gotten nowhere in terms of information."

Eli chuckled at that.

"And if the person is no longer here in Italy?" Norah countered.

"Then I guess I'll strike this job from my budding résumé." I smirked, reaching for more bread. "Okay, so what about Arlo's disorder? Do you remember anything about it?"

She frowned. "I was very, very young when that happened. My parents wouldn't tell me anything—not even when I was older. I grew tired of asking after so many years and finally dropped it. It was just something we didn't speak of—ever. And when I *did* try to ask, they'd become angry at me."

I glared at Eli. "What do you know about it all?"

"Who? Me?" He leaned back in his chair, his arms crossed. "Couldn't say. But something tells me Arlo has a few bread crumbs for you to follow."

"You *are* Arlo. You're part of him!"

"No, I'm Eli. I'm my own person. Keep up."

"Well, can't you just procure those bread crumbs from inside you some-where?" I looked pointedly at his fifth piece of bread.

"Touché. But no."

———

When we arrived at Ibisco after the filling dinner, I trudged up the stairs to my temporary room, turned on the light, and jumped. "Holy crap! What are you doing in here?"

"Hey!" Jessa said, pushing herself off my bed. "How was dinner?"

"Uh . . . it was fine." *There's a girl on my bed. A strange girl I have said five words to. Sitting here. Being weird.*

"Why don't we go for a walk?" she asked. She wore a white dress with orange and purple flowers on it—the most color I had seen in the Delgado house since I arrived.

I scratched the back of my head. "I think I'll pass."

She walked closer to me, her head cocked. "Why?"

"Why? I just . . . uh . . . I don't know why. Just wanted to rest, I guess."

She stood on her tiptoes. "Are you afraid I'll bite?"

My mouth went dry, and I changed the subject. "I take it your run went well from this morning?"

"So great!" she squealed. "I was sweating like a pig and got done earlier than I thought I would."

"And today's tour?"

"*Magnifico.* Anyway, ready to go?"

I rolled my eyes. "You're not going to take no for an answer, are you?"

She shook her head.

"All right. I'll go. Hey, by the way, why were you in here?"

She rolled those violet eyes and said, "I was snooping around." As if to say, "Duh, Sherlock." And with that, she walked past me, grabbed her hoodie from the hallway, and I followed like a little puppy.

———

Sorrento at night smelled like summer. And I don't mean that in some Shakespearean, poetic, don't-really-know-what-I-mean way. It smelled like wet grass and melted ice cream and fresh flowers and a hint of sweat. The streets came alive with laughter, music, and lights, and Jessa was the most talkative she'd been since we met. I liked the sound my feet made as they hit the stone road, making me think of the thousands of Romans who had traveled these same streets, their sandals strapped tightly to their dusty feet.

Jessa pulled at her long locks and began braiding them as she walked. She stopped right as we entered the line for the gelato shop and opened her mouth wide. "I have something to say."

"Okay." I treaded lightly. She looked like she could either be my closest friend or kill me, and I'd be fine to experience either.

"Yes, I know who you are—or who your parents were—but you should know that I don't hate you like everyone else does. In fact, I didn't know a thing about you or them until Mom clued me in. So then I read a lot about your parents, and how everyone seems to take out their anger on you. And if they're not hating you, they're coming up with these insane conspiracy theories. I don't hate you. You had nothing to do with what they did. I think you should know that."

"Uhhhhh. Yeah, wow. Thank you. Sorry, but I haven't ever really had anyone say that to me, so I'm not sure what to do."

"Just smile and be happy I'm not a jerk. Or one of those crazy conspiracy theorists."

"Got it." I gave her my cheesiest grin as we approached the counter. I handed the man two euros, and I bit into the *stracciatella* gelato that tasted like heaven on a cone. It reminded me of chocolate chip ice cream but way sweeter. We walked and talked and ate our gelato.

"I know you probably get this a lot, but do you think the cure still exists?" she asked. "What was it called?"

"NovaVita. And no, I don't." When I said this, I must not have sounded very convincing because she cocked her eyebrow and rolled her eyes. I realized she knew very little about my parents and the cure. "I don't see how it possibly could've survived the explosion." I know this because I watched their lab explode on live TV, but I didn't tell her that.

Jessa reached up to my lips and wiped off gelato that had stuck to my cheek. I shuddered and turned away, hoping she wouldn't notice. "Do you need a bib or something?" she asked.

For the first time since I met her, I heard Jessa giggle, and it was contagious.

We strolled down the street until we came to a bench that overlooked the ocean. I heard the gentle lull of the waves, and I liked the way she looked with her hood pulled over her head, with those stupid little braids sticking out, with her bright-as-a-rainbow dress that looked like it belonged in another time period.

"If you say the cure doesn't exist, then I believe you." She looked serious enough. "It's just strange that a cure that important can just be gone like that"—she snapped her fingers—"it's sad. All those people who died from the Raven Virus, you know?"

I replied, "Lots of things about that day are sad. It was destroyed in the fire. Everything was. Even the computers that had the formula on them just disintegrated. Not even I could do anything to fix them."

She met my bulging eyes with a curious grin. "What do you mean, *not even you?*"

"I . . . uh . . ."

Say something. Say something. Anything.

"What does that mean?" she asked.

Say something. Literally anything right about now other than staring at her with your mouth open, your eyes twitching.

"Earth to Knox!"

Oh my Lord, this is the longest time anyone has ever gone without saying something. Please for the love of—

"Good evening."

I turned around and saw Arlo. I don't know how I could tell, but it was him. Maybe it was the straitlaced outfit, his hair combed and his sleeves down. Arlo was back. I jumped off the bench and hugged him, grateful for the interruption. The hug, by the way, was completely unintentional. I'm not much of a hugger, but I was just so glad Eli was gone—so glad someone interrupted us so I wouldn't have to explain the whole Suicide Tree thing. "I can't believe I'm saying this, but I've really missed you, Arlo."

He smiled and nodded toward Jessa. "What are you two up to?"

"Just eating some gelato," she answered, getting up from the bench, her eyes still on me, wondering what I hadn't told her.

"So how did you get Eli to leave?" I asked.

"There's no on-and-off switch, my boy. He just decides on his own, I suppose. Gets bored." He looked around, his hands in his pockets. "Now, where do you suppose I could get some gelato? I've been craving it for decades."

CHAPTER 11

Drugs and Gelato

Pensacola News Channel 5

Quinn: *You're watching News 5 and I'm Quinn McGeorge. Tonight, we're doing an exclusive interview with Dr. Ellis, an expert on diseases. She'll be discussing the Raven Virus and how our nation should prepare for this epidemic. Dr. Ellis, thank you for joining us tonight on this special episode.*

Dr. Ellis: *It's my pleasure to be here, Quinn.*

Quinn: *Let's jump right in. What is the Raven Virus?*

Dr. Ellis: *The Raven Virus is a disease that affects the immune system. It starts out much like the flu: fever, body aches, mucus buildup. However, as the virus grows, the infected individual will begin coughing up black blood—*

Quinn: *Why is it black?*

Dr. Ellis: *The more oxygen in the blood, the redder it gets. If there is a decrease in oxygen, then the blood turns darker. In other words, there's no circulation of blood in the veins. But coughing up black blood isn't the end for the infected.*

Quinn: *So coughing up blood sounds like tuberculosis?*

Dr. Ellis: *No, tuberculosis is caused by a bacteria. It isn't viral. In fact, scientists are hard at work to understand how or why the Raven Virus is turning blood black and prompting people to cough it up.*

Quinn: Is this lethal?

Dr. Ellis: I'm afraid so. Because the virus is found in the organs, primarily the lungs, it eats them from the inside out, slowly diminishing their capacity, causing the chest cavity to fill up with blood and the liquidy remains of the lungs. The lungs, now in liquid form, are sloshing around in the chest. Eventually, liquid completely replaces the lungs, the suffering patients cannot get enough oxygen, and respiratory failure occurs. They can no longer breathe, and they drown.

Quinn: What an awful way to die. How did the Raven Virus come about?

Dr. Ellis: This is still an ongoing investigation from what I understand, but to answer your question, it was due to an accident in Waco, Texas. Two men were conducting a low-budget lab experiment on birds for various diseases. But something went wrong and they tried to isolate the disease. However, they were unable to do so and there was an outbreak.

Quinn: What about a cure? Is there one?

Dr. Ellis: That's tough to answer right now. At the moment, the CDC has brought in Doctors Benjamin and Athena Kevel to create a cure for the Raven Virus.

Quinn: Do you think they will succeed?

Dr. Ellis: God, I hope so.

———————

After Arlo satisfied his craving for gelato, we went back to Ibisco, and I asked if I could speak to him alone. After making hardly any progress during dinner, I knew I needed to make the most of my time with him.

Arlo needed to start talking.

We made our way to the bedroom upstairs, and he closed the door.

"Look," I said, opening the window to let in some fresh air, "you're back now and I'm glad. I didn't really like Eli. He was a tool. But I need answers now. I came all the way to Europe to help you track down some lunatic, and I need you to start giving me some clues about where to start. Maybe even more important than that: you know my parents, and I deserve to know how."

The cool breeze made him shiver, so he grabbed a blanket and threw it over his lap as he sat down. He rested his palms on his knees. "Knox, there's something you should know about that. About all of this."

"Okay, yeah, I want to know everything." My legs hung off the bed while I leaned back on the wall.

"I don't exactly know *everything* about your parents. I just know . . . a few details from their life before. There are lots of puzzle pieces, and it's going to take time for me to put them all together. My . . . way of life jumbles things around a lot. It's hard to remember. Nearly impossible. Sometimes, I'll have a flash of a memory, and nothing else."

I drew in a slow, steady breath. "Arlo, what are you saying?"

"I'm saying what I said." He scratched the back of his head. "And I promise I'm doing my best. I've been working with a therapist for a while now, and we've made some breakthroughs. But again, things are . . . in disarray."

My body tensed, and I clenched my jaw. "You brought me to Italy to find some crazy woman, and then you decide to drop this bomb on me that you knew my parents—and now you're trying to convince me you don't remember the details?" My voice was surprisingly calm for someone who was about to strangle another human being.

"I can tell you what I do know. And don't act like I conned you. I do have some answers, just not *all* of—"

"Then start with what you do know."

He rubbed his eyebrows. "All right, then we must start at the beginning, when I met your parents." He cleared his throat. "My family came to Sorrento, Italy, because my father was stationed outside of here. He was a marine, and when he was here on duty, he fell in love with this place. He met my mother, and after he finished his tour, they got married and started a family."

"I know. Norah told me that."

"Well, did she tell you about my father's little problem?"

"What little problem?"

He lowered his gaze and in a hushed tone, said, "That makes sense. She probably wouldn't remember. My father developed epilepsy when I was a teenager. Norah was probably four. The seizures were terrible. It was awful to watch him suffer. This strong, capable marine—a hero—convulsing on the kitchen floor. And there's nothing you can do to help him."

There was an unnatural stillness in the room, and I wanted to put my arm around Arlo and tell him I was sorry. But I didn't know how and I wanted to be angry at him for taking me on this wild goose chase.

He continued: "My mother had children to take care of. She needed a cure."

My eyebrows squished together. "There isn't a cure for epilepsy."

A grim smile met my eyes. "I beg to differ."

I urged him to continue.

"We were out shopping one day, just wanting to get out of the house. My dad had an episode that was . . . difficult to watch. At first, it started with his body jerking, but it quickly escalated to convulsions. Then the smell hit us. He had soiled himself. It was the worst episode he'd ever had. My mom sobbed as she tried to hold him, to comfort him. People laughed." His voice cracked, and his eyes were glossy, like he was watching a movie about his life. I felt my eyes mist too. "But he started to come out of it and flailed as it finally ended. I watched as the two of them sunk down to the ground, crying. It was then that a mysterious woman approached my parents and handed my mother a card."

"Like a business card?"

"Right. And my mother took it and looked up at the woman and said, 'What do you want?' The woman walked away without answering. Later that night, I saw my mother at the kitchen table holding the card, her hand on the phone. She was hesitant at first but then dialed the number, and I sat and listened from the stairs."

"What did you hear?" I asked. And somehow, I could envision this young Arlo, from a different world, hiding at the top of the staircase, eavesdropping on his mother.

"The mysterious woman who handed her the card offered to cure my father. That's what I heard."

I threw my hands in the air. "But how is that possible?"

"That's what my mother asked. But she went to meet this person anyway, and they changed my father's life. They cured him."

"How?" How does one find a cure for epilepsy? Perhaps the same way two scientists found a cure for the Raven Virus—I don't know. It was still a difficult thought to grasp. "I just don't understand how. How is that possible?"

"With her, anything is possible." It sounded like a mantra the way he said it. The way one might say the slogan of an insurance company.

I felt the coldness from the night sweep through our room, and suddenly I wanted a blanket too. "Her? A woman cured him? So . . . this is the same woman who did this to you, right? Is that where you're going?"

He nodded. "My father took one drink of this gross-looking olive-green concoction. Within a few days, there were no signs of any seizures. He was healed."

"That's . . . unbelievable. And you don't even remember her name? You remember these details, but not her name?"

"My parents would never utter her name. We weren't allowed to ever speak of this. They were furious when I even found out about this woman, but how could I not? My father was healed. I had to know more."

"So she cured him, and then what?"

"Selling your soul to the devil always comes with a price." He pulled the blanket up further, up to his neck almost. I wanted to get up and close the window, but I couldn't move. "They would one day have to return a favor for her. They didn't know when or what it would be, but they would one day have to serve her."

"It sounds like you're talking about the mafia, Arlo."

He quickly shook his head. "No, no. That's kids stuff. This woman was twisted, demented, and the favor was just as deranged as she was."

"What was the favor?" I asked.

He looked down at the floor and shook his head, his shoulders hunched. "I was the favor."

A gasp left my throat. "What do you mean?"

"Because this woman cured my father, she came along later and experimented on me. My parents had no choice. That's why I am the way I am. She did this to me."

I rubbed my weary eyes. "Arlo, that's terrible. So you remember all of this, but you don't remember the woman's name or her doing this to you?"

"Not really. Just flashes."

"But I don't get what this has to do with my parents?"

"The drug they gave my father?"

"Yeah?"

He leaned forward and took his time before answering. "There were two young doctors who came to our house that day to administer the drug that would cure him—two employees of hers. Their names were Benjamin and Athena Kevel."

CHAPTER 12

Breakfast

It was through science that my parents fell in love.

They both attended the University of West Florida, continuing on for their doctorates there before they settled in downtown Pensacola. For years, they shared cafeteria lunches, the same halls, the same professors. Day after day, my father, always the romantic, carried his girlfriend's books to the next class or to her dorm. In the yearbook there's a faded photo of them together—dissecting a frog or some other helpless slimy animal.

I thought that if anyone could smile that big while cutting into something dead, then there was nothing that could tear them apart.

Their marriage was a happy one—and as their child, I'm grateful for that. My dad wasn't exactly the one to throw a football around with his son, but he did teach me about organisms and the world that lived beyond our own, invisible to the naked eye. Always teaching me the proper way to hold beakers, how to clean them.

The two of them were superheroes to me.

So you can imagine my great surprise when they decided that NovaVita belonged to them and them alone, refusing to cure the millions affected by the Raven Virus.

When they received the momentous news that they got the funding to cure the Raven Virus, I knew they would go down in history as the most famous scientists who ever lived. I just didn't realize it would be for infamy. After weeks of no sleep and nothing but service to this cure, they finally figured it out. They created a cure, and then they died.

Just like that.

When I questioned them about why they wouldn't just hand over the stupid cure, they refused to explain. They told me it was none of my concern. They completely blocked me out when it came to their work, to *this* work. Kind of like Norah when she'd asked her parents about the woman who ruined Arlo's life. Nothing but crickets.

So I let them handle it on their own. I let them barricade themselves into their lab downtown. I let them die a fiery death, watching on live television as flames consumed their building, the cure, and their bodies. I let them.

————

After Arlo turned my world on its back, I probed for more details, but he couldn't remember anything else. He brought his hands to his temples and said he had a headache coming on. Turning off the lamp and rolling over, he said he'd give me more details later—if he could.

But the biggest mystery was this woman's name. Who was she?

Arlo's cliffhangers irked me to no end. But when you have $250,000 sitting in your back account, you try not to push your luck too much. And truth be told, maybe I didn't want to know all the details about my parents. Maybe that's why I didn't hound him so much, begging for more information.

Maybe I just wanted to remember my parents as I always had: two brilliant scientists who loved me.

The next morning, I awoke to the smell of freshly brewed coffee, sizzling *prosciutto crudo*, and homemade bread. My typical breakfast in Pensacola consisted of a protein smoothie I whipped up or leftover pizza. Okay, usually pizza. But I could get used to this kind of cuisine.

"Hey, Norah," I said, reaching for the newspaper. Not that I could read Italian, but I had to do something with my hands—anything to distract me from memories of last night. I rubbed at my weary eyes.

"*Buon giorno.*" She set a plate in front of me that had to be over a thousand calories, and I dug right in. "Best to fatten you up while you're here."

I chewed my bite and swallowed it down before asking, "Where's Jessa?"

"Out for her morning run." The prosciutto sizzled as she pressed the spatula into it. It smelled so good that I was salivating while I already had some in my mouth. "Never have trusted someone who volunteers to sweat like that each morning, but she seems to enjoy it."

"You don't trust your own daughter, huh?" I took a sip of the dark coffee, its steam billowing under my nose.

"No, and you shouldn't either." She winked at me, and I gulped a little slower, wondering if she knew about Jessa's snooping around in my room the previous night.

A moment later, in walked Arlo. He was on the casual side today: jeans, a nice polo, and white tennis shoes. *"Buon giorno, sorella."*

"And good morning to you, *fratello*. How do you like your eggs?"

"In the trash," he answered with a chuckle.

Norah lightly smacked him on the arm. "Come on. You hate eggs? You are an adult, Arlo. Adults eat eggs."

"Speak for yourself, but I know where they come from and I don't want it in my mouth." He elbowed me to laugh at his joke, and I relented.

I skimmed the newspaper, shoveling more food down my gullet. "Norah, what does *Maggio* mean?"

"May. Why?"

"Oh. There's a festival in Amalfi is the last weekend in May—uh, I think. That's not far from here, right?" Not that I knew the maps of Italy all that well, but there hadn't been much else to do on that ridiculously long flight. "What's Amalfi like?" I asked.

"Colorful," Norah answered, whipping up the eggs with a fork. "There are thirteen villages in Amalfi, and perhaps my favorite is Ravello. No speaking English there, I'm afraid. They're all quite old school in their traditions."

"That shouldn't be a problem." I smiled at her. "I have my own personal translator."

I had seen pictures of Amalfi and knew it was an all-day trip to travel up the mountains. Which meant, all day with Jessa.

That is, *if* she'd be interested in going.

A moment later, Norah set a plate of eggs and prosciutto in front of her brother.

"Are you wanting to go to Amalfi?" Arlo asked, pushing the eggs to the side of his plate and taking a bite of the hot prosciutto.

"I mean, I wouldn't mind. There's a festival in Ravello this weekend." I looked at him with "please can we go?" eyes.

"Ah, yes, the Wagner Festival," Norah said, scooting the eggs closer to Arlo with a fork.

"Wagner?" I asked.

"Yes, after Richard Wagner, the composer. It's what we call the festival. You'll like it, Knox. We should all go as a family. Lots to do. Lots of wonderful food, art, and music."

Italy was all of those things and more. The ocean, the laidback villagers with their brightly painted villas. The romance, the history.

Yet I was here to track down some psycho instead. Kind of put a damper on this little vacation.

"We aren't here to gallivant around villages, my boy. We're here to accomplish a job." He brought a forkful of eggs to his mouth, sniffed, and gagged.

Not that getting the largest sum of money in my life was something to complain about, but I needed more than just money. I had spent months doing nothing. I needed to live a little.

"Actually, Arlo, I was thinking." I wiggled my eyebrows. "It'll be a reward."

He left the table to get more prosciutto from the pan. "A reward? How so?"

"Yes, *mi amore*, how so?" Norah asked, picking at Arlo's uneaten eggs.

"Well," I began, "we have the rest of the week to make big progress on this, right? I know we can do it, so once we've made a big leap in the right direction, then the festival can be our reward." I leaned back in my chair, proud of myself for coming up with that idea on my feet.

Arlo returned to the table and grinned. "We can go," he said. "I very much like the idea of a reward. But let's not forget why we're here." He gave me a stern look, something my father would've given me in a lived not that long ago.

I brought my attention to my plate, scooping the last bits into my mouth. "Yeah, you're right."

I must've looked glum because Norah spoke up: "Let the boy enjoy his youth, *fratello*. You've got plenty of time to find your persecutor. Live a little while you're here, and enjoy your family. You know? The ones you haven't seen in decades."

He grunted but relented. "All right, all right. But how about you and I do some research *today*? Then we'll go to the festival this weekend as our reward."

"Okay. Where do you want to start?" I asked, setting the newspaper down and reaching for my coffee.

"With my parents' house."

CHAPTER 13

Slowly, Carefully

To get to the Jensons' home, we had to take a ferry to the island of Capri.

"Isn't it mostly rich people who live in Capri?" I asked Arlo as we headed down the stairs. Sorrento was set on a high hill and was a strange but oddly satisfying shortcut from Norah's villa to the marina was to take 307 steps down to the docks. I counted every last step.

It hadn't occurred to me, however, what misery would lie before me when it was time to trek back *up* the stairs—with Josie in my messenger bag.

"Not only rich people live there, but many rich and famous vacation there. My boy, you might pay ten euros for a shot of espresso, but it's worth it to be sitting across from a celebrity. Plus, you'll love the view." Arlo flew down those stairs like it was nothing. Surprising for a man his age.

We approached the marina and purchased our tickets. "*Grazie.*" I tucked the ticket in my pocket, and we walked down the dock to board. It must've been a slow day on the ferry because there weren't many people on board.

Arlo and I took our seats as the ferry gently took off on the waves. Arlo's attention was directed toward the navy-blue waves that hit the mountains. Colorful villas worth millions lined the side of the mountains, as if they had naturally grown there like dandelions. "You like Frank Sinatra?" Arlo asked out of the blue.

"Of course. Who doesn't?"

"Well, he wrote a song called 'Isle of Capri.'"

"Yeah?"

He nodded. "Yep." Suddenly, he burst into song, an upbeat, buoyant tune: *She whispered softly, "It's best not to linger"*

And then as I kissed her hand I could see
She wore a lovely meatball on her finger
'Twas goodbye at the Villa Capri.

I smiled. "You have a pretty good singing voice, Arlo."

He pretended to tip an imaginary hat. "Why, thank you, my boy. Tips appreciated."

I shook my head and laughed.

The bell rang, and the boat slowed to a stop as we approached the dock. I slid out of my chair, and we walked out into the blazing sun. Pushing my sunglasses to my nose, I took in the scenery: restaurants, coffee bars, and shops. Tourists in their swimsuits. Arlo walked as if he knew exactly where he was going.

"Over here," he called out, motioning toward a dock.

But the only thing there was a gray-haired man behind a little podium that said BOAT RENTALS in rainbow paint. He leaned over it absentmindedly. "*Buonasera, signori.* Great day for boating!"

"A boat?" I whispered. "Arlo, I think we're at the wrong place." I pulled out the directions Norah had scribbled for us. She didn't mention anything about needing a boat.

"I assure you we are at the right place," he answered. "We'd like to rent the speedboat right there. How much?"

"Four or eight hours?" the boatman asked.

"Four should do it."

The man pulled out a waiver. It appeared Arlo would have to sign his life away to rent the boat, and I prayed we wouldn't wreck it. "That'll be eighty euros. Going to the grotto today?"

The Blue Grotto was a sea cave on the coast of Capri. Only accessible by scuba gear or kayak. But something told me we wouldn't be exploring it. I shoved Norah's directions back into my pocket.

"Maybe. Just doing some sightseeing." Arlo gave him a reassuring smile, but I didn't feel reassured at all.

"*Molto bene!* Just sign here, and we only take cash."

Arlo signed his name and dated it and then pulled out the exact amount.

I thought about asking for a plastic bag to wrap up Josie in, but asked instead, "Any sharks out there?" and boarded the boat. Not that I was particularly concerned, as Pensacola Beach was known for some of the most brutal shark attacks outside of Australia. But I liked to be prepared.

"Only a shark named Michael, but he won't hurt you." He guffawed at a joke he probably used on every tourist here.

On second thought . . . "Do you have any plastic bags I could borrow to keep my laptop safe?"

He gave me a wry smile, reached under the stand, and brought out a plastic cover. "Five euros."

I dug into my pocket and handed him the money. I wrapped up Josie and put her back in my messenger bag.

The man gave us a five-minute rundown of how to steer the boat, and off we went. People spent more time learning to ride a bike than they did a boat in Capri.

The close-up view of Capri's sapphire-blue water was mesmerizing. It glittered—the way the sun hit the water made it look like a precious stone. As we came upon the Bay of Naples, Arlo pointed to colossal rock formations protruding out of the water and into the sky. "*Faraglioni*," he said. "These stacks you see have names here. That's Stella, Mezza, and"—he turned around, his hand loose on the steering wheel—"Scolopo."

We jetted past the famous rock formations until the boat sputtered to a stop. Arlo pointed above us. "That's where we're going."

I peered up to see a white villa on the edge of the mountain, and my eyes bulged out. "Arlo, buddy. No. First of all, no. Second, you're out of your mind."

"Beg pardon?"

"Why didn't we just drive up there?" I shouted, my anger rising up as I steadied myself, the boat pulling with each current. Who rents a boat when we could've just driven right up to the villa?

"You must learn to control your shouting." He tightened his shoelaces. "The front entrance has a locked gate, yes? Whereas, the backyard is wide open. My parents would've assumed no one would be stupid enough to go up the steps on the side of the mountain."

"Why didn't you just get the key to the gate? Or hop the gate?"

"Do you see a key on me, boy?"

"Norah! Didn't Norah give you a key?"

"You're going to learn a lot while on this trip, Knox. The first thing to learn is that my parents didn't trust anyone. Not even their own children. Norah doesn't have a key. Never did."

"Then how the heck did she expect us to get in there?"

He steadied himself. "I told her we had a way in, which we do. Now stop your moaning and groaning."

He whistled as he dropped the anchor to the bottom of the sea. It took several minutes before it finally hit the bottom, making me feel uneasy. Our boat was parked right up to the mountainside.

Arlo pointed above us. "Now, it's really very simple. There are stairs on the side of the mountain, you see?"

Sure enough, Arlo was right. Stone steps etched into the mountain like a timeless statue zigzagged their way up to the villa.

"You can follow them right up to the back porch." His tan skin looked even bronzer out on the ocean.

I steadied myself on the boat, the wind swaying it back and forth. "So what's to stop someone from breaking into their house?" I asked, dumbfounded.

He reached under the steering wheel and threw some rope at me and crossed his arms in front of his chest.

I turned around, holding the rope in my hands, and glanced at the stairs once more. Yes, those were stairs, but they ended about forty feet before touching the water.

"Arlo, do I look like a mountain climber to you? Please, can we just freaking take a car? A moped? Anything but this."

He rolled his eyes and tied the rope in a loop and swung it as hard as he could. The loop just barely grazed the bottom of the steps, so he threw it once more, and it hooked perfectly on the rail. He pulled down on it and stared at me with a stupid grin.

"Let me guess. Me first?"

He nodded. "Someone's gonna have to hoist my fat body up there."

I stifled a laugh and grabbed my bag. I prayed I wouldn't fall—not necessarily because of the fall itself but because of what the water would do to Josie.

Arlo gave me a boost. Climbing four stories up a rope wasn't easy on the hands, and it certainly didn't make me look inconspicuous. I took my time, putting one hand in front of the other. "How am I doing?" I yelled down.

"Fine, just fine. I'm coming in behind you." Arlo snatched the rope and began pulling himself up. He caught up to me fast, and before I knew it, we were two stories up. Minus how sore my muscles would be later, it wasn't too hard to climb the rope. It was like gym class all over again. Easy.

Until I looked down.

All in all, it was a rookie mistake. To be fair, I didn't even know I was afraid of heights until that exact moment.

My eyesight blurred before my hand slipped. "Arlo!" I yelled. The rope burned through my skin as I slid down into Arlo's face, sneakers first.

"Steady, steady," he said calmly, pushing my feet away from his face. "Knox, mind over matter, my boy." I could see his fist shaking in the air.

I shook my head, trying to literally scare the fear out of me. Finally, I held on tight and closed my eyes as I shimmied up the rope, one foot at a time.

"There ya go! Overcome it. That-a-boy."

Nausea swept over me, and I tried to subdue it. Before I knew it, I was gasping for air. "Arlo, we have to stop. Get my inhaler."

"Inhaler? Right, right. We'll get it when you're on the steps. Only a few yards to go."

I kept pulling myself up, the wicked hands tight on my lungs, squeezing and squeezing until there was barely any oxygen left. I was ready to just fall and let it be over. Until my hand hit metal. "Ow!" I opened my eyes and saw the stairs. I pulled myself up and considered kissing the dirty steps. "Arlo, come on! I'll help you up."

I grabbed onto his arm and helped him onto the steps, where we both sat down for a moment. Before either of us could say anything, my inhaler was in my mouth. After a couple puffs, I looked below to see the waves as they splashed against our boat, rocking it to and fro. To avoid hurling into the sea, I focused in front of me, forty feet high, where the Tyrrhenian Sea took over the world.

Arlo patted my shoulder. "You did it. Just took some motivation."

I narrowed my eyes. "I could've died."

With a pointed finger to the sky, he said, "But you didn't."

And so we began the trek up the mountain's steps. The farther we walked up the stairs, the stronger the wind blew. We carried on until we reached, as Arlo said, the back porch.

Completely and utterly wide open for the taking.

Their backyard wasn't so much a backyard as it was an Olympic-size pool overlooking the ocean. Expensive patio furniture and umbrellas lined the pool, and a stone pathway led us to the back door. I wondered how Arlo's parents had afforded all of this.

"Arlo," I said, "what did you say your parents did for a living?"

"Owned a small grocery store." Arlo walked past me with a determined smile on his face and crept up to the sliding back door. He waited for a moment, listening with his good ear. He didn't hear anyone (and why would he?).

To be perfectly honest, this entire hush-hush adventure was starting to get on my nerves. It seemed like a lot to do for so little payoff. Then again, what were we expecting to find?

Arlo put his hand on the handle and pulled. It was unlocked. Jehovah is Lord, the stupid door was unlocked.

He tiptoed in, and I followed.

The villa had a minimalist vibe with pricey modern statues and abstract art decorating the ivory walls. All the lights were off in the villa, but a lavish chandelier hung over the dining room table. From the living room, I could see the ocean. I wondered why I wasn't floating in it, enjoying the cool blanket of water on such a humid day. I approached a crystal vase, empty of any contents. I was afraid to touch anything. The villa reminded me of a museum.

Arlo headed toward the kitchen, where he opened the refrigerator door. I socked him in the arm. "What do you think you're doing?"

He looked at me like I was born yesterday. "I'm hungry. That was a work-out for an old man—all those stairs."

I studied our surroundings and saw a door across from the living room that had to lead to a study or office. "Maybe we should start there."

He nodded as he grabbed a bowl of leftover spaghetti. To my surprise, he reached for a drawer that had a fork in it—on the first try.

"Arlo, that spaghetti probably has mold in it. Throw it away."

He looked underneath the bowl, scrutinizing the noodles. "Nope. No mold." Then he shoveled more pasta into his mouth.

We headed to the study's door, and all I could hear was Arlo's slurping. I slowly turned the knob and opened the door. It creaked open.

I walked to the bay window first. Once I opened the curtains, the bright sun lit up the room. Books lined the walls, and a large oak desk sat in the middle. "Do you remember this room, Arlo?"

He scoffed. "Unfortunately, yes. I remember it was my father's study and we weren't to bother him."

I looked around the room and set down my bag. I pulled out Josie, placing her on a small end table. As I powered her up, I asked, "So what are we looking for exactly?"

"Clues, Watson."

I sighed. "Anything specific?"

Arlo stood still, closing his eyes, as if he were in a different place, or a different time. And I prayed he wasn't transforming right now, because I needed Arlo, not Eli or Todd.

"Well, to be honest, I don't think we're looking for anything specific, my boy. But we are looking to trigger some memories in my distorted old brain."

"Okay. That's a start."

"If we can trigger some memories, maybe it will help me connect a few more dots."

"Let's start looking then," I said.

And so we did. I was hoping if I toppled over enough books, one of them would be a secret lever for a secret entrance, Scooby-Doo style. Instead, we spent half an hour going through everything we could with no such luck.

As I moved my fingertips along every crevice, in search for anything hidden, I asked Arlo, "If this house, which is in Capri, belongs to your parents —and this house is clearly not cheap—then what exactly *did* your parents do for a living? And don't say they owned a grocery store, because there is no way a grocery store would afford this lifestyle."

He chuckled at that. "They *did* own a grocery store. Norah told you the truth about that. When I was very, very young, we lived in Sorrento. But we moved to Capri when I was a bit older, after my father won a settlement against the military for an injury. Rather a long and dull story. Anyway, we lived here in this big house on the ocean and swam in that gargantuan pool out there."

"What happened to their grocery store in Sorrento?"

"Oh, they still ran it. Just because they had money didn't mean they wanted to be bored all day. They'd take a ferry like we did and take care of the store. Then Norah took over."

"Hmm. So what'll happen to this house now?"

Rather than answering my question, Arlo dusted off his hands on his pants and said, "We've looked all over the study. Maybe we need to try a different room. Nothing is really triggering in here for me."

I nodded. "All right. Let's look in their bedroom then."

Arlo walked to the study door, and there was a subtle creak in the wood floor I hadn't noticed before.

"Arlo, stop!" So he did.

"What's the matter?"

"Move over." I got down on the floor, my jeans rubbing off the dust that had accumulated over the weeks. I spread my hands over the floor and moved them around until I felt it: slits in the floorboards. "Arlo, this is it. This has to open. Just like Scooby-Doo."

"What?"

"N-nothing. Uh, but this should open. See?"

He studied where my fingertips were and nodded. "I suppose you're right, my boy. But how? How do we open it?"

I studied the room, looking for anything I hadn't noticed before. I tried to wrack my hacker brain, trying to think of what I'd do if I didn't want anyone inside this opening. I went back to the shelves, running my hands over every little crevice once more.

"We've already done that. There's no secret lever or any such thing in this room."

I went to the desk and pushed it over with all my might. It toppled over on its side, and I used my phone's flashlight and my excited hands to find the answer. But there was nothing. I grimaced and then stood up.

"Don't worry," Arlo said. "We'll figure it out. If we have to hammer that thing to death, we'll open it up."

"Maybe the way to open it isn't in this room."

Arlo stroked his chin, contemplating the thought. "Well, I suppose, but—"

I raced out of the study and into the living room. I looked all over the place, knocking decorations over and pulling at this and that. "Is it moving?" I asked from the living room.

"No, my boy. It's not."

Feeling frustrated, I walked back into the study and just looked around, trying to take in the bigger picture. On the wall next to the study door, I noticed something. "Why would this one room need air conditioning?" I asked, pointing to the thermostat on the wall.

Arlo shrugged. "I honestly don't know. He was quite the control freak so maybe he wanted to control the air in his own study."

I walked to the thermostat. I knocked it around a bit, but nothing happened. Until I popped it open with my fingernail and exposed a keypad instead of the typical wires and knobs found in a thermostat. *Oh, glory.*

"My boy!" Arlo exclaimed, patting me on the back. "You did it!"

"Not yet. We don't know the code."

"That's why I hired you. I want you to break into it."

And the pressure was on.

Except, it wasn't really that hard the more I thought about it. In fact, it's what I'd call a soft hack. Most keypads have a default code that make it easy for police or firefighters to get into. I surmised that Arlo's father didn't know this, and I typed in 0911.

I received an ear-piercing beep and a pulsing red light.

"My, that's quite annoying," Arlo said. "How do you shut it off?"

"By typing in the right code, which I don't have, but I'm going to get." Whoever set up this little system sure knew what they were doing.

I ran to the desk, pushed it upright, and placed Josie on top of it. Pulling a chair up, I sat down and got to work. The name on the keypad was Secu-reIT. Since I didn't know the code, I'd have to create my own code for that keypad to unlock it. All I needed was to get on the WiFi, which was set to public, and then send command through SecureIT. Since I didn't have their login and couldn't do any phishing (on the count of, they were dead), I took a quick visit to the dark web and purchased a well-known program called UnlockIT. Within a few seconds, the program was up and running, and I pinpointed the location of the keypad I wanted the program to unlock. I typed in the command and my new code. I walked to the keypad and typed in 4312 and voila.

The secret door slid open just like that.

Arlo's hand met my shoulder and he patted it once more. "Excellent job! Just excellent. Now, let's see what this thing has in it."

We both knelt down on the ground and found . . . stairs. More freaking stairs.

"Oh, no way!" I said. "You are smoking crack if you think I'm walking down a flight of creepy stairs like that. Uh-uh."

"Have courage." Arlo rolled up his sleeves, swiped my phone, and turned on its flashlight. "Let's see what we can see."

He led the way, and I followed until we reached the last step. "So it's . . . a basement?"

"It is."

"A creepy hidden basement only accessible by a hidden keypad? I swear if we see Frankenstein's monster down here, I'm bouncin'."

"Shh." He shined the light around the basement.

"Arlo," I whispered.

"I know. It's empty."

CHAPTER 14

The Devil Herself

We stayed down in the basement for longer than I had intended, searching empty shelves and little crevices, looking for anything at all that might've been left here before everything was cleaned out. The dusty shelves hadn't seen fingerprints in months. It seemed like no one ever came down here. Strange, since Arlo's parents passed mere days ago.

It was unusual being in a basement again. Back when I was younger, my parents had a basement they used as their lab. Of course, they had their own lab at work, but they loved to bring work home. I used to swivel around in a chair as beakers clanked and strange concoctions boiled.

I backed away from a shelf, my body suddenly cold, and pointed my phone's flashlight on the ground. I saw something I hadn't noticed when we first walked in. I ran halfway up the stairs so I could get an aerial view.

"Arlo, move over." I gestured with my hand, as if pushing him myself.

"Huh?"

I motioned with the flashlight. "I want to see what's underneath you."

Arlo's head bent down, and below his tennis shoes was a large dark spot on the cement. His face turned grayer than his hair, and I snapped a few pictures from above with my phone. "What is it?" I asked.

He stooped to the ground and ran his fingers along the chilly cement, his fingers trembling as he did so. "It's a stain."

Noticing the faraway look on his face, I asked, "Do you know what the stain is from?"

He nodded but kept touching the cement, as if to wipe it all away. "It's . . ."

I carefully walked down the steps and studied the stain. Right in the center of the room was a Frisbee-size dark-brown stain, aged over the years. "Is it . . ." I trailed off, unsure of how to say it—afraid I might trigger something within Arlo. But wasn't I supposed to? Wasn't I supposed to help him remember everything?

"It's blood," he said, confirming my thoughts. "Least . . . it looks that way, doesn't it?"

I squeezed my eyes shut, trying to think. "Okay, Arlo. We don't have to do this if it's too much for you. We can come back."

He shook his head, still caressing the cement, as if touching it would transfer over the details of what happened. "No, I'm okay. I was prepared for this. That's what we're here for, right? Clues? Piece the puzzle together?"

I walked up to him and put my hand on his shoulder. "Do you remember anything? Do you remember this room or this stain?"

He absentmindedly stroked his hair. "I think so." He thumped his head twice, as if to knock the memories out of it. "But it's . . . hard to recall. It's like I can feel it, my boy, but nothing is clicking."

We couldn't leave this place without something—anything. And a decades-old stain wasn't going to cut it—if the stain actually had anything to do with Arlo in the first place.

"So do you think your parents took whatever was in here . . . out? I mean, clearly this place was used for something. Do you have any idea what it was used for?"

He shook his head. "I didn't even know we had a basement. There's just no telling what it was used for. Too bad we can't ask them," he said with a sigh.

We both sat down, feeling useless. Spiderwebs blanketed the corners of the basement, and the coolness of the day caressed my skin.

Arlo rested his feet on top of the table and leaned back, his head resting in the palms of his hands. "Maybe if I take a nap, I'll remember something about this place."

"I don't think a nap will work."

"Why can't you just use your hacker magic to find the person responsible?" Arlo asked, almost wistfully.

"Because I don't have a name, remember? If I had a name, it'd be a different story. How does no one know this woman's name?" I wanted to get out of this creepy basement. It was a good find, but it wasn't doing us any favors. This place was cleaned out. Nothing but a cryptic stain staring back at us. I suggested to Arlo that we go back up the stairs and—

"What was that noise?" Arlo perked up, and so did I.

"Arlo! I thought you said your parents were the only ones who lived here."

"They were. They sold it."

"Wait," I whispered. "This isn't their house anymore?" I hissed. "Is that why Norah didn't have a key?"

He hesitated. "Well, in a manner of speaking . . ."

I jumped out of my chair. "Arlo, you swore I wouldn't wind up in prison. If the feds find out I'm breaking into houses now, I'll—"

He put up his hands. "Slow down, my boy. We've got this handled. Just trust me."

I put my hands up in defense. "How? How do you have this handled? We don't even know who's here. It could be the owner."

"Calm down," he said with an eyeroll. "Just follow me."

"Fine."

Arlo led the way back up the stairs. Eyeing the plastic cover, I wrapped up Josie and shoved her in my bag. I grabbed the bowl and fork from Arlo's spaghetti, which he was going to leave in the study had I not grabbed it.

As we entered the living room, we saw a short man. He did not look happy to see us. I discreetly set the bowl and fork down on an end table by the door.

"Who are you?" he asked, reaching for what I hoped was his cell phone. "You're not supposed to be here."

Arlo pointed back to the study. "Well, it's a good thing we got here in time, isn't it?"

"What?" the man said, visibly shocked.

"I want to know how it passed inspection. That's what I want to know."

The man shook his head. "What do you mean? *What* passed inspection?"

"You just purchased this house, right?" Arlo asked.

The man nodded. "Not for me, but for my client."

"Well, you better tell your client that you've got an infestation of roaches."

The man's eyes bulged out, and mine followed suit. *What is he doing?* "No! That can't be right. We had this place combed to death for insects. Are you sure?"

"Do I look like I'm fooling around? They're in the walls, and it's going to take some work to kill them off. At this rate, they might as well pick up the house itself and take it off that cliff." He gestured to the cliff, and the man's fear-stricken eyes followed.

The rotund man suddenly pulled at his collar. "Oh, this is bad. This is so bad. My client's going to kill me."

"Now, now. We can help you get rid of these vermin. Tomorrow?"

He pulled out his smartphone, probably looking at this calendar. "Tomorrow morning, maybe by eight. That's the earliest I can be here. But you swear you can get rid of them?"

"Of course. Every last one."

He vehemently shook his head. "Good, good. They just all have to be gone. No trace of them, or my client will flip."

Arlo stuffed the paper in his back pocket after having jotted down the date and time. Or scribbled for all I knew. He patted the man on the shoulder and said, "Don't worry. We'll get you all taken care of."

But we both knew there would be no one here tomorrow morning to kill the imaginary roaches.

We started to walk away, and I couldn't believe we actually got away with it. That was some fast thinking for an old man. My hand was on the back door and as I pushed to slide it open, I heard, "Wait."

We both held very, very still.

Without turning to look at him, Arlo said, "Something the matter?"

"Why are you going through the back door?"

I let out a big breath. "Oh, just to check the outside on our way out. Make sure there aren't any . . . nests?"

Oh, brother. Do roaches even have nests?

"We'll hurry!" Arlo said as he followed me.

The man must've peered into the study to see the basement, because the next thing he said was the last thing we wanted to hear. "Stop!"

Arlo gave me an incredulous look. "You didn't close up the trap door?"

"Go! Go!" I yelled, taking off through the back door, running as fast as my scrawny legs could carry me.

Arlo was right on my heels. "You're over your fear of heights, yes?"

"No! Yes? I don't know!" I ran as fast as I could, out the sliding door and past the glimmering pool, approaching the stairs that led to the water below. I skidded to a stop, the dirt clouding around us.

"No time, my boy." Arlo grabbed my shoulders and right before the idiot pushed me off a forty-foot cliff, he said, "Hold your breath!"

––––––––––

I held it all right. Right as I plunged into the water. When I came up for air, I heard the splash next to me. Then I heard gunshots.

"Hurry!" Arlo said. "He seems a little vexed!"

"Ya think?" I paddled as fast as I could and pulled myself up into the boat. What I wouldn't give to be my gross, unshowered self right now. I started reeling in the anchor as Arlo turned on the engine. No matter how fast I reeled, the anchor was taking a lifetime to reach me.

"*Fretta! Fretta!*" Arlo shouted.

"Yelling at me in Italian is not going to make me go faster!"

I heard another gunshot right as the anchor made its way to the surface. "Go, go, go!" I shouted. Arlo sped off toward the west side of the mountain, and I promptly vomited into the most beautiful ocean I had ever seen.

After wiping the chunks from off my lips and realizing we were far, far away from that maniac, I actually felt happy. We had gotten away without any real damage. I pulled Josie out of the plastic, and sure enough, she was dry. As we sailed back to the dock, I was relieved to have never met a bullet, the police, or Michael the shark.

I felt a firm hand on my shoulder, but the look on Arlo's face was anything but stern. "Knox, good job."

I scowled. "We have no information! You literally pushed me off a cliff, Arlo. *And* to top it all off, we just got shot at."

"Thankfully, he missed." He winked. "And besides, I saved your life."

I narrowed my eyes. "How did you *save* my life?"

"By throwing you off a cliff. Now quit your fussin' and help me navigate."

————————

My parents were passionate about their work. Obsessed, if I'm being honest—an attribute I borrowed from them in my own work. When they found out they'd be in charge of curing the Raven Virus, they jumped up and down together like little kids, holding each other's hands as they celebrated. That was the happiest I had ever seen them, and even as a kid, I was so proud of them.

I wanted what they had.

I knew their hard work would one day pay off. What I didn't know was that it would all disappear with nothing to show for it but a tombstone with a clichéd epitaph and a legacy built on infamy.

But maybe I could change that. I couldn't pay for my parents' sins, but maybe I could redeem our family name somehow. Maybe, just maybe, I could find whoever did this to Arlo, put his mind at ease, and stop this woman from doing it to more people.

Arlo and I dried off on the ferry. I would officially smell like a fish for the rest of the day.

"I remember."

I peered up at him. "You remember who did this to you?"

"No, no." He shook his head. "I remember the rest of the story."

"Oh, you mean the story about how you knew my parents and they administered a life-changing drug to your father? That story?" I was a little irritated to say the least. My clothes were soaked, I was shot at, and I was starving.

"Do you want to hear it or not?" He sat back, arms folded.

I sighed. "Yeah, of course I do. You just now remembered? Out of nowhere?"

He tapped his head. "Something about being at my old house, I suppose. It sparked some memories."

"Good. Then . . . it was worth it. Tell me the rest of the story, Arlo."

He leaned forward and folded his hands in front of him. "Your parents were brilliant, you know that?"

I toyed with a string at the end of my shirt. "So I've been told."

"Don't get smart with me," he scolded. "They *were* brilliant. I knew even as a young man that they would change the world one day. They did this . . . woman's dirty work, and I don't know why. But the fact of the matter is, they worked for the devil. When they came to our home that day, they were quiet, kind, comforting. In fact, it was at that very house on the cliff in Capri. That's where I met them.

"They were gentle with my father. All he had to do was drink that nasty-looking green stuff, and they'd run a few tests, and he'd be a normal man again. So I was around them for a few days while they monitored his progress. At first, they politely declined our invitation to eat lunch with us or have a cup of coffee. My mother insisted, and you'd be crazy to tell her no."

"Was she a lot like Norah?" I asked.

"She was graceful like Norah. Weird like Norah. But she was determined. Norah tends to accept whatever life brings—whatever the universe offers. Not my mother. No, no. She was a fighter."

I could see the marina up ahead. The ferry was close (and those 307 steps), but I didn't want anything to interrupt this conclusion. I had traveled so far and still had so few answers.

"Anyway, your parents finally relented and had lunch with us. Your mother would laugh at every nerdy joke your father told. Jokes I could never understand—but she laughed. They were beautiful together."

"I'm not trying to change the subject," I said, "but it had never occurred to me to ask: if this woman created this drug to cure epilepsy, why didn't she just sell it and make billions of dollars?"

"At that time, she had more money than she knew what to do with. She didn't want money. She wanted *favors*, remember? She wanted power. I had mentioned the favor that my family would one day have to owe to her."

I had wrapped the loose string from my shirt so tightly around my finger that my skin was turning a different color. I unraveled it, waiting for the conclusion to his story as the ferry anchored.

"My mother and father had no choice but to do one thing for that vile woman. We thought it would be months, years down the road before she'd ask. But she came to our home one evening, just days after the drug had eased my dad of his seizures. She was wearing a red dress, and I thought she truly looked like the devil. She sat on our couch and put a photo of little Norah on the coffee table. It was a photo taken from far away, from the street. It was a zoomed-in shot of Norah in her bedroom, playing with her dolls."

Arlo cleared his throat, and the bell whistled, signaling for us to deboard. I put up my hand to stop him from standing up. "Finish the story."

"She looked at my parents and said, 'You owe me a favor, don't you? You have seventy-two hours to make your decision.' Of course, as I said, I was the favor. The favor was that my parents had to let that woman experiment on me. I remember she got up from the couch and pulled her jacket over that horrible red dress. 'Oh,' she said, 'if you don't do it, I will come to your house and walk up those steps to Norah's bedroom, right there on the left. And while she sleeps soundly, cuddling her favorite doll—Bella, isn't it?—I will take the sharpest of knives and cut her from her little head to her little toes until she is unrecognizable.'"

CHAPTER 15

Trigger

I walked off the ferry and began my ascent up the 307 steps that led back to Ibisco. Fog covered my sunglasses, and I was suddenly reminded of Florida's humidity. I didn't think I could possibly miss that place, but strangely enough, I did. Maybe a boring life wasn't so bad, after all.

I couldn't get the image of little Norah out of my mind. Knowing that she wasn't *really* alone in her room when they snapped the photo. Arlo couldn't muster much more after that, so I didn't push it and didn't want to make him grumpy—certainly not grumpy enough to trigger an alter.

When we got back to Ibisco, Norah greeted us at the door and called out to Arlo, "You need a haircut."

"Woman, I don't need a haircut." He waved her off, walking past her. "I'm exhausted and I just want to go to bed."

She folded her slender arms. "You look unkempt."

Arlo smirked. "That's the look I was going for."

Norah rolled her eyes. "Well, aren't you two going to tell me what happened at Mom and Dad's?"

Arlo and I both stared at each other, but neither said a word.

She grimaced. "You've been gone all day long at their home, and you have nothing to tell me?"

"Actually, yes," I finally said. "Your parents' house is sold, which *someone* didn't tell me about until it was too late. Fun fact for ya there. Then, since we were hoping to trigger some memories about the woman who administered the drug, we got lucky and Arlo *did* remember some helpful details."

"We're going to discuss the fact that their house is sold at a different time, but for now, these things Arlo remembered? They'll help you get closer to finding who did this?"

I nodded. "That's right."

"Good, good. Well, you have plenty of time then. Arlo, about your hair . . ."

I left them to bicker and went to my room and locked the door. And there was Jessa sitting on my bed again. If this trip started with gunshots but ended with Jessa waiting for me, then I guess it wasn't so bad after all.

"You have *got* to stop doing that." I set plastic-covered Josie on the bed and walked to the chest of drawers, rummaging through them for a clean T-shirt. "So I went to your grandparents' house today. Pretty sweet place."

"In Capri? Yeah, so I've heard."

"You've never been?" I asked, closing a drawer.

She picked up Josie and opened her. "No. Mom didn't have the best relationship with them. This is such a nice laptop." She stroked the stickers I had on the top and stopped at one with a budding white flower. "A flower?" she asked. "No guys I know ever have flower stickers on . . . well, actually, I don't know any guys who have stickers on anything, really."

I blushed. "Oh, yeah. That's . . . a plant, really. I mean, it blossoms, but uh . . ."

She gave me a quizzical look. "What's it called?"

I gulped. "*Cerbera odollam.*"

"Hm. Cool name."

"Speaking of names," I said, slowly taking Josie from off the bed. "I named my laptop Josie."

She giggled. "Josie? I like that. I don't have anything important enough to name."

"Well, we'll just have to find you something to name then." I ran my hands through my hair. "I got shot at today."

"You did?" she asked excitedly. I wondered if she actually was worried or if she wanted to see a gunshot wound.

"No, no. Just shot *at*. No bullet wounds to show off, sadly."

Her excitement deflated. "Oh."

"We don't have a lot of information yet. But we will." I sat down on the bed next to her, apologizing for sitting on her skirt. After she pulled it out from under me, she reached up to my face, and for a moment, I thought she was going to pull me toward her. But her fingertips grazed my hair instead and pulled out a teeny tiny seashell.

"Wh—why is there a seashell in your hair? Who shot at you—Poseidon?"

"No. And he doesn't shoot people—he'd probably harpoon me to death, maybe."

She elbowed me, and I returned the favor.

"So now what?"

"Um, I guess we keep trying and researching until something triggers in Arlo's brain. We need a name, and I need to find her. That's why I'm here."

"Well, are you all right?" she asked.

I looked into her violet eyes and smiled. "I'm all right now."

––––––––––

Downstairs in the living room, Arlo sat with a large black towel covering his neck down. Norah held scissors in her hands as she circled him like a shark.

"Talked you into it, huh?" I teased, plopping down on the clawfoot couch.

"Yeah, yeah." He gave me the stink eye. "No need to torture me anymore."

"*Silenzio!*" Norah said, lightly tapping him on the head with her scissors. "You need a haircut. You look like a homeless person."

Jessa had ditched the flowy skirt and was pulling on her running shoes. I've never seen anyone exercise so much. It was exhausting just to watch her.

As less and less hair covered Arlo's head, I noticed a strange circular scar above his left ear.

"Hey, Arlo," I said, pointing. "How'd you get that scar?"

"What scar?" he asked, twiddling his thumbs. "Where?"

"Up above your ear."

He reached for his right ear and felt around.

"No, other ear."

His fingertips made contact with the raised scar, and I thought for a moment I saw them tremble. "Oh. I'm not sure. Can't recall. Just something from childhood, I suppose." But the confused look on his face said otherwise.

"Hmm." I made a mental note of the scar. I had quite a few scars from stupid childhood incidents, and I always knew when I got them and how. It was strange to forget such an odd scar like that.

"So tell me more about Mom and Dad's mysterious basement," Norah said, snipping at Arlo's hair.

Arlo continued, "Everything was fine until some man showed up and crashed the party. They had good spaghetti."

Norah swept off loose hairs from Arlo's shoulders and then went back to trimming. "A man?"

"Yeah, that was a nice surprise, seeing as how we weren't supposed to be there." I glared at Arlo.

Norah bopped Arlo on the head once more. "You shouldn't put your . . . employee in danger like that."

Arlo rubbed his head. "He was perfectly fine. And he's being paid well."

"Threw me off a cliff," I muttered.

"So now what?" Norah asked. "How will you find this woman if you have no clues?"

"That's the rub, I guess." I grabbed a broom and started helping sweep up Arlo's hair. "I'm going to keep talking things out with Arlo to see if anything else gets triggered."

"Well, it's been fun," Jessa said, checking her wristwatch and setting a timer. "But I need to go for a run."

"Bye, darling," Norah said. "Stay in lighted areas."

She bolted out the door, her steps fading the faster she ran.

"Oh yeah, did he mention we got shot at?" I said, shaking out Arlo's hair into the trash can.

Norah stopped snipping. "Do you have any bullet wounds?" Her eyes beamed with excitement, and it was like I was looking right at Jessa.

"Uh. No. Sorry to disappoint you."

She shrugged. "Well, maybe next time," she said with a wink.

The next morning was blurry. My eyes hurt from lack of sleep, and I don't remember that Arlo ever came into the room. I pulled on a pair of jeans and brushed my teeth before meandering downstairs. Everyone was gone for the day, according to a note that was left for me. Arlo had gone with Norah to see the grocery store, and I assumed Jessa had a tour today. I left a note on top of theirs.

Going to explore. Will be back by evening.

—Knox

I decided to enjoy the solitude. Hopefully, some quiet time that didn't include creepy basements, gunfire, or jumping off cliffs. I needed to be away from people and try to piece together this mess. Maybe doing something fun would help me concentrate.

Pompeii was just a forty-five-minute drive away. I had wanted to see it for years now, so I called for a cab and headed to the ruins.

As I entered the ancient town, I rolled up my sleeves and put on my sunglasses. I knew I needed a tour guide, so I went to the booth to see if there were any available. Imagine my surprise when I heard, "Well, hello, Knox."

Jessa beamed at me, and I couldn't help but smile back. She wore a tight polo with the tour guide company's logo on it. Her brown hair was pulled away from her face. "*This* is where you work?" I asked.

She nodded. "I work all over, but they needed extra help today in Pompeii, so here I am." Her violet eyes mesmerized me, and I wanted to swim in them. Her olive skin beckoned to be caressed, but I wasn't here for that. I had to try to stay focused. "You don't need a tour guide, do you?"

"Actually, that's exactly what I need."

"Lucky for you, I'm available." She grabbed a pamphlet with a map on it and handed it to me. "You ready?"

I said yes and followed Jessa down the trail at the beginning of our tour.

We stopped under a tree for some shade. "I get so sweaty on these tours," she said, laughing. "I figured some shade wouldn't hurt." She wiped her brow with the back of her hand. "Now, over there is a type of oven they used to bake bread. See how the flour would pour out onto the counter? We even have a perfectly preserved loaf of bread from before the volcano."

Italians were proud of their history. And I saw it in her eyes that Jessa not only loved telling tourists about the city of Pompeii but also wished she could've lived to see it in its glory days. Pompeii had an amphitheater, an ornate water system, and even a solution to sewage. There were stores and gorgeous homes for the wealthy.

Jessa stopped under a tree to show me the mosaics. "As you can see, sometimes there will be empty spots here in these homes, where mosaics were. Many of them are now in the museum on display. But isn't this one beautiful?" She must have seen the wonder in my eyes because she asked, "Amazing that one act of God could eliminate an entire thriving city, hmm?"

I nodded. "I can't believe how intact it still is. I wonder what it must've been like around here when the volcano erupted."

"Chaotic. Terrifying." She whispered the last word. "Women screaming, looking for their children. Just absolute terror." Suddenly, I wasn't just talking to my new friend; I was talking to a living, breathing piece of history. She was so convincing that I thought perhaps she had been there during Mount Vesuvius's eruption, long, long ago. She was radiant even when she was sad for people she had never met. "Why do you think the volcano erupted?"

"Why?" I shrugged. "Just a natural disaster."

Little beads of sweat slid down her olive cheeks. "Just a natural disaster?" She leaned in. "Do you want to know what I think?"

I laughed. "Of course I do."

She pointed up to the sky. "I think it was God's revenge."

I stifled a laugh. "What? What do you mean?"

"Let me show you something." She walked a few yards until we were back on the main street, where shops and cafes once stood. On our right was a small building with frescoes lining the top of the walls. Erotic ones at that. There were four, maybe five, rooms with concrete slabs for sleeping.

"What is this place?" I asked, glancing at the ceiling.

"This is what you would call a brothel. You see up there?" She pointed to the ceiling, bringing my attention back to the erotic images. "A man, perhaps a traveler, would walk in, point to which sexual act he wanted, and head into this room here with a woman of his choice."

I blushed at having heard Jessa say something like that to me. "That's . . . well, that's pretty gross."

"That was only the beginning of Pompeii's immorality. And I believe God had had enough. He allowed Vesuvius to swallow them whole. Most historians point to the volcano as the villain. But don't you see? Vesuvius wasn't the villain, and neither was God. The only villain in Pompeii's history was its people. They brought this on themselves."

"But look how many villains there are in the world today," I countered. "They don't always get their just desserts. Some of them still walk the earth, hurting and killing people—just like the woman who ruined your uncle's life. Why won't God take his vengeance on them?"

Since their deaths, my parents had been known as villains. Always and still to this day. They were not heroes for creating NovaVita—they were villains because of their refusing to offer it to those who needed it, to those who were dying. A volcano didn't swallow them whole, but the explosion's flames enveloped them. Maybe the explosion was the earth's way of getting rid of bad people. Maybe God took vengeance on them. And maybe I'll just never know.

She stood next to me, looking up at the paintings. "The lifelong question. Why do bad things happen to good people?" She brought her water bottle to her lips, taking a long chug. "I'm certain that karma, whether you believe in it or not or call it by a different name, finds its way to every bad person on earth. We just might not see it."

My eyes caught hers. "Yeah, maybe you're right."

"Of course I am." She winked. "Now, let's go to the museum so you can get a discount on the souvenirs and buy me a snack."

———————

When my parents knew they had found the cure to the Raven Virus, they cried uncontrollably. I had never seen anything like it. They sobbed and laughed and embraced. Benjamin and Athena Kevel were the most famous people in the world.

Until they decided not to share NovaVita with those who needed it. That's when they became villains.

After the media got wind of their plan, it was only a few hours before the threats came in and just a few days before the protests started. I had to move out of my childhood bedroom and move in with Aunt Jane so I could be safe. My parents stayed in their lab, unrelenting, untouchable.

I was with Aunt Jane when the explosion happened, watching it live. She went berserk, yet for some reason, I stayed still. Calm. Expressionless. I went into shock. My body jolted back and forth as my aunt shook me, trying desperately to wake me from my trance.

I never could forget that moment. Suffocating on my own fear. Drowning. Dying.

They said the explosion was so hot, so intense, that it melted absolutely everything. Nothing could be saved.

So sometimes, when I really need help, when I'm feeling stuck, I talk to them. I'd like to think that maybe they hear me. And even if they don't, it makes me feel better.

On the taxi ride home from Pompeii, I talked to them. Not audibly, of course. I didn't want to startle the driver or Jessa. But I told them how I felt. How I missed them and how I was worried I couldn't find this woman for Arlo. I told my parents that no matter what everyone said, I didn't think they were villains.

Maybe they weren't the bad guys after all.

The taxi driver made his way to Ibisco. I tipped him generously, and when I walked through the door, Norah was already waiting for Jessa and me.

"Norah, look who I bumped into—"

"Knox, darling, it's best you probably sit down." Norah was more somber than usual. Her tight black dress clung to her slender frame, hugging what curves it could find.

I plopped onto the chair. "What's up?"

"Arlo's gone."

My heart skipped a beat as I realized it was probably my fault—from triggering him. "Where did he go?"

"Well," Norah said, "he's kind of still around."

"Who is it? Eli? Todd?"

"Actually," Norah said. "It's Dean."

CHAPTER 16

Meeting Dean

As I sat across from Norah, my body grew stiff. No matter what I did, nothing could be accomplished. Nothing could get done because Arlo's alters were always one step ahead of me.

"There are a few things you need to understand about Dean," Norah began. The lights were dimmed in the living room, and all I could hear was the faint *drip-drip-drip* of the leaky faucet in the kitchen and the *thud-thud-thud* of my skittish heart.

"Okay, go ahead," I said, mentally preparing myself for an alter I had never heard of—heh, didn't even know existed until now.

"He's not like the others." Her hands were folded in her lap, and she was surprisingly pleasant for someone who sounded like she was telling a ghost story. "He is violent, Knox. I know you don't want to hear that about Arlo, but I remember. I remember what it was like."

An evil Arlo? I thought.

"While some alters like this hurt people without realizing it, he harms others because . . ." When she trailed off, her mind left the room for a moment. She was somewhere else, somewhere dark. All alone.

"Because what?" I asked.

She shook herself out of the trance, and her eyes lifted to mine. I hadn't noticed until now that they were green—a bright green just like my mom's. "Because he enjoys it."

"*Enjoys* it?"

"This version of Arlo"—she shook her head—"every bad thought and memory that Arlo has comes out in Dean. He won't listen to reason. I have to find him, restrain him, and wait it out." Norah's leg began to shake—a nervous habit? Her dainty hands bobbed up and down to match the rhythm of her legs.

I rubbed my forehead. "When did this happen?"

"About an hour ago. I knew it was him because . . ." She trailed off once more.

"Because?"

"His eyes are different when he's Dean. I know it's been years, but I'll never forget those eyes. There's just something about them."

My hands grew clammy. "Back when I first met you, you said Eli wasn't the worst of the alters. Is this what you meant?"

She nodded. "Yes. I just didn't think it'd happen here. It's been so long since I've been around Arlo that I . . . I guess I got so caught up in seeing him again that I disregarded the bad memories."

"Mom," Jessa said, joining our conversation. "You knew he had this . . . violent alter, and you let him stay here?"

Norah winced. "I'm sorry, darling. Like I said, I just hadn't seen him in so long. This was a good thing for me to see him, for you to meet your uncle. I didn't think Dean would show up. Honestly. I thought it was a thing of the past, long forgotten. I was wrong."

"Well, he's here now and we need to deal with it. Right? And you don't have to go alone. We'll go together. Where is he?"

"Absolutely not." Norah pointed to us both. "You're not coming."

"Why not?" I asked. "If you say he's violent, then you shouldn't go alone."

Jessa glanced at her mother. "He's right, Mom. And this morning, he had said he was going to see his parents."

"Like, their graves?" I asked.

She nodded. "That's right. But that was Arlo talking at the time, not Dean."

"Okay, then I'll go there." I got up from the couch. "Hang on." I ran upstairs to grab my inhaler from my drawer. When I came back down, I asked Norah: "If he was Arlo earlier today, then how do you know it's Dean out there right now?"

She was gripping the armrest so hard her knuckles turned white. "He turned into Dean not too long before you got here. He was in the kitchen, we were chatting, everything was fine. I left to use the bathroom, and when I came back, it was Dean. He said in a strange voice, 'If you follow me, I will hurt you.' So I obeyed. I let him leave the house. I couldn't possibly overpower him."

"Where is it? The cemetery?"

"Wait," Norah whispered. "We need to protect ourselves just in case. Take this." She got up from her chair and went to the china cabinet where she opened a small drawer. She turned around, and I felt the cold metal hit my hands. I nearly dropped the weapon on the ground.

"Are you nuts? I'm not going to shoot Arlo! Er, Dean. No one. I'm not shooting anyone." I shoved the handgun back into her palm, but she wasn't having any of that.

Norah pulled me close and brought my face to hers. Her long fingernails dug into my skin, but her eyes begged me to stay calm. "He's dangerous. This isn't Arlo anymore, Knox. He's someone else. Someone *bad*. Whatever that woman did to him . . . to make him become Dean . . . it's really bad, okay? We have to be prepared. We can't just leave him out there."

I had to find Arlo, but I certainly wasn't going to shoot him. My parents were scientists, so I had seen some bizarre stuff before. I could handle it. I grabbed my hat and held the gun in my hand. "Is it loaded?"

She cocked an eyebrow, as if to say, "Really?"

"Well, wait. Why can't you do it if we have to . . . stop him?" I asked.

She grabbed her jacket off the coat rack and put it on. "I'm a terrible shot. I have shaky hands."

I checked to make sure the safety was on before tucking the .40 into my jeans and then pulling my hat down low. "You're not wearing that, are you?" I asked Norah.

She looked down, holding the hem of her sable dress in her hands. "What's wrong with it?"

"Well, nothing. Except, you want to go capture Dean in a cemetery and you're wearing a long dress."

She sashayed past me and said, "I don't need a man to tell me what I can and can't do in a dress."

———————

On the way to the Jensons' graves, I was reminded of my own parents' graves. I wondered if the daisies I had planted had blossomed or wilted. That day seemed like a hundred years ago, yet it had been only mere days.

"You'd think my memory would be fuzzy after all these years," Norah began, "and maybe it still is, but I remember the first time I met Dean very clearly."

"You actually remember that?" Jessa asked. It was at this moment that I wondered, *Did Norah ever tell her daughter about the uncle who lived in America? About their lives together before he was sent away?*

"Yes, *bella*. I do. We were young, of course. It was a typical day. Nothing out of the ordinary, except for coming to grips with the new version . . . er, versions . . . of my brother. Anyway, I distinctly remember playing with my dolls in the living room. Mama was cooking dinner. It smelled divine. She always was an exceptional cook. Arlo came in—or at least we thought it was him—and he walked straight into the kitchen from the front door and grabbed Mama's fresh vegetables from the store and began to throw them everywhere. It was like he was having a temper tantrum. Then, once out of produce, he slammed his fist into the wall. I couldn't believe he didn't break his knuckles, but he sure broke that wall. Of course, Mama was screaming at him to stop, asking, 'What is wrong with you, Arlo?' Looking back, I always wondered if she thought it was strange to ask that question. We all knew what was wrong. Then Arlo looked at her, his fists clenched, and said, 'I'm not Arlo! I'm Dean.' By then, I was cowering with my dolls behind the couch, hoping he would leave. My own brother! I wanted him to leave because I was scared of him."

I chewed on my lip. "What did your mother do when he told her to call him Dean?"

"She didn't hesitate. She said, 'Okay, Dean. It's nice to meet you. Are you hungry?' But he only laughed, throwing his head back. He laughed all the way out of the house, and we didn't see him for days."

"For days?" Jessa asked, tilting her head. "Where did he go?"

Norah shrugged. "To this day, we don't know. He just came back to the house one day, and he was Arlo again. Mama asked if he remembered Dean. He knew of no such thing."

I rested my head in my palms, trying to make sense of this. Trying to understand how I would be able to get us out of this mess—a mess I didn't even create.

"Knox," Norah said from the driver's side, "are you okay?"

"Am I *okay?*" I echoed. "Well, let's see. I'm in a foreign country on a job that has yet to be completed, headed to a cemetery to hunt down the evil version of my employer. Yes, of course I'm fine."

Norah slammed on the brakes and we all jolted forward. She threw the car into park and turned around to face me. "Knox, we do not know each other well enough for you to talk to me like that. I'm just as scared as you are, perhaps even more so because he is my brother. No one forced you to travel here and take on this job. You could've said no when Arlo told you about his disorder. But you're here. You're here with us, and we need your help, not your scorn. Can you handle this? Can you?"

My cheeks burned with Norah's lashing out, especially with Jessa's hearing every word. But I had it coming. I was pissed. I was pissed that this job was turning into a failure, that we kept getting sidelined by something Arlo had zero control over. I had to put my emotions aside and deal with Dean.

I rubbed the back of my neck. "I'm really sorry, Norah. And you too, Jessa. I'm here and I'll help. I promise."

Norah gave me a curt nod and put the car back into drive. "Good. Because I didn't want to have to kick your butt out of the car and onto the street. I might feel bad about it later." She gave me a wink through the rearview mirror, and we turned into the cemetery.

———————

We found Dean not by his parents' tombstone but a few yards across from it, leaning against an oak tree. He tinkered with a bottle of bourbon, swishing its contents back and forth. He wore slacks, a wrinkled button-up, and a gaudy watch. I wasn't looking at the man I had gone on an adventure with or the man who pushed me off a cliff into the sea. I was staring into soulless eyes that belonged to a monster. Norah was right. His eyes—you don't forget them.

It was somehow fitting to see Norah in a cemetery. The fog licked at the edges of her dress, making her ghostly pale body look as if it floated around the tombstone. Jessa and I followed behind her.

The first time I heard Dean's voice, it was a howl of laughter. "Look who brought the cavalry," he said, laughing and sputtering. "You're just in time. You see, I was feeling bored and poor dead Mom and Dad didn't have much to say to me." He brought the bottle to his mouth, smirking before he took a hard chug, the bourbon running down his chin to his neck.

"Dean, I'm not afraid of you," Norah said. Her voice was even, stern. "I don't know why you're here right now or what triggered it, but it's time to bring Arlo back. Tell Arlo to come out."

He pushed himself off the tree, taking a broad stride in front of us. His red-rimmed eyes caught mine for a brief moment. "Oh, of course, of course." He swaggered left and right, zigzagging toward us. "Absolutely. I don't mean any harm, *sis*. Only . . ." He walked toward Jessa and me, firmly gripping the bottle's neck. He was just a few feet away from Jessa, and I could smell the alcohol on him—had he drenched in it? It nauseated me. And it always had. I don't really know why because no one in my family drank, and I never went through that teenage phase of drinking on the beach with friends. "There is just one other thing I need to do before Arlo comes back. You don't mind, do you?"

"Okay, we'll help you do it," Norah said, giving him a reassuring smile.

Dean lifted up his hands in agreement. "As you wish." In an instant, his hand shot out and grabbed Jessa by the collar of her shirt as he broke the bottle on a tombstone. Shattered glass struck my jeans, and I shouted at him, but it was too late. He held the jagged bottle to Jessa's neck, pressing deep into her skin.

"Dean, no!" Norah screamed, the tears making their way down her ashen cheeks. "Let go of her, I swear to God. She hasn't done anything. Take me. Take me!"

He chuckled, like it was a silly game—like he was enjoying it. Like he was *winning*. "I promise you, Norah: if you take one more step, I'll kill her."

The way he talked was nothing like the monster I had envisioned. Each word was spoken as casually as if he were speaking to an old friend.

"Mom! Help! Please!" Jessa's cries were the most terrible sound I had ever heard. Her hands held onto Dean's arm, her nails puncturing his skin.

"Jessa, it's going to be okay." Weeping turned into sobbing as Norah's shoulders quaked. "I won't let anything happen, darling. Tell me what you want, Dean. I'll do it. You don't really want to hurt your niece. Just talk to me."

Sweat glistened on his brow and his eyes, I could've sworn, were as dark as Norah's dress. "My niece?" he spat, a string of saliva on his chin. "I don't have a niece. Arlo has a niece. Now tell me something, Norah."

"I'll tell you whatever you want to know." Norah was pleading, begging. Seeing this strong woman entreat such an evil version of Arlo was more than I needed. I reached behind my back and felt the metal handle.

But that wasn't the only thing I felt. My chest heaved up and down, constricting me every second.

"Why did they save you and not me?" he asked, his voice more somber somehow, different.

Norah's head bent down, and she wiped the snot from her nose. "Who? What do you mean?"

Jessa whimpered, so Dean pushed the bottle further into her throat. Tiny drops of blood trickled down her flesh, and I tried to swallow the bile that made its way up my throat. "That woman got to experiment on me and ruin my life solely because she threatened to cut you up a little bit. Mom and Dad chose you over me. They let her do this to me." He narrowed his eyes.

"Why do you think that is?" He feigned surprise, bringing his hand to his mouth, gasping. This was all just a sick, twisted play, and he was the star, the cemetery his stage. "I guess they just loved you more, didn't they? They didn't care that that woman experimented on me like an animal, as long as you were nice and safe. They could've sent *you* off somewhere to live. Like, I don't know, America. Like they did to *me*." He shouted the last word and threw the bottle across the cemetery. He held Jessa in a headlock, her blood oozing down his arm.

Now was my chance.

Norah stood up straight, wiping the tears from her eyes. "I can't change their decision. What happened happened. It doesn't change anything. They were scared. What else were they supposed to do? How could they have known what that woman was going to do to you, Arlo?"

Spittle built up in the corner of his mouth. "Don't call me that!" he yelled. "That's not my name. That's not my name!" He whined when he said this, and it was like watching a tired two-year-old holding a bottle of liquor. I expected him to stomp his feet on the ground and throw a hissy fit. "They chose you over me! They didn't give a crap about me, and you know it."

Norah threw up her hands. "Fine! Fine then. Let's say that's true, Dean. What do you want me to do about it? What will hurting Jessa do to fix it? Tell me."

"*Balance*." He took his time enunciating the word. "Why not take this opportunity to balance out the world?"

I tightened my grip on the gun, praying that physics wouldn't betray me. Slowly, I pulled it out of my jeans and ensured Dean's eyes were solely focused on Norah. When I was sure he didn't notice where my hand had landed, I hurled the gun right at Dean's head, knocking him out before he had time to flinch. He fell to the grass—barely missing a tombstone—and Jessa fell with him.

I had just knocked out my boss. Er, a version of him.

Norah ran to her daughter and we were all on the ground, surrounded by death, crying and shivering. Everyone, except for Arlo, who might have suffered a concussion.

Jessa sat up and looked at us without saying a word, her trembling hand touching the cuts. Blood covered her sun-kissed skin.

Norah held her daughter close, squeezing tight. She ripped the hem of her dress and took the cloth to soak up the blood on Jessa's neck. I guess the dress did come in handy after all.

"Why didn't you use the gun?" Norah shouted, flames in her eyes.

"I did!"

"*Idiota!* You threw it! That's not using it."

"I wasn't going to *kill* him." Then I looked at the blood on Jessa's neck and realized I would've had to, had I waited much longer.

And that's when my lungs could take it no more. Suddenly, I collapsed to the ground, grasping for air when none would come. I was a fish out of water, flopping around, begging for just an ounce of oxygen.

"Knox!" Jessa yelled. "Mom! What's wrong with Knox?"

Her words were muffled, but I felt her hands around me, trying to hold me.

"He's having a panic attack." Norah helped to prop me up and calm me, while I tried to tell her my inhaler was in my pocket. That it wasn't a panic attack, but something far worse. But no words would come. I faded in and out of consciousness until I was no longer in that cemetery, no longer with Jessa and Norah.

At least not the Jensons' cemetery. I was back at the cemetery in Gulf Breeze, standing under the cedar tree, next to my parents' graves. Where hundreds and hundreds of daisies thrived all over the graveyard. I couldn't even see the tombstones there were so many flowers. The ones I had planted.

I heard a voice. Behind the cedar tree were my parents, alive and healthy. "Knox," my mother said, "what are you doing here?" She was flawless. Her onyx hair flowed behind her. Her blue eyes sparkled in the sunlight. Without the crooked smile, I truly was the spitting image of my mother.

"Mom!" I shouted, running to her, stepping on the daisies all the way, until I fell into her arms. "You're alive."

She held me and ran her fingers through my hair, the way she used to do before . . .

"Son," I heard my dad say, "it's not time yet." He put his hand on my shoulder, and the grip seemed stronger than I remembered. Was he always this strong?

"Time for what?" I asked.

"It's not your time to go yet. Those people need you. They need you to wake up."

"No, no. I'm fine," I cried. "I'll stay here with you guys."

My mother shook her head. "You have a job to finish. Help them."

"No! This is where I want to be."

My mother gently kissed my forehead before releasing me from her loving arms. "It's time to go. I need you to wake up."

"What?"

"I need you to wake up. Wake up, Knox. Wake up!"

I jolted out of my dream, sweaty and teary-eyed, unsure of my surroundings. Until I saw two familiar faces hovering above me. I was still in the cemetery, and Jessa's bloodied neck snapped me to attention. "Where's Dean? Arlo! Where's Arlo?"

"He got a little sick and vomited. He's rinsing his mouth out by a hose nearby. He saved you."

"Wh-what? How?"

"We all thought you were going to die," Jessa said. "I didn't know you had asthma, and neither did Mom. We thought you were having a panic attack and tried to calm you. Then Arlo woke up and saw what was happening. He ran to you and pulled the rescue inhaler out of your pocket. You . . . you wouldn't take it at first, but finally you did. It was almost immediate—like you realized what he wanted you to do. When you took your inhaler, you woke up. Then Arlo . . . well, he was really upset and got sick again and now here we are."

I was leaning against a tombstone, which would've creeped me out had I not been so out of it. Norah reached out her hand to help me, and I obliged. Norah and Jessa steadied me as we walked to the car in silence, Arlo leading the way.

CHAPTER 17

Done

I don't even remember the ride back to Ibisco.

I just remember racing up the stairs, grabbing my duffel bag, and opening up Josie to search for the quickest Delta flight out of this hellhole.

Don't get me wrong: life sucked in Pensacola, but it didn't suck *that* much. I'd welcome Aunt Jane's clinginess with open arms compared to the circus of crazy around here.

Yanking open the wooden drawers, I grabbed all of my clothes, which wasn't much, and shoved them into my duffel bag. No sense in spending time folding them. I marched into the bathroom and pushed all my hygiene products into my bag all at once, not bothering to check if they all had lids. I went back to the room, and Josie had up the latest flights.

If I hailed a cab, I could get to the airport in an hour, and then my flight would take off a few hours later, around 6:00 a.m. Fine by me.

The price? Not so pretty. But that didn't matter. I still had Arlo's money in my account.

For now, at least.

But someone interrupted my thoughts.

"Please don't go." Arlo stood in the doorway, and just looking at him made my blood boil.

I turned around to face my employer. To face a man I had grown fond of. "What kind of psychopath hires an ex-hacker to aid him on a wild goose chase, only to try to kill his own niece with a broken bottle?" I yelled at Arlo. I don't know that I had ever done that. My quivering muscles and beet-red cheeks must've surprised him. "You were going to kill her. You know that?"

"No, I wasn't," he replied, somber. "Dean was going to. Not me."

I rolled my eyes. "Whatever helps you sleep at night."

He rubbed the back of his neck. "I just wanted to know who did this to me, and instead all I've done is ruin everything for everyone, especially you."

"Especially *me*?" I screeched, kicking my duffel bag across the room, its contents spilling on the carpet. And those bottles definitely didn't have lids on them after all. "How about Jessa—huh? Your niece! What about her? I think she could've done without the future scar on her neck. You know what? You're just an idiot. That's all. You're an idiot who ruined everything. You wasted my time and you hurt your family."

He squeezed his eyes shut as if trying to rid himself of my words. "What if I leave?" he asked. "What if I leave, and you stay? You could find her without me. I'm not much use anyway, since I can't remember everything."

My hands were on my hips, and I felt like my mom, standing in the sand, yelling at me to watch out for jellyfish. "That doesn't even make any sense, Arlo. Just . . . what am I supposed to do, huh? I can't help you when you're like this and making everything a nightmare." I cringed at my own use of "like this." To be fair, it wasn't his fault. It's not like he had any control over Dean. But I was just so angry; I didn't care. I wanted to hurt him. "It's not worth it. None of this crap is worth the money. I don't care if you never find the woman who did this to you."

I turned my attention to Josie and closed the laptop. I'd purchase the ticket when I got there. But right now, I needed to leave and get away from this house of horrors.

"Just take out the money from my bank tomorrow, okay?" I said, pushing my clothing back into my duffel bag before zipping it up. "And tell Norah and Jessa I said goodbye." I walked past him without a hug, handshake, or pat on the back. Heck, not even a middle finger. There was nothing else to say to this man.

I flew down the stairs and outside the villa, where I was already on the phone with the taxi service.

"There's a cabbie in your neighborhood, sir. He should be there shortly."

"Thank you."

I sat on a bench, debating whether to text Aunt Jane and let her know my plans. I was sick to my stomach I was so angry. An asthma attack was one thing, but nearly killing Jessa? I couldn't be here another minute. No more crazy antics. No more Italy. No more Arlo.

"I don't have a lot of friends around here, you know." I looked behind my shoulder to see Jessa approaching me. Her hair lay in waves down her shoulders, the first time since I got here that I saw her hair not in a ponytail. "Scoot over," she said. And so I did. She sat next to me, and there were bandages along the nape of her neck.

"I don't either," I said. "Have friends, anyway."

"Well, you could've had one if you would've hung around a little longer."

"I'm sorry, Jessa. I just need to go home. I made a bad decision in coming here."

She nodded, noticeably displeased. "Probably. But I think you're giving up too soon."

"And how would you know?" That came out curter than I intended.

She shrugged. "You don't seem like the type to just give up on something this big."

I laughed. "Maybe. Maybe not. I know I'm not dumb enough to hang around here and risk getting shot at again or having an asthma attack or . . ." I stared at her neck, the bandages red from soaking up her blood. "How's your neck?"

"Gross," Jessa replied. "But it's cool, because if anyone asks, I'll just tell them I got bit by a vampire."

"One second," I said, forgetting about my dilemma. "You're telling me that a vampire bite is cooler than an evil alter ego attacking you with a broken bottle of bourbon?"

"I didn't say *cooler*. Just more believable." She smiled right at me, and I wanted to reach out and grab her hand and pull her into the cab and take her away with me back to Pensacola.

The cab pulled up, and I reached for my duffel bag, wrapping my fingers around the handles. And that's when another hand wrapped around my own.

"Knox," she whispered, her plum-colored eyes staring back at me. "Please don't leave."

My fingers loosened their grip, and the cabbie yelled for me to hurry. To hurry so we could get to the airport, where I'd fly back to the US and back to my boring life, with my weird aunt and her stupid new husband and the locals who thought up wild conspiracies about me—about my parents. Back to Pensacola, where I survived on leftover pizza and wore the same clothes for three days. Or was it four?

"*Fretta! Andiamo!*" the taxi driver yelled out the window.

"Please," she whispered once more, "if anyone should be hightailing it out of here, it should be me. I was the one hurt. Don't go just because of something stupid. Something out of your control—out of Arlo's control. Stay here. With me. Finish what you started."

I thought back to the dream I had had during my asthma attack. The dream that had felt so real. What would my parents think if they knew I deserted Norah, Jessa, and Arlo when they needed me the most? What would they think if they knew I disobeyed them? *"Stay here. They need you. Help them."*

Maybe it was her pleading violet eyes, the rush of her fingertips on my hand, or the way I felt because she needed me that way, but in that instant, I changed my mind. "No thanks," I yelled to the cabbie. "I have to stay here!"

The cabbie flipped me the bird and sped off. I let go of the duffel bag and interlocked my fingers with hers. "You really want me to stay?"

"Yeah, I do," she said. "I want to get to know you better. Besides, I know hardly anything about you. Like what you do in America and what you do for a living."

I looked down, trying to think of a good response. "I'm self-employed." *Okay, that wasn't quite as smooth as I was thinking, but it's better than the web designer bit.*

She stood up from the bench, still holding my hand when she replied, "Self-employed, hm? Do all hackers pay taxes too?"

I pulled back my hand, still lingering in midair. "How did you—"

"Overhear you yelling 'I'm an ex-hacker!' to Arlo a few minutes ago before you stormed out? Well, I have ears, for starters. Not to mention, the other day when I was snooping around, I found your passport. Julian Taylor?"

"Okay, I guess I made it pretty easy for you to figure it out."

She shoved her hands in her pockets and balanced back and forth on her heels. "So you wanna tell me about that career of yours since you're staying? Or do I have to beg?"

There are few things in this world that could keep my attention. Coding, and maybe the ocean. But Jessa Delgado never bored me. I could watch her do literally nothing for days, and I'd still feel like it was the most exciting time of my life.

So the fact that she knew my secret didn't exactly faze me. I kind of wanted her to know that part of me—to know everything about my crappy life and who I was in another world. I wanted her to be a part of it, and I wanted to bore her to tears with all my crazy stories about the hacker world. I wanted to introduce her to the Suicide Tree.

But somehow, just these few steps would work for now.

"Yeah," I replied, pulling her toward me. "Why don't I tell you over some gelato?"

———————

Nighttime in Italy is full of stars and warm air and footsteps on those centuries-old streets. We sat on the fountain in the piazza, licking our gelato and watching as people ambled around, with nothing to do but tell stories and make each other laugh. Life was different in Italy, and as I sat there with Jessa, I thought I could spend the rest of my life here.

"How did you get caught?" Jessa had chosen the raspberry gelato, and it was redder than a rose. She wasn't even dainty when she ate it, like most girls. I mean, not that I had been around that many girls, but the ones I had been around just ordered a crouton and water whenever we went out. But Jessa? She didn't care. She ate the way most Italians eat: like their lives depend on it.

"Well, nothing is worse than having the feds knock on your door, I'll tell you that. But I basically fell into one of their traps, and they found me and came after me." I was eating a rendition of cookies 'n' cream. There was enough gelato on the cone to send me into a diabetic coma, but I didn't mind.

"What kind of trap?" she asked, her lips bright red. And suddenly, I found myself wondering what they tasted like.

"Knox?"

"Huh?"

"I asked you what kind of trap?"

"Oh, right, right. Okay, so do you know how people contact hackers?"

She shrugged. "Is there, like, a hotline for you people or something?"

I laughed and stowed away that idea for a hilarious comic book. "No, no. In chat rooms, usually. Like gamer chat rooms and stuff. They find your handle and hire you."

"So what's your handle?"

I remembered sitting in front of Arlo not too many days ago when he said my handle, and I thought how strange it had been to hear it out loud. "Suicide Tree," I said.

"Like the plant?"

Marry me. Marry me right now, you crazy fool.

"Uh, yeah. How'd you know that?" I asked.

"My mom has this book of poisons"—*of course she does*—"and I was reading up on it. Goes undetected in autopsies. It's like the perfect murder weapon." She crunched into her waffle cone, and I visualized what our children would look like.

"Y-yeah. You're right. Exactly. So anyway, I was in a chat room, and I had a guy hire me, and once I started the project, the guy just sort of disappeared. Within minutes, I kid you not, feds were banging on my door."

Her mouth gaped open. "Oh, that's not good. What was the job?" she asked.

"Just stupid political crap."

Political campaigns were quick, easy money. A man by the name of Jack Anderson was running for office at the time and wanted the dirt on his opponent, Ron Upchurch—"Stop Your Search! Vote for Upchurch!"—but it didn't look like Jack could win. That's when Jack hired me to . . . persuade some of Ron Upchurch's backers to change their minds, if you will, and start supporting Jack instead. All it took was finding dirt on Ron's backers, letting them know I had the dirt, and then telling they'd be squeaky clean if they switched sides.

"So once you were caught, what happened?"

"To be honest, I was charged with cybercrime, but your uncle got me off the hook."

"Well, that was nice of him." She winked at me. "So now that the charges are dropped, I'm guessing you can use a computer again but not for evil?"

I chuckled. "Right, but I'm definitely going to be using it for that."

"So that's why you brought—what's her name?—*Josie* with you? To help you help Arlo?"

A cute girl just willingly called my laptop Josie. This was romance.

"Yeah, but I've only used her once to help me. We haven't really needed her yet since I've been too busy corralling Dr. Evil over there."

Jessa wiped her sticky hands on her jeans and left me for a brief second to throw away her napkin. When she sat down again, she nuzzled up to me. "Dean is definitely terrifying. But Arlo isn't. They're polar opposites."

"I know."

"We all have our demons, I guess."

I mustered enough courage to lift up my arm and gently place it on her freckled shoulders. "Some more than others."

She tilted her eyes up to mine, and I wondered if this was where I'd kiss her for the first time. On this fountain on this warm night, in this ethereal city.

But instead, she simply stared into my eyes and said, "Yes, some more than others."

CHAPTER 18

Ravello

Jessa and I didn't get back to Ibisco until way past everyone's bedtime. Before I went into my room, hoping not to disturb a snoring Arlo, Jessa grabbed my hand at my door and whispered in my ear, "Tomorrow is the festival in Ravello. Do you still want to go?"

I thought about all the research we needed to do and the puzzle pieces that just kept getting farther and farther apart. And I thought about my parents working for the devil herself. But I also thought about Jessa's sweet-smelling perfume and her strange flowing dresses and the bizarre way her eyes lit up at the sound of something macabre.

"Yeah, maybe everyone could use a little bit of a break."

She squeezed my hand and went to her room, where I daydreamed for just a moment that I had followed her there, where my strong hands would grab her dainty arms and I'd press my lips against hers like those heroic Fabio-type guys I'll never in a million years be anything like.

Instead, I whispered good night and crawled under the covers and closed my eyes and dreamed of what it would be like to spend the day with a beautiful girl who knew my secrets and didn't mind one bit.

———

The next morning, before I raced down the steps to see what breakfast Norah had in store for us, I heard a familiar voice call my name. "He-hey, Knox, you got a minute?"

I stopped at the bedroom door and turned to face him. "Todd?"

He nodded. "You're here. You d-didn't leave."

I glanced at my feet, trying not to make too much eye contact. "I decided to stay and help."

"We want to ask for forgiveness, Knox. We're so terribly sorry for—"

"Todd." I walked toward him, my hands in my pockets. "I forgive you . . . uh, I mean Arlo. All of you. You can't control Dean. He's his own person. And I think he came out because Arlo was triggered from being at his parents' house and everything else. I know none of the other alters would ever hurt Jessa on purpose. I'm here and I'm staying."

He smiled. "Th-thank you, Knox. We appreciate that."

"Now, can we please hit the road? Because I want to see Ravello."

———

The Ravello Music Festival was in the mountains of Amalfi in the little village of Ravello. After an hour and half driving through the Amalfi mountains, with the road's twists and turns, we finally made it to the festival. According to the brochure I had picked up back in town, we were to visit the Annunziata Building. "Built in 1281 by the Fusco family, it became part of the Rufolo family estate. Located just beyond the Villa Rufolo Park, the building is famous for its garden and domes overlooking the town and sea," I read aloud from the brochure. After finding a parking spot that was closer to Florida than it was to Ravello, we fought our way through the throngs of visitors and locals, until we approached the building—a recital hall accessible only by taking ninety steps.

Oof. Thank God I was starting to bulk up my scrawny legs while I was on this trip.

We approached some little shops. They were thriving with delicious produce and goods for sale—from pasta to pepperoncini to lemons bigger than my head. I couldn't get used to all the cigarettes, though. Everyone in Italy smoked.

"*Quantos?*" I asked a shopkeeper.

She eyed the lemon and replied, "*Due euros.*"

I reached into my pocket and paid the lady two euros. I took my lemon and had no idea what I was going to do with it, but it was so cool that I'd have to have been an idiot not to get one.

Jessa walked next to me, and the glisten on her forehead made me feel a little better about sweating through my shirt so soon. She wore a peasant blouse that hung off her shoulders just a bit. "What's with the lemon?"

"It's a souvenir. And you can't have it." I held the lemon in front of her face, taunting her with it.

She pushed it away, scrunching up her face. "I don't want it anyway, weirdo."

"It's a giant lemon. How can you not be fascinated with this?"

She simply rolled her eyes and waved to Todd and Norah, who were in the piazza.

A younger Italian man offered two tiny cups of some yellow drink to Todd and Norah—probably lemonade. The cups were smaller than a shot glass—almost like the cap you get with cough medicine. Probably samples.

"*No grazie*," Norah said to the shopkeeper, fanning herself with a Ravello Music Festival pamphlet. She brought her attention to some peppers at another stand.

Todd reached for the cups. "Sure, I'll t-take one." Then, as he realized how small they were, he said, "Actually, l-let me get a few of those if you don't mind. I'm qu-quite parched." He gulped down two cupfuls and then reached for two more, downing them in an instant.

"Uh, Mom?" Jessa grabbed Norah's arm. "Isn't that—?"

"Oh, for heaven's sake!" Norah snatched the fifth—sixth?—cup out of Todd's hand. "Todd! Don't drink that!"

"Why not?" he asked, jerking away from her.

"Don't you know what that is?"

He squinted and pursed his lips. He had that look on his face when people bite into a sour lemon. "Oh no."

"What is it?" I asked, amused by his scrunched-up expression.

"That is *limoncello*," Jessa answered matter-of-factly.

Confused, I asked, "Is he, like, allergic to lemons or something?"

She let out a groan. She might as well have muttered *tourist* with a roll of the eyes. "It's alcohol. Homemade versions around here are usually forty percent. So, it's like a headache in a tablespoon. Except he had more than a tablespoon."

"Arlo doesn't drink alcohol, but does Todd?" To be honest, it was very confusing trying to figure out which alter did what. Maybe a spreadsheet would've helped keep track.

"I'm guessing by the look on his face that he doesn't drink, either."

Norah threw her hands up in annoyance. "This is just marvelous, Todd! We've been here for ten minutes, and now you're going to be hammered the rest of the trip."

"I'm s-sorry." He tossed the tiny cups into a nearby trash can. "Am I going to be okay? I've never had any alcohol before."

Jessa laughed. "You'll be fine. Just a little tipsy, that's all."

"You remembered where the silverware drawer was in a house you hadn't been in in decades," I recalled, "but you forgot what *limoncello* was?"

Todd looked at me funny. "I don't think th-that was me."

I sighed. "Oh, right. Sorry."

Todd started heading toward the concert, walking down a dirt hill.

"Well, might as well get to our seats," Norah said, slumping her shoulders. "This is going to be a mess."

"I'll b-be fine," Todd called out. But we didn't seem convinced.

––––––––––

I was annoyed that we were still nowhere in terms of figuring out who the mystery woman was and I still didn't have the information I wanted about my parents, but I really wanted to be at this festival with Jessa. I know my priorities were a little messed up, but when you spend the most exciting years of your life stuck inside all the time, you kind of miss the simpler things.

Like walking around an Italian village with a gorgeous girl who's totally out of your league.

We made it to our seats and past the throngs of Italians and tourists.

Drunken Todd tripped only twice on the way to our seats, but at least he managed not to fall over.

"How are you doing?" Norah asked Todd. We all leaned in to await his answer.

Todd looked her dead in the eye and replied coolly, "I'm fiiiiiiiiiiiiiine."

Norah narrowed her eyes. "You're fine, hm?"

"That's what I shhhhaid. I'm fiiiiiiiiiiiiiiine." He brought his attention to the stage.

"Norah," I said, nudging her, "shouldn't we get him some water and food? Maybe that'll help?"

She sighed. "That's exactly what I was going to do, but they all closed their windows since the concert is starting. I couldn't get him anything."

After formal introductions and the typical fundraiser thank-yous, the symphony started. Violinists played as sweetly as I had imagined they would. The crowd applauded after every piece, and Todd snored through half of the concert.

That is, until he woke up.

"I don' shfeel sho good." Todd tried to stand up, but Norah pulled him back down, urging him to take his seat. She mouthed apologies to those he disrupted. "Please, Todd, sit down. Just go back to sleep." She gave a polite smile to the other guests, hoping they'd ignore him.

"My head hurts." Todd rubbed last night's knot on his head and belched so loudly that I think the conductor heard him. A younger woman dressed in a sleazy gown glowered at us.

"Uh-oh" was the last thing heard from Todd before a shower of projectile vomit shot out of his mouth like the Trevi Fountain. Chunks of food I did not recognize sprayed the row in front of us, hitting expensive suits and dresses. Women screamed while cowardly men shielded themselves from the onslaught, using their women as safeguards. The orchestra halted, with the maestro turning around and scanning the crowd for his victim.

"Get him out of here!" Norah hissed as she pushed Todd on top of me. "*Mi dispiace*," Norah said to the angry crowd, as I led Todd out, hoping and praying they wouldn't come after us with pitchforks and torches. Although, I was going to need a torch to burn off the terrible smell on my clothes.

I guided him to a nearby fountain, and he washed himself off. "I peel better." His drowsy eyes rolled back and forth, and he fell in front of me. I caught him as best as my weak arms would allow and guided him toward the ground. We leaned up against the fountain's stone wall, where we sat there catching our breaths. Todd dozed off, and I listened to the symphony start from the beginning, hoping I imagined the few mumbled curse words that came before the symphony began.

Jessa jogged up the hill and found her way to us. No, she really jogged—peasant blouse and skirt and all. She plopped down next to me and handed me a bottle of water. "Here ya go. It's getting hot out here."

"Thanks." I guzzled half of it down in a few seconds. "Where'd you get this? Thought the shops were closed?"

"They opened one up for me. I dazzled them, I think." She gave me a cheesy smile. "That was pretty gross, though. Like, probably the grossest thing I've ever seen."

I stared wide-eyed. "There were just . . . so many chunks."

She giggled and lightly shoved me. "Stop it. Talk about something else."

"You talk about something else," I countered. "Tell me about Ravello, O Tour Guide Goddess."

She beamed when I called her that. "Okay, I've got a fun fact for you. One of my favorite things about Ravello is an ancient legend that my mother used to tell me."

"Italy and ancient legends? Sounds fake." I winked at her, and a contagious smile blossomed.

"You'll like this one." She sat cross-legged and faced me while Todd snoozed behind her, drool trailing down his chin. "Do you remember how Satan tempted Jesus three times in the Bible?"

"Yeah, I guess so."

"Satan took Jesus to the world's most beautiful places—regions that no one could resist, like a paradise, I guess. Well, the second time Satan tempted

Christ, he told him to jump from a pinnacle and to rely on the angels to catch him. It's said that Satan took him here, to Ravello."

"And do you believe that?" I asked, quizzical.

She shrugged. "It's hard not to believe in the legends around here. They take a hold of your soul, and it's hard to shake them."

"That's not the only thing."

Smooth, you idiot. Where did you get that line from? A Lifetime original movie?

"What?" Jessa giggled again, and I wasn't sure if that was a good sign or a bad one.

"I just meant that—"

A groan escaped Todd's lips, interrupting us, and I was surprisingly relieved. Todd had a pretty good knack for rescuing me from my own stupidity.

Impeccable as always, Norah came up the hill, her black dress caressing the ancient stone walkway. Suddenly, Jessa jumped up and grabbed my hand, pulling me toward her.

"What are you doing?" I asked, my knees bent and my butt just barely lifted off the ground.

She held her hand in mine and firmly tugged on it. "Mom, he's right here," she yelled, pointing to the ground above Todd's head. "We'll be back!" And she took off running, dragging me with her and leaving Norah to deal with the smelly mess that was Todd.

Jessa still held my sweaty hand as we ran together. We ran past the shops, past the Italians drinking *limoncello*, and far away from the vomiting man, until we came to a stop to catch our breaths. Okay, to catch *my* breath. I wasn't a runner like Jessa, so quick sprints were a good way to get me to barf. There had been enough barfing for one day.

"Where do you want to go?" she asked, pressing her two fingers to her wrist.

"Are you seriously checking your pulse right now?"

I finally caught her blushing. She replied, "No! Well, yes. Answer my question!"

"I think this way." I held her hand tight and headed down a dirt hill. We walked for a few minutes in silence until I saw the glimmer of the ocean. For so many people to be here for a festival, the water sure was clear of them. We pulled off our shoes, heading to the bank.

"We don't have a change of clothes," she said, tossing her shoes behind her.

"It's hot. We'll dry off fast. Plus, I still have vomit on my clothes." I took off and dove into the cool water, immersing my body.

I came up for a breath and called out to Jessa. "Okay, scaredy pants. Where are you?" I looked around for her but didn't see her. "Hilarious. Did you leave?" I paddled back toward the bank, panic setting in. "Where did you go?"

And that's when my head was pushed under water, giving me just enough time to hear Jessa's cackling.

When I popped back up, she was already long gone, swimming as fast as she could. Was she just good at every sport?

"You suck!" I yelled. "I could've drowned."

"Don't be such a baby," she called back. And with that, she threw her soaked head back, laughing in the sparkling, intoxicating water.

As I swam toward her, I knew I was being hypnotized not by the little village in Italy, not by the unsolved mysteries, but by the strange girl who told me even stranger stories.

"Cake with hot sauce."

"No way!" I said. "You'd rather eat cake with hot sauce than ice cream with ketchup?" We floated in the water, staring up into the clouds as we asked each other stupid questions. I couldn't remember the last time I just goofed off with another person and actually enjoyed it. To be honest, I enjoyed being alone. I didn't have to try to impress anyone or force a conversation. But with Jessa, nothing was forced.

"I love spicy food. Probably wouldn't be so bad." She floated next to me and bumped against my leg. "Would you rather fight a zombie or a vampire?"

"Oh, that's easy. Vampire," I answered.

"Me too. But why?"

"Because I have the option of turning into a vampire if I play my cards right. Whereas, with a zombie, I'm going to die. Or sure, I could turn into one, but being a vampire would be ten times more fun than being a zombie. People would taste gross."

"How would you know?" she asked, flicking water at me.

"Hey! Well, I don't. Just using logic."

For a moment, we stopped asking each other questions, and I let my feet touch the sand as I bobbed up and down. I hovered over Jessa, who was still floating. She reminded me of a snow angel—her arms and legs sprawled out. "You know," I said, "I could push you under water right now, but you'd probably act like a total girl and start crying."

She snickered. "Go for it. Just remember: I'll retaliate." She closed her eyes and gently moved her arms back and forth, floating away, completely unafraid of what I might do. "And you won't like what I'll do to you," she threatened.

I lay on my back again, staying afloat, trying to relax my body, when I saw something flying in the air, careening down from the sky, getting bigger and bigger, soaring, soaring, until my giant lemon landed directly onto my gut. "Oof!" I went underwater and popped back up.

"Oh, did I interrupt?" Norah's voice echoed toward our ears, and Jessa skimmed water, splashing me the whole way back. I followed behind her, and then stopped. I swam back and went underwater, only to find my glorious lemon waiting for me in the sand. I grabbed it and came back up for air.

We walked up the shore, wringing the salty ocean out of our clothes. Thankfully, whatever puke was left on my pants had now made its way to the fish. Yummy.

"You'll be happy to know that after a few cups of coffee, Todd is feeling better." Norah stood with her arms crossed, looking anything but pleased. "I couldn't have done it without you. Oh, wait!" She slapped her hand to her forehead. "I did."

Todd sheepishly waved, his smile apologetic. I felt like that's all he did: apologize for doing stupid things.

"Not that you two seem to care. Off gallivanting around. You missed the rest of the symphony. Not to mention lunch."

My stomach growled, and she was right. All that swimming made me hungry.

"Sorry, Mom." Jessa opened her arms wide, a puddle of water encircling her. "Would you like a hug to make it all better?"

"You smell like a salty wet dog." She handed Jessa her shoes. "Now get your shoes on. We've got plenty of sightseeing to do."

———

With my bulbous lemon safe and secure in Norah's oversized purse, I eyed the different shops and stands. What else could I take with me as a souvenir? The plump bright-red chili peppers looked like a winner to me, but Norah insisted they were too spicy for my poor American tummy.

"I personally would like some chocolate," Jessa said, pointing to a tiny shop on the corner.

"You two get some chocolate while Todd and I pick out some things for tonight's dinner. We'll meet up in an hour."

"Where should we meet?" I asked.

"Anywhere," Norah said with a shrug. "Ravello is quite small, *mi amore.* You couldn't get lost if you tried."

We waved goodbye, still giggling like little kids as our waterlogged shoes squeaked along the ground, leaving wet spots behind us. A trail for Norah to find us if we got lost. Impossible or not.

The bell rang as we entered into the bar, and the shopkeeper waved. *"Buon pomeriggio."*

Jessa told him *good afternoon* as well and began salivating over the various bon-bons and pastries. She pointed to one wrapped in gold and asked for two. "What would you like?" she asked me.

"Is that tiramisu?"

She nodded. "It's delicious. *Un tiramisù, per favore.*"

The shopkeeper put our decadent treats on white plates as Jessa pulled out a few euros. My hand stopped her. "I've got it," I said with a wink.

We found a cozy corner in the back with a window and sat down, the tiramisu making its way to my mouth before my butt had even made an imprint.

"This is by far the most delicious, creamiest piece of heaven I have ever experienced."

She giggled and propped her feet up on the window seat. "Just wait until you try this!" She held the chocolate in her fingers, suggesting I take a bite right there. It felt a little too romantic, but I wanted to be romantic. So I took a bite of the chocolate.

And her finger.

"Ouch! Knox!" she cried.

"I'm so sorry! I didn't mean to bite your finger!" I reached for her hand, but she pulled it away.

"Goodness, I didn't realize you were *that* hungry." She laughed it off, still rubbing her index finger. "I can't imagine what you would've done if I were holding a bite of steak."

"I probably would've taken the whole hand."

"So when you're not practicing cannibalism," she said with a scoff, "what exactly do you do all day in America?"

I lifted my eyes to hers. "It's not pretty."

"Not much in life is unless you have a positive perspective."

"Can't argue with that, I guess." I licked my fork, willing myself to steer clear of the plate. "Well, since my parents are dead and I can't hack, I watch a lot of old DVDs and have my groceries delivered so I don't have to be around too many people. I dream all day about being on the computer, about doing something worthwhile. But the one thing I love more than anything is the only thing that will land me in prison. And it really sucks, because I have this totally ridiculous, yet absolutely amazing idea, but I can't do it because that would mean I'd need to use Josie for evil, as you said, and that would be against the rules."

Working on her next piece of chocolate, she asked, "You mean, it *used* to be against the rules. You're off the hook now, aren't you?"

"Oh yeah. That's true. I guess with everything going on, I hadn't thought of that." *Of my freedom*, I almost said. "But I still probably shouldn't hack. Despite the charges being dropped, I'm sure the feds have me on their bad boy list. If they find out, I don't think Arlo can save me again."

"But . . . that's in America, right? You can't hack in America?"

"But I'm not supposed to be *out* of America. If my IP shows that I'm here, they'll know I left the country. If I reroute my IP to America—well, I'll be 'hacking in America.'" I pondered this for a moment. "Though, I suppose I could work on just the *non*-hacking bits of it."

"So what's the totally ridiculous yet absolutely amazing idea?"

"It's pretty experimental. Like, there's a huge chance that there's no way it would ever work, but if it did, the outcome could be insane."

She leaned in, her violet eyes searching mine. "Tell me. I want to know." And she did want to know. I could tell she was genuinely interested in this crazy scheme of mine.

"All right, so you know how a hacker can send a virus to someone via email or an attachment or a link? And if you click it or open it, your computer will be susceptible to whatever I want."

She nodded. *A good sign—she gets what I'm saying.*

"Well, viruses have always been meant to do something specific, although malicious, to the computer. What if there was a program that acted like a virus and could do something to the *user?*"

"What do you mean, to the user?"

I think I'm losing her.

"Like, what if the program didn't affect the computer? What if it affected you personally?"

"Give me an example," she said.

"Okay, well," I began, "what if a criminal, say a drug dealer, opened the program and it prompted him to tell me, the creator, the truth to anything I asked. If he watched the hypnotizing program I created, I could then ask him where he's been getting all his drugs to sell, and he would have no choice but to tell me the truth because he's been infected."

Her eyes bulged and a smile warmed her face. "That is an incredible idea. So this potential program would be like a polygraph test on steroids—if the polygraph test could force you to tell the truth?"

"Exactly! Sure, some pretty bad things could happen in the wrong hands, but there are good possibilities too."

"How close are you to figuring this out? To making it a reality?"

I sighed. "I was really close until I got busted. There were just a couple final touches to add, and then I could test it."

"So this idea of yours. This hypnotizing truth-serum computer program—it's never been tested on anyone?"

"Nope."

She thought for a moment before saying, "What if you could use it on Arlo?"

My breath hitched. "You mean, hypnotize him into . . . remembering her name?"

"Yes, why not? What do you have to lose?"

"Jessa, that is an amazing idea. I don't know why I never thought of that. That's what we need to do. Try it on Arlo and see what information we can get from him. You're a genius!"

"And you have chocolate powder on your cheeks."

I rubbed off the mess with a napkin, and we thanked the shopkeeper as we walked out into the sun.

"Aw, my shoes aren't squeaking anymore," I said. "I guess they finally dried out."

"That means Mom will be way more excited to see us."

"Where do you think they are? Back at the car?" I asked, looking around at the mountains surrounding us.

"Probably. Let's take our time heading back, though, so we don't have to carry all that produce."

"Deal."

On the way home, in the back seat of Norah's tiny car, I watched the sun touch the water as we descended on the narrow mountain road. In front of the setting sun were two out-of-place boulders resting in the water.

"Look carefully," Jessa whispered, pointing at the large rocks. "What do you see?"

I turned to look at her and found myself whispering too. "What do you mean?"

With one finger, she pressed it to my cheek and pushed my face toward the boulders.

"The two boulders look like a woman floating in the water. Do you see it? Her head and her chest."

And I did see it. But I still felt the touch of Jessa's finger playfully pressed into my cheek. So I held my breath and reached for it, gently guiding her finger away from my face.

It was then, in the twilight, on this balmy day in a little village, that our fingers interlocked. While it wasn't the first time her hand had touched mine, it was the first time she didn't pull away in a bashful rush.

CHAPTER 19

Spaghetti and Coffee

"I-I'm not sure I'm understanding you, Knox." Todd fidgeted while I explained the new idea. His shyness never seemed to waver. Every time I thought he was warming up to me, he'd go back into his shell. He grimaced before he asked, "You want to take your laptop and have it have it *brainwash* me?"

Jessa interjected. "It's not as bad as it sounds. And it's not brainwashing you. Think of it like hypnotizing, but with a twist. It happens through the computer rather than some guy swinging a pocket watch back and forth."

"*If* I can get it to work," I corrected. It wasn't that I doubted my abilities, but this kind of thing had never been done before; so I wasn't sure what the consequences would be. "I'm going to need to test it and make sure it's safe. We really don't know if this will work."

"It has to," Jessa said reassuringly.

"I hope it does, but what if Todd doesn't know the answer? What if Arlo is the only one who knows?"

Todd wrung his hands together. "Can't we wait until Arlo gets back? I-I don't think I want to take part in this."

Jessa reached out and patted his hand, but he flinched. "Todd, you can do this."

"Wh-what does it do? W-walk me through it."

"Well, basically, I created a program that has one goal: to get you to do what we tell you. You see, right now, if we asked you who was responsible for injecting a personality disorder into your brain, you wouldn't be able to tell us her name. But it's still there in your mind—er, one of the alters' minds, I guess. Deep, deep down, you know her name because you've heard it before, many years ago. The answer is there in your brain right now—we just have to extract it. This computer program will basically make you tell us who did it to you. If it works, anyway. Think of it like a truth serum through hypnotism."

Slowly, Todd nodded, trying to make sense of it all. "Will it hurt?"

I shook my head. "No, of course not. You'll be in a trance, basically. Then I pull you out of it."

"Th-then you should finish it. Make it. Maybe by the time you're done, Arlo will be back."

"You want me to get started now?" I asked.

"Time is of the essence, right?" He got up from the couch and headed for the stairs. "I'm going to get some sleep now. Good night."

We all said good night to Todd, and Norah headed to the kitchen. Jessa and I followed her, wondering why she wasn't heading to bed too. "Whatcha doing?" I asked her.

"Making you a strong pot of coffee, *mi amore*. You've got a long night ahead of you."

Jessa tapped my hand. "You know I'm staying up with you, right?" she whispered.

"Well, if you want to . . . but aren't you going to be tired or bored?"

"No, I'll be wired thanks to Mom's coffee and totally fascinated with this project. I want to see how it works, and maybe you can test it on me first." She was bouncing on the balls of her feet, a gleam in her eye.

Me. Jessa. Caffeine. Solitude. All night. This was going to be the best night ever.

"Some food too, perhaps?" Norah said, reaching for a pot.

Jessa and I both sang an affirmation in unison.

"What would you like?" she asked, turning on the stove.

"Something *very* Italian," I replied.

———————

With two heaping bowls overflowing with spaghetti and red sauce, Jessa and I got to work in my makeshift work space. Todd was sleeping, so we had to work in the study. The one with all the books, and apparently a good place to do yoga.

"Has your mom read all these books?" I asked, hooking up my charger to Josie. There had to be close to five thousand books in the study, maybe even more. All of them old and worn, obviously read time and time again.

"I know you won't believe this answer, but yes, she has. She's read every last one and continues to add more to her library."

The green light on my laptop indicated that Josie was ready to go. "How many have you read?"

"Me?" She scoffed. "Not even a fraction. I'm working on it, though. One day I will have read that many."

With my desk set up and Josie ready to go, I sat down, pulling a chair next to me for Jessa. The spaghetti tasted like heaven, and I gobbled it up, nearly forgetting my manners as bits of marinara flew toward Jessa's face.

"Hey!" she said, wiping the sauce off her cheeks.

"Sorry!" I took my sleeve to wipe the sauce from my skin. "It's just so good. I can't eat it fast enough."

"Now you know why I run all the time." She twirled the spaghetti in her fork onto her spoon. "With Mom feeding me nothing but carbs, I have to run them off every day."

"But your mom eats carbs, and I've never seen her exercise, except for yoga."

"Yeah, but she has a high metabolism. She's one of the weirdos who can eat whatever all day long and not gain a pound. I did not inherit those genes. Must've inherited my dad's." Delicately, she placed the perfectly coiled spaghetti into her mouth.

I gulped down a bit that was far too big. "Well, I think you look beautiful and . . . uh . . . you know, you don't have to run at all."

She blushed. "Thanks, Knox." She cleared her throat and turned her attention to Josie. "So what do we do first?"

"The first thing is to pull up the old file from when I first started on this and see what's left to work on. I got so close to finishing it once, before the feds came along and all that. So most of the work should be done."

"If you've had Josie stowed away all this time, why didn't you ever go back and finish this?"

"Well, remember, I was heading to trial and probably prison. I couldn't go near it. And since Arlo got me off the hook, I actually haven't had time to work on it, let alone think of it."

She nodded, setting down her fork. "Makes sense. Good thing I gave you a nudge, huh?" She winked at me, and I smirked.

"Yeah, good thing. Hey, here it is." I opened the file and the code popped onto my screen. As I studied it, a wave of nostalgia washed over me. I don't remember what I wore that day or what I ate or anything except for the feeling of near-complete satisfaction. I had been just moments away from completing this for testing when the condo door flew off the hinges.

Shaking off the memory, I looked for discrepancies in the code. As I scanned the code line by line, Jessa slurped up her remaining spaghetti, careful not to soak my face like I did hers.

The idea for this program, like so many things in my life, was inspired by my parents. After their deaths, I always wondered who was responsible for the explosion. Although no leads ever showed up, I wanted to be ready if they ever did. I thought that if I could somehow get a confession from the perpetrator, I could have them thrown in prison for life. Of course, since I wasn't in the FBI, I found a loophole.

Still no perps in terms of my parents, but at least I'd get to test it out on Todd.

"How come there's a semicolon there off on its own?" Jessa asked, pointing to the screen with her reddened fork. "Looks funny."

I leaned in extra close to the screen, examining it. "Oh, uh, actually, it's not supposed to be there at all. I have no idea how that got there." I deleted the semicolon. "Nice catch."

She smiled, looking very proud of herself.

A couple of hours passed, and our bellies were more than satisfied. As the code was finishing its compiling, the coffeepot was ready for another round, so Jessa went to the kitchen to get us fresh coffee. By the time I heard her open the door, Josie let out a loud *ding*, indicating that the file was complete—ready for testing.

"Is it time?" she asked, holding two steaming mugs of coffee.

"Yeah, yeah. Come sit down."

She sat next to me and saw the file. "What are you going to call it?"

I shrugged. "I don't know. Any ideas?" I stretched my arms high above my head and heard the crack of my spine.

"You should call it *Ibisco*"—Jessa stifled a yawn—"after the villa. Its birthplace."

"That's an awesome idea. Ibisco it is." I looked at her. "Hey, you finally got to name something, remember?"

She laughed and said, "Yay me."

I renamed the file and pressed enter. "Are you ready to test it?" I asked, nervously.

She nodded a little too excitedly. "Yes, let's get this going!"

"Uh, should I take the coffee away from you?"

"Probably." She handed me the mug, and I stole a sip of her steaming coffee.

"All right. So if you were Todd, then I'd have this program ask you, 'Who injected you with a mental disorder?' Then hopefully, you'd have no choice but to answer me. But since you're not Todd, I'm going to tell the program to ask you something else."

"What are you going to ask me?"

"Something I know you don't know the answer to, but technically you would know the answer."

She scrunched her eyebrows. "Good luck with that."

"Let's see if Ibisco can get it out of you. Also, please don't kill me if this all goes terribly wrong, okay?"

"No deal," she said with a smirk.

But before I launched, my finger hovered over the button. What if this *did* go terribly wrong? What if Ibisco hurt Jessa's brain somehow?

"What's wrong?" she asked.

"Just . . . maybe I should be the one to test it."

She crossed her arms. "Why do you get to have all the fun?"

"No, it's not that. I'm just worried that it could fry your brain or something."

She rolled her eyes. "Oh, give me a break. I'll be fine. If I'm not, then we'll cross that bridge when we get to it. Now, do the thing!"

I sighed. "Okay. Here we go." I implemented the code and saved the file. I brought it up on the computer screen, where all Jessa had to do was open it.

"Ready?" I moved behind Josie so I could watch Jessa but not see the screen.

"Ready as I'll ever be." She clicked the button, and her eyes lit up. "Wow. There are so many colors."

I had programmed it to where every color in the rainbow would swirl and twirl in front of her face. It looked like typical fractal loops, but my hypnosis code was embedded in it. It must've worked because she looked entranced. She reminded me of the first time I saw a 3-D movie with my parents. I had thought my eyes were going to pop out of my head.

I stayed silent, not wanting to interrupt this process. Jessa didn't say anything else, but her mouth was slightly agape and her eyes were glossed over. I prayed I wasn't frying her brain as she watched the dazzling, whirling shapes.

"Jessa?" I said.

She nodded her head, but no response.

"I'm going to ask you a question. But I need you to keep staring at the screen. What is your dad's middle name?"

Her eyes broke away from the screen and met mine. "Alessandro."

A squeal left my mouth, and I was super glad Jessa was in a trance so she wouldn't remember that. "Holy crap, it works! Okay, now to get you out of this little trance." I walked around the desk and picked up a glass of water. "Please don't hate me." I threw it directly in Jessa's face.

"Hey!" she shrieked. "What'd ya do that for?"

"What's your dad's middle name?" I asked.

She raised her eyebrow. "How would I know? I literally know absolutely nothing—" She stopped as her eyes grew wide. "I answered you, didn't I?"

I nodded. "Alessandro."

She gasped and jumped up to hug me. "It worked? It really worked? I told you!"

"It really, really worked."

We both smiled at each other, our stomachs and hearts full. "But . . . I swear to you on my life I don't know his name. I've never asked my mom. I didn't want to know anything about him."

I shrugged. "You knew his middle name. It was told to you at one point in your life, or perhaps you saw his middle name somewhere. But remember, your brain stored it way deep down inside. Ibisco just helped you pull it out."

She shook her head. "That is insane."

"You're telling me."

Now we both knew what had to happen next: we had to wake up Todd.

CHAPTER 20

Who Is She?

"**S**hould we wake up Norah too?" I crept up the stairs, with Jessa right behind me.

"I know my mother seems kind and poised, but she will rip your head off and eat it if you wake her up," Jessa whispered.

I turned around, stopping at the last step. "Okay, so just Todd then. Got it." Then I thought for a moment. "Wait," I whispered. "If it's Todd, what if it doesn't work? What if we specifically need Arlo to make it work?"

Jessa bit her lip. "I mean, they're the same, but they're not. One body, totally different people. Should we wait until Arlo comes back?"

I let my head drop to my shoulders and popped my neck. "No. Let's just try it."

Gently, I opened the door to the room Todd and I had been sharing all this time. There was no point in being so quiet, though, because Todd's snoring could probably shake the whole house. Jessa turned on the lamp while I nudged Todd. "Hey, wake up," I whispered.

"Huh?" Todd sat up and looked around, squinting his eyes. "Wh-what time is it?"

"Very early in the morning. But I have good news. Ibisco works, and we need you to try it."

Confused, he asked, "What do you mean Ibisco works?"

Jessa piped up. "That's what we named the program that's going to hypnotize you into telling us who injected you—er, Arlo—with a mental disorder."

I arched my eyebrow. "Thanks for the subtlety, Jessa."

She grinned. "Anytime."

Todd's legs met the carpet, and he reached for the glass of water on the nightstand. He took a quick swig and declared, "I'm terrified. Do I have to do this?"

Jessa sat down next to him and held his hand. "Todd, we're here. We won't let anything bad happen to you, and I already tested it out."

He squeezed her hand and said, "Okay, just . . . let me calm down for a moment. I'll be right there."

We tiptoed back down the stairs and made our way to the study, where the marinara sauce had begun to crust on the plates. Our coffee was cold now, but I figured we were hyped enough to get the job done. I sat down on the chair, pulling up Ibisco on Josie. Once it was ready on the screen and Todd was in the room, I motioned for him to take a seat.

As I did so, I had a sinking feeling this wasn't going to work. What if I wouldn't be able to get an answer? What if the answer were so deeply embedded into his brain that we'd never find the truth? Besides, the test with Jessa was fairly simple. This was certainly more complex.

"Hey," I whispered to Jessa. "What if this doesn't work? Like, for real?"

Without a second thought, she quipped, "What if it does?" I realized then that maybe Jessa was more like her uncle than she realized.

"Todd, I'm going to initiate Ibisco, and I don't want you to take your eyes off the screen. Then I'm going to ask you a question."

"Then he's gonna pour water in your face," Jessa mumbled.

"Wh-what did she say?" Todd asked.

"Nothing. Nothing. Anyway, before I initiate it, I want to ask: Do you know the name of the woman who injected Arlo with a personality disorder?"

He shook his head. "No, I d-don't."

With that, I pressed the ENTER button and stepped back like before. Just like it did for Jessa, the screen illuminated with bright colors and crazy shapes and images. Todd didn't speak, however. He leaned in closer to Josie, captivated. Josie beeped. *Here goes nothing.*

"Todd," I said softly. "Who injected Arlo with a personality disorder?"

I didn't have to look at Jessa to know we were both holding our breaths, waiting and hoping and praying that Todd would respond. That he could dig deep and give us the answer.

His eyes met mine, and he said with finality: "I do not know."

I turned and looked at Jessa, unable to say anything.

"Ask him something else," she suggested.

"Who knows the name of the woman who gave Arlo a personality disorder?"

Wide-eyed, Todd said, "No one knows her name. We never knew it." A bitter smile crossed his face. "We weren't allowed to utter her name in the house because she never told us her name."

I swallowed hard and pressed my fingers into my temples. Massaging them, I tried to practice a quick moment of steady breathing.

"Okay, we're done here," I said.

Jessa moved toward the desk and grabbed a glass of water. "Well, time to wake up, Todd."

She threw the water in his face, and he jumped up, wiping the liquid from his eyes. "Wh-what was that for?" he yelled.

I touched his arm. "We had to get you out of the trance, buddy."

In a hushed voice, he asked, "Who did it?"

"We still don't know. You said no one knew her name because she never told anyone."

Todd sat back down in the chair. He covered his hand over his mouth and looked past me, past Jessa, past everything. It was like he was looking into another world. He shook his head, in disbelief clearly, and finally muttered, "How will we e-ever find her then?"

––––––––––––

The sun touched the tips of the villas, a breathtaking sight, but my thoughts were clouded with problems that had no solutions. My genius idea to use Ibisco blew up in my face. This woman, this devil, was nameless. How could I find someone without a name? Heck, even a first name would be better than no name.

Todd and Jessa sat quietly in the living room, talking with each other. I could've joined, but what would I have said? I had nothing of value to offer. I eavesdropped anyway.

"So do you talk to the other alters?" Jessa asked.

"S-sometimes. I mean, we c-communicate with each other."

"Are you all, like, friends?" Jessa asked, sounding perplexed.

Todd chuckled. "I guess so. We're not enemies."

"Can you do things that Eli or Arlo can't do?"

He thought on this for a moment before responding. "I can draw two circles simultaneously c-clockwise and c-counterclockwise."

Jessa widened her eyes. "What! No way."

An infectious smile blossomed on his face. "Y-yes way. And none of the other alters can do it. Bring me some paper, and I'll prove it."

Jessa jumped off the couch and ran to the desk in the study. I heard a drawer slam and she whizzed past me. She shoved the contents into Todd's lap and said, "Okay, show me."

He set two pieces of paper on the coffee table, took a pen in each hand, and proceeded to shock and awe Jessa as he drew two circles simultaneously.

"You're brilliant," Jessa said. "You should put this on YouTube."

"W-what's that?" he asked, setting down the pens.

While Jessa explained the subtle nuances of the world of YouTube, I snickered every now and then at Todd's queries. "How do the videos get on there?" and "But what if people can see them?" and my personal favorite, "Why would anyone watch these videos?"

Then a thought struck me—one so galvanizing that I stood up. When Todd said, "No one knows her name. We never knew it," he was talking about the alters. The alters didn't know her name because Arlo wouldn't let them speak her name. I had asked the right question to Todd.

But I had asked the wrong person.

CHAPTER 21

Ask Me Anything

I dashed into the living room and interrupted Jessa and Todd's conversation about YouTube. "Todd, I need you to get Arlo."

He furrowed his brow. "Why?"

"It's really, really important. I need you to ask him a question for me, or ask him to come out. Can you do that?"

He pressed his lips together and looked down. "I-I don't think he'll come out right now."

"What's this all about, Knox?" Jessa crossed her arms and waited for my reply.

"I know how to find out who did this to Arlo. But I need Arlo to come out. Or . . . maybe if Todd can ask Arlo a question, it'll work. I'm not really sure."

Jessa patted Todd's hand. "Do you think we could speak to Arlo?"

Todd shook his head. "I w-want to stay here, please."

I rolled my eyes. "Fine. You can stay. But I need you to ask Arlo something for me. You can communicate with him, right?"

Todd caught my eyes. "Yes."

"Great. I just need you to ask him a question. Let's go back into the study so you can ask him." I started to walk away, but Todd wasn't following. "What's the hold-up?"

"Why can't we ask him in here?"

"Because I need you to use Ibisco again. It's very, very important, Todd. Please."

Jessa lovingly placed her arm around him and pulled him to her. "Todd, I'll be right there by you. Just think of it as a redo."

"A r-redo? Redo. Redo. Okay. A redo." He stood up and followed me to the study, with Jessa right on his tail.

I fired up Ibisco and offered the same chair Todd had used moments ago. "Okay, buddy. Just sit right here and I'm going to start Ibisco."

He did as he was told but held on to Jessa's hand like a child about to cross the street. "I'm ready," he said.

"Great." I pressed enter and stood back. After waiting a moment or two, I asked, "Todd, can you ask Arlo a question for me?"

Todd nodded.

"Please ask Arlo the name of the woman who gave him a personality disorder."

At this, Todd twitched. And twitched again. Something was clearly agitating him.

"What's wrong with him?" Jessa asked, concerned.

"I don't know. Just wait."

Todd reached for the scar above his ear, the one I had seen during Arlo's haircut. He rubbed it as if it hurt. I held my breath and waited for an answer. Finally, Todd opened his mouth, and I leaned in to hear his response.

"Odette," he said. "Arlo said her name is Odette Cleary."

————————

Despite our efforts not to have Norah chop off our heads, we woke her up anyway. Begrudgingly, she wrapped her black robe around herself and met us in the living room. It was like a family meeting, except I was the only one who wasn't related. Norah sat in her chair while the three of us squished together on the clawfoot couch.

Apparently, asking to speak with Arlo must have coerced him out, because Arlo was back again.

Norah was the first to say something. "So the woman who caused all of this—her name is Odette?"

"Odette Cleary, to be exact," I said. "And I don't know if we dug too far or what, but apparently, it's caused Arlo to remember more than just her name. I think it triggered a lot of memories, actually."

She nodded, trying to make sense of something that isn't supposed to make sense. "*Fratello*, I want you to start from the beginning, and please, for the love of God, speak slowly while I get through this cup of coffee."

Arlo cleared his throat, his hands on his knees. "The beginning it is then."

Jessa and I sat close together, and I thought about casually putting my arm around her; but I figured this wasn't a romantic moment. So instead, I folded my arms across my chest while she sat crisscross applesauce.

"After my father was cured of epilepsy, I had many questions, as I'm sure you can imagine. But our parents would never answer them. No matter how much I pried, they refused to divulge any information. Looking back, it was probably to protect me. I remember Odette telling my parents that night— the same night she threatened to kill Norah—that they owed her a favor. Me—I was the favor, of course. For decades, I didn't know what it was. Then I worked with a therapist in the last year, and that he helped me figure that out. After the therapist helped me figure out that my parents had allowed some strange woman to experiment on me, we got stuck. We couldn't make any more progress. Everything has been buried so deep inside my mind that I knew I needed help from more than just a therapist. I needed to go back to Italy and track down the person responsible, even though I had no way of knowing if those memories would come back. Thankfully, some things have been triggered over the last few days, and I remember more." He hesitated.

Norah spoke up, balancing her coffee cup on her knee. "Take your time. I know it must be difficult to bring up these terrible memories. So you were the favor, as we know."

He nodded, but for the first time since I'd met him, despite all the awful things that had occurred, I saw Arlo swipe a tear from his eye. But this wasn't a sad tear. This was an angry tear. "I was Odette's little science experiment. I was the lab rat. And what better option than some young man whose dad had used her experiment to cure him of epilepsy? I was a *free* lab rat, I should say. She could've used anyone in the whole world. But she used me. She used me to test her disorder because our parents allowed her to do so."

Jessa spoke up. "Do you remember when Odette . . . did this to you?"

"Yes," he replied. "Now I remember. Our parents took me down into the basement—the same one we went to the other day, Knox. Why we couldn't have done this at Odette's stupid facility, I don't know. But it happened in our own home. Maybe it was a sadistic control thing for her. She entered our home with her goons, and I remember overhearing her talking to Mom. 'You made the right choice. It's a simple experiment with minimal side effects. Better side effects than what Norah would experience.' My mother cried, but she didn't stop it. I don't know how they could've overpowered Odette and her goons. So we were in the basement, and I remember crying because I didn't understand what was happening. I thought I was in some sort of trouble. No one would tell me what Odette was going to do to me. I don't think our parents even knew what that woman was going to do."

I asked, "Why couldn't your parents have left? Just ran away from Odette?"

He shrugged. "I don't know if I'll ever uncover the answer to that, my boy. I just don't know."

"But there's something I just don't understand. After she did this to you, wouldn't she have wanted to monitor you? But your parents eventually sent you off to America."

He lowered his gaze and finally said, "She visited us one more time before I left for America. They did some lab and some reports. Then she said, 'Well, this looks to be a success. You're all done now, Arlo.' And that was it. It was like it was just for fun. Just to see what would happen if her experiment worked, and then she was bored with it all."

"W-were my parents there?" I asked.

He shook his head. "I expected them to be there at the lab or even when they did their final reports on me, but they were never seen again after they helped cure my dad of epilepsy. Guess they had moved by then.'"

"Is there anything else you want to share, *fratello*?" Norah asked. "Anything else you remember?"

"She shaved my head," Arlo said, almost remembering it all over again.

Then he touched the side of his head, just above his ear. His fingers swept over the scar—the same one I had asked about during his haircut. "She shaved it off and then made an incision under my earlobe. She pushed down on the piston and injected me with a serum. After that, I woke up with stitches and this scar. She had done something to my brain. To my mind. She made me . . . what I am now. And our parents watched, Norah. They were there, and they didn't stop her."

Norah stood up straighter, trying to show how strong she was. I knew she wanted to cry, but she held back the tears.

"And then I slept for a very, very long time. I slept for an eternity, I remember. And when I woke up, I was someone else. And no one knew what to do with me."

Suddenly, the room fell very silent.

CHAPTER 22

Vallone dei Mulini

Someone knocked on my door at 6:30 in the morning. "Go away," I growled.

Jessa swung open the door. "Good morning!" She was wearing her bright running shoes and jogging in place while checking her pulse.

"Oh, Lord. Morning people. You know everyone hates you, right?" I covered my head with my pillow only for her to yank it off me.

"You missed a beautiful sunrise."

She bent down and touched her toes, and I willed myself to look away but miserably failed.

"So what's on the agenda today?" she asked.

"Sleeping." I pulled the covers over my head, hoping she wouldn't jerk them off.

I was wrong.

"Nope!" She yanked the sheet off my head and plopped down on my bed, and for a girl who just ran Lord knows how many miles, she didn't even smell bad. "Sleeping isn't on *my* agenda, though. Why don't you take a break from all your little research for a while and clear your head?"

"Oh yeah?" I sat up in bed, suddenly very aware that I was wearing only boxer shorts underneath the thin blanket. "Gee, I'd love to take a break, but that's all I've done is take breaks. We finally have a name, so now, I need to get to work on finding her."

"You know, when trying to solve a problem, it's best to do something mundane or fun to take your mind off everything. Then when you come back to the problem, you'll have clarity."

I raised my eyebrow. "Is that so?"

"Mhm. So! I can show you some of the hot spots in Sorrento. That's what we'll do."

I eyed her suspiciously. "All right. You win. But promise me after our little adventure time, we'll get back to work?"

"Deal." She opened my closet to grab a clean shirt. "Do you need pants too?"

"I . . . uh . . . I can get them."

"Fine. Hurry it up and get dressed and we'll do some sightseeing."

"Okay, but *you're* driving Norah's tiny car." I threw my pillow at her and she grimaced.

"Actually," she said, throwing the pillow back with full force, "we'll be taking my Vespa. See you in five."

———————

Thanks to the god-awful rom-coms my aunt made me watch, I always thought riding around in a Vespa looked adorable and romantic, but that's impossible because Italians drive like they're on fire. Italians on Vespas make New Yorkers look like ninety-year-old grannies. They just go fast and hope to God they don't hit someone. And if they did, they'd probably just turn back to make sure the pedestrian was still alive.

Jessa sped around curves like she was born to do that and that alone. Weaving in and out of alleyways, sputtering across the stone streets. I clung to her as tightly as I could, trying to remember if there were any rom-coms where the *guy* clung to the woman's waist. Nothing came to my mind, but I took what I could get.

We slowed down and Jessa was off the Vespa before it stopped. She kicked the kickstand and took off her helmet, setting it on her seat. I threw my leg off the motorcycle and readjusted my jeans. My hands were numb from holding onto Jessa for so long.

Beneath us was green vegetation crawling up and around a strange stone building. "What is this place?" I asked.

"*Vallone dei Mulini.* It means Valley of the Mills."

A stone building stood in the middle of a ravine. Lush green ferns hugged the building and even protruded out of the open windows. Sunlight hit the stone just right, and it truly was one of the most least-fascinating landmarks I had ever seen. "So it's just a mill then?" I asked, trying to gauge its importance or relevance.

"It's an *abandoned* mill, actually." She headed toward some bushes, and I followed behind. There was a narrow and steep trail that led down the ravine.

"Of course it's abandoned. I don't know what else I was expecting." I hunched over to avoid the branches hitting my face. "Is this the right way?"

"It's a shortcut." Jessa brought her index finger to her pouty lips. "Don't tell anyone."

Mouth agape, I nodded and crept along the dirt pathway. "Are we supposed to go this way?" I whispered.

"It's not for tourists. Be careful—the pathway slants down, so bend your knees."

I steadied myself, and we skidded down the path, leaves and brush scratching my bare arms. Jessa pulled back a large branch, revealing the mossy building. Sparrows perched on the open windows, singing a melody. We had to jump over a muddy creek to get to the mill, so right before Jessa took the plunge, I yelled, "Boo!" She missed and landed right in the middle of the creek, soaking her feet up to her shins.

"You suck!" she yelled. Then she bent down, scooped up a handful of mud, and chucked it at me.

"Oh, that's how you wanna play?" I chased after her, but she took off running toward the mill. I rounded the corner, close on her tail, and found myself entering the abandoned mill.

But no Jessa in sight.

"This is Ravello all over again. Seriously, you have got to stop hiding. Jessa, where are you?"

Sunlight shone through the open windows, and the silhouettes of the sparrows stood still, like gothic statues.

"Hello?" My voice echoed. "Not impressed!"

"Boo!"

I jumped but didn't screech like a woman this time. "Okay, all right. We're even?"

"Yes, even," she said with a wink.

"So why here?" I asked, looking around the interior of the mill. The sun shone brilliantly through the rounded windows. Ferns in every shade of green engulfed the exterior, but branches crept through the windows, inviting onlookers to come back outside. "Why'd you decide to come here? Do you do tours here?"

"Because you wanted a taste of Sorrento, and it's a historical site. Plus," she said, caressing the walls, somehow damp in this hot weather, "it's, like, super creepy." Her eyes lit up when she said this, and I found her love for the macabre to be endearing, clearly a trait she borrowed from her mom. "And I don't do tours here."

"Is that why there aren't any tour guides outside of this place? Are we even allowed to be here?" My guess was no.

She glanced at me, wandering around the large room. "That's all relative, don't you think?"

I shook my head. Jessa headed up some narrow stairs, kicking away overgrowth that had made its way into the mill. "Wait up!" I said, trailing behind.

We made our way to the top of the mill, and I was certain there had to be at least twelve freaky insects crawling on me. The sun poured out over the roof, and Jessa sat down, leaning against the wall.

"Would you believe I come here when I need a break from life?" She crossed her legs. They were so toned from all that running that it was hard not to stare at them.

"Really?" I said, kneeling down beside her. "You do seem to know the place really well."

"Well, no one ever comes here, obviously. And it's quiet and weird and pretty."

"Like you." Another smooth line from yours truly.

She nudged me, smirking. "That's not true."

"Oh?"

"Nope. I'm not quiet."

"But you're pretty."

Her cheeks turned as red as an apple, and I felt good about myself for having made a cute girl blush—twice in one week. I could hunt down the cell phone number of the president of the United States, but making a girl blush was close to impossible for me.

She clapped her hands together, breaking me from my trance. "So! Are you ready for your amusing Italian story time?"

"Yes, please." I sat back and closed my eyes.

"This ravine is said to have been created by an earthquake after a prehistoric volcanic eruption."

"Kind of like Pompeii?" I asked.

"Sure, kind of like that, but with fewer fatalities, I would imagine. Fast-forward to the thirteenth century, the flour mill had a great advantage with the constant stream at the bottom of the valley. The Sorrentine people ground all the types of wheat they needed. As time grew on, the milling of flour shifted to nearby pasta mills, and unfortunately, the sunken area of industry became largely obsolete. The mill was closed and abandoned in the forties."

"But this place looks like it's been abandoned for hundreds of years," I said.

She nodded. "Right. They were soon overgrown with vegetation and plant life that thrived in the humid crevasse, giving them the appearance of having been unused for centuries rather than decades."

"Wow," I said. "That's actually pretty cool."

"Not to mention," Jessa said, with a mysterious lilt to her voice, "a man died here."

I snorted. "Yeah, sure."

Her eyes glimmered, and a devious smile stretched across her face. "Oh, you think my ghost story is a lie, do you?"

"I think it's probably just a little legend you were told when you were young that probably has little veracity to it."

"I tell you what. I'll tell you the story, and when we get back home, you can research it yourself on Josie and see if I'm lying."

I narrowed my eyes. "All right. Deal."

"Twenty years ago," Jessa began, enjoying story time just a little too much, "there was a Welsh man who came here for vacation with his family. The Valley of the Mills is a beautiful tourist attraction, but most people are discouraged from visiting the area. This man, though, loved danger and felt even more persuaded to tour it after a few too many drinks.

"So he came this way with a few of his buddies and threw one leg over the edge you see there." She pointed up high to the ledge with a guardrail that kept passersby safe. "As soon as he did, though, he lost his balance and slid down the ravine. One hundred fifty feet, to be exact."

I tried to think of how long it would take someone to slide down one hundred fifty feet, but it made me queasy just thinking about it as I recalled my brief moment on a rope in Capri.

"He lay down at the bottom of this ravine, his face planted into the very stream that kept this mill going for so many centuries. The one you pushed me into?" I chuckled. "Yeah, that one. But it was too late for anyone to save him—he had suffocated in a pool of water."

I shook my head. "Where do you guys get these stories?" I asked, bewildered. "Is it passed down from generation to generation, or is there a book you get when you move here that explains it all?"

She giggled and lightly smacked my arm. "Hey, no matter how we hear them, they're all good. They add character, history to the landmarks."

"Speaking of history," I said, trying to change the subject. "You don't talk about your dad. Is he completely out of the picture?"

"I guess so," she answered. "I mean, I've never met him."

"Oh." I had remembered this from Norah at our first Italian meal, but I wanted to hear more from Jessa.

"Yeah, he left when he found out Mom was pregnant. She never heard from him again."

"Was he from here?"

She nodded. "In Italy? Yeah, born and raised in Sicily."

"Well, you're better off without him." Our eyes locked for just a moment, but it was the longest moment of my life. If I had had the guts, I would've grabbed her face and kissed her. But sadly, I was about as smooth as a jagged rock.

"What about your parents? I mean, I know the story from what Mom told me, but tell me something I don't know."

I raised my eyebrows. "Such as?"

She shrugged. "I don't know. How did they get started with NovaVita and the Raven Virus?"

"That's a *long* story."

"We've got time."

I grinned. "All right. Well, after the outbreak started in Texas, the CDC called up my parents and hired them to create a cure. They got funding through some bigwig research corporation too."

"Why'd they pick them? Like, how did they know to call them up?"

"To be honest, that's always eluded me. They were already well known for their involvement in medications that cured things like the common cold."

"Your parents were the ones who did that?"

I nodded. "Yep. Cured the common cold. So the CDC came along, and Mom and Dad accepted the opportunity under one condition: they could stay in Pensacola, Florida, to create it. The people funding this said yes and gave them a lofty amount of money to get on it—and fast."

"How long did it take them to come up with the cure?"

"Well, the whole nation was freaking out, so the heat was on from the moment they were chosen. Plus, there was so much media coverage of the disease. Imagine if we had had social media back when tuberculosis was a big deal. It was crazy seeing the videos of people coughing up black blood and wasting away. So it took them about three weeks. By then, hundreds had already died. They basically didn't sleep for three weeks."

"They sound amazing. It's sad that the world hates them."

I rolled my eyes. "Tell me about it."

"So if they had this cure, then why wouldn't they turn it over? That's what they were hired to do."

I studied her for a moment. "I don't think I'll ever know the answer to that."

"Did you ever know anyone who had the Raven Virus?" she asked in a hushed tone.

"Honestly, I knew of mutual friends who had it. But it didn't affect anyone I knew personally. You?"

She shook her head. "No. It got pretty contained in the States, right?"

"Yeah, that's right."

"Do you think there will ever be a . . . well, *another* cure for it?" she asked.

I reflected in serious thought before answering. "There has to be. I mean, I know people are working on it, but no one has come close to what my parents did. They were geniuses. I know there are plenty of geniuses out there, but they were different."

She leaned her head on my shoulder, stifling a yawn. "I'm kind of sleepy."

"So go to sleep." I cautiously moved up my arm, resting it on her shoulder. Finally, a smooth move.

She nuzzled up against me, and the warmth of her body heated me up like a furnace. Just having her near me was enough to make me forget all of my problems. Forget about Arlo. Forget about this mess.

———————

Jessa and I returned to Ibisco, where Arlo and Norah were waiting for us. They sat in the living room, Norah on the clawfoot couch and Arlo on the matching chair.

"Where have you two been?" Norah asked, pressing mute on the remote.

Jessa answered, "He wanted to tour the mill. Just being hospitable to our guest, Mom."

Norah pursed her lips. "Mhm. Well, I think Arlo's been waiting on you, Knox."

"My boy, are you ready to get to work?" Arlo asked. Today he wore jeans and a nice polo and those old man tennis shoes.

Jessa ran upstairs to take a shower, and I sat down next to Norah. "Yes,

I am. Now that we have a name, I guess it's time to actually find her. But I have to ask, once we find Odette, then what?"

Arlo grinned. "I want to meet her."

I glanced at Norah. "Do you think that's the best idea? Meeting the woman who did this to you? Once we find her and know she's still here, then what?"

Arlo didn't hesitate to answer. "Then I want her in prison for life for what she has done to me."

"*Fratello*, under what grounds? It's your word against hers. From a million years ago, no less."

I nodded in agreement. "Yeah, and if she's this wicked person like you say she is, I'm guessing she has friends in high places. There's no way she would actually serve time."

"Actually," Arlo began, "once again, that's where you come in. I want you to prove that she is up to no good so we can get her thrown in to prison for life."

"But don't you think scores of people have probably attempted that and failed?"

"You won't, though. Your job, now that you know her name, is to find out everything you can about her and get proof that she's still up to her evil tricks. Then, once we have the proof, I'm sure we can find someone who'd love a shot at taking down a tyrant like Odette."

"Okay," I said. "Then I guess I better get started with stalking Odette Cleary."

CHAPTER 23

Phishing

I stayed up through the night while everyone slept. At first, finding Odette Cleary online proved to be a challenge. Although I was able to find the basics about her online, I needed more than just the boring Wikipedia specs. I wanted the dirt. I knew some guys on the dark web who could probably help me.

It took some patience, but I finally had a buddy in Europe who had heard of Odette Cleary—the *real* Odette. Apparently, she had got to every cop in Italy paid off in some way. If they're not paid off, he said, they have deadly threats hanging over them to keep quiet. He said that Odette was the president of Cleary Research Facility, founded in 1975 by Wayne Cleary (her father). Back then, it seemed to have a good reputation for funding the research of infectious diseases. Now? I wasn't so sure. Everything seemed to be quite secretive about the facility's activities.

My friend said Odette had been president over the facility for the last few decades but that she basically had permission to do whatever on earth she wanted, thanks to her notorious favors. He was helpful, but it still wasn't the dirt I needed.

I rubbed my weary eyes and signed off. After a little bit of sleep, I'd wake up and go see this Cleary Research Facility for myself.

———

When I was little, my dad would wake up at 5:00 a.m. to get dressed for work. Somehow, my internal alarm clock sounded at 5:30, and I'd creep into the kitchen to say goodbye to my dad. He'd sit at the table, reading his Bible and sipping his coffee. He drank from a huge, faded convenience store mug.

"Can I have some?" I'd ask, peering up at him.

He'd look around to make sure my mom wasn't around. "Yes, one sip. But don't tell your mother."

And somehow, strong black coffee always tasted wonderful to me, even at the age of five.

I guess that's why even now, I love the smell of coffee early in the morning. It makes me reminisce back to a time when my parents weren't the hated scientist couple of the universe.

So when Norah slid my first shot of Italian espresso toward me, a feeling of nostalgia swept over me. She also handed me a tall glass of water.

"You'll want to drink this, *mi amor*, after you finish your shot." She smiled at me with concern, almost as if to say, "I hope this espresso doesn't kill you."

I reached for the tiny glass and took the shot in one gulp. Lightning bolts coursed through my veins, and I tried not to choke on the thick, deliciously evil liquid. I fiercely shook my head, trying to overcome the feeling of being slapped in the face.

"So you like it then?" Norah asked, patting my shoulder.

"Dear Lord. That was intense." I reached for the glass of water and poured its contents down my burning throat. "How do you drink that all the time?"

"Oh, it's an acquired taste." She turned back to the kitchen counter, making a plate of ham, cheese, and crackers.

The door swung open, and in came Jessa, jogging in place and wiping the sweat from her brow. "Eight miles!" she said. "I'm a beast."

Norah set the plate of food on the table. "*Molto bene.* Now, my little beast, come eat your food so you can recover."

Jessa stretched for a few seconds before plopping down next to me. Eyeing the shot glass, she said, "Oh no. How'd you like the espresso?"

"It felt like someone punched me in the face." I felt jittery and knew I was bobbing up and down in my seat, but I couldn't stop myself.

"Yeah, it's a lot like that. I don't know how Mom drinks it all the time."

She reached for the ham and cheese and vigorously stuffed her mouth. "I tried it once or twice, and that was enough for me."

"Hey, losers," we heard a voice say. "So what's on the agenda today? Something stupid?"

Eli had returned.

"I just don't see why I have to go, that's all." Eli was anything but happy. He wanted to roam around Sorrento and drink and eat and chase women.

Not to say I didn't want to do that, either, but still. We had a purpose for being here, and he was going to have to suck it up and help me.

"You need to go because . . ." *Well, wait. Why does he have to go?* I needed Arlo, not Eli. Arlo was the one who needed to go. "Because of reasons," I finally said, unsure of what good it would do to take Eli with me. "Just want to check one last thing before we go." Under the name Cleary Research Facility, I hit the Maps option on Google to locate them once more so I could save their address and know where on earth we were going.

"So we go to this place where this woman—"

"Odette," I said.

"Right, whatever. *Odette.* We go to her work and then what? Ask her, 'Hey, lady—did you cut open a guy named Arlo and inject him with some crazy concoction that gave him multiple personalities?'" He rubbed his temple, seemingly annoyed. "I'm just saying, I shouldn't have to go."

"Eli," Norah began, "Knox needs you for moral support. I know that concept is difficult to understand, but he needs you and you're going. That's final."

Eli crossed his arms and rolled his eyes. "Fine. But I'm going to complain the entire time."

I couldn't help but notice a slight smirk when he said that.

Norah dropped us off at the train station in Sorrento and hugged us goodbye and told us to eat at a restaurant called *Vecchio Carlino* near the piazza. Something about ordering *arrabiata*, whatever that was.

First-class tickets on the train got us window seats, beverages, and little cookies. It was going to take a couple of hours to make the trek to Florence, so Jessa and I researched Cleary as much as we could while the train sped by breathtaking landscapes.

"So what's her name again?" Jessa asked, sipping her Coke.

Swiping on my phone, I responded, "Odette Cleary."

"I like her first name," Jessa said. "So archaic."

"Jessa. She's a psychopath." I drank the rest of my Coke and unwrapped my cookie when Eli set down his newspaper.

"Well," she mused, "some psychos have cool names."

"Crap. Stocks are dropping today." Eli slapped the newspaper with reproach. "Unbelievable."

"Eli, that newspaper is like three weeks old," I said, eyeing the date.

"Oh. Let me borrow your phone then." He reached across the table for it. I smacked his hand. "Ow! What's your problem?"

I glared at him. "Don't touch my phone."

He rolled his eyes. "*Touch*-y." He glanced out the window. "So we're off to Florence, huh? That's where that famous statue is. What's it called? What's that guy's name?"

"*David*," Jessa said.

"Yeah, yeah. That's the one."

I know, I know. I was surprised to hear Eli the stockbroker mention Renaissance art too.

"He's mesmerizing," Jessa whispered, almost wistful. "He's unlike anything you'll ever see. Well, maybe right underneath the Sistine Chapel. That beats everything else you'll ever see in this country."

"If we have time, maybe we can go see him." I smiled at the girl who sat next to me, taking in her flowery smell and her light-brown hair. "In the meantime, we need an appointment with Miss Cleary." I pulled Josie out of my bag and powered her up.

"How are you going to do that?" Jessa asked, swiping Eli's cookie package and opening it.

"I'm going to do a little . . . phishing."

"What's that?" Eli asked.

"It's a way of getting personal information from someone through an email."

"Oh, that's clever," Jessa said. "But who will the email go to?"

"The secretary."

"But won't you need to create a login page and domain that looks just like the scheduling program she uses?"

I narrowed my eyes, surprised at her knowledge in this area. "Right . . . exactly. Thankfully, I've done this before. I've already got a login page saved for the scheduling app the secretary uses."

"How do you know what she uses?" Jessa asked, intrigued.

"Believe it or not, the Cleary Research Facility website told me." I pulled up a domain-hosting site to create a domain name similar to what the secretary would see. "It said something like, 'To schedule a tour of the facility, please call our secretary, Jenny, to schedule through Calendar To-Go.'"

"Wait," Jessa said, swallowing her stolen cookie. "But if we need an appointment, how will phishing get us one?"

"Easy. I get her to go to this link and login. Then it'll send me the info she inputted: her login and password to the scheduling app."

The train jolted a bit, and we leaned forward a little too hard into the table. I steadied Josie and got back to typing. I stifled a laugh when Eli's drink spilled a few droplets on his slacks.

"How are you going to get her to open the link?" Eli asked, drying the Coke with a napkin.

"Watch and learn." I picked up my phone and typed in the Cleary Research Facility phone number.

A way-too-high-pitched voice answered. "Thank you for calling the Cleary Research Facility. This is Jenny. How may I help you?"

"Jenny, this is Drake with Calendar To-Go. It looks like someone tried to hack into your account. I'm calling to make sure everything is okay."

Jessa's eyes bulged, wondering what on earth I was doing. Eli tried to feign apathy, but I could tell he was curious.

"Oh no!" Jenny said. "I had no idea. What should I do?"

"Well, first, do not log in to the program like you've been doing. I'm going to have you confirm your password, okay? Check your business email—I just sent over a secure link from Calendar To-Go."

I could hear typing in the background. "Okay, I've got it. I just type in my login and password?"

"That's right."

"I think I did it," she said. "Now what?"

I checked my email to see if the login and password information was collected properly. It showed up in my inbox. Boom. "Now I want you to shut everything down and restart your computer, and you'll be good to go. We've added another layer of security to the scheduling app, and the hacker has been blocked from causing further damage."

Well, I mean, he's right here, but whatever.

She profusely thanked me and I hung up. "See?" I said. "Easy. Now we have her info and I'll log in and get us an appointment."

Jessa rolled her eyes. "I don't know what scares me more: that you made that woman believe you or that you actually know how to do that stuff."

What I did was just a bit of social engineering and a simple technique. I didn't dare begin to tell her all of the other not-so-simple things I could do.

"I got a question."

"Yes, Eli?"

"What's the objective again? Not that I give a flying crap, but I guess I better be in the know in case you screw it all up."

I clenched my jaw. "Meet Odette. Distract her. Get the contents from her computer. Prove that she's up to something terrible. Use that proof to take her down for good. Get justice for Arlo. Complete my job."

He nodded. "Gotcha."

As the train pulled into its station, we grabbed our bags and headed out into the sun. Florence was so different than the low-key Sorrento. It was modern and minimalist, with brand-new skyscrapers and high tech oozing at almost every corner. All the beauty of Italy with a big dose of modern technology.

My fantasyland.

We caught a cab and headed to Cleary Research Facility.

Hidden behind tall trees and a sleek metal sign, the facility left nothing to the imagination. Chrome lined the all-glass building, which must've been at least thirty stories high. Audis, Fiats, and Porsches crowded the parking lot. Men and women in suits and lab coats exited the doors for their lunch break. A water fountain welcomed newcomers to the atrium as well as a blast of cool air.

"Fancy schmancy," Eli said with a whistle. "This is the life right here."

Looking up at him, I asked, "Do you know where you are? You're in the devil's lair."

Jessa giggled, and we followed her to the main desk.

"May I help you?" the secretary asked. She was wearing a black tie with her blazer and a headset. It was definitely high-pitched Jenny.

I whispered to Jessa, "Follow my lead." They stood behind me as I introduced myself. "Hi, I'm Julian Taylor, and we have a meeting with President Cleary at two p.m."

"Julian Taylor?" The secretary scrunched her eyebrows and began touching her screen, searching for my appointment. Surprised to find it, she said, "It's . . . oh, it's right here. The fill-in secretary must've scheduled you. Yes, top floor. There's a waiting area. Here are your badges."

We clipped our badges to our clothing and headed to the elevators. Jessa pushed the thirtieth-floor button and up we went. When the elevator door opened, we were welcomed by a man in a suit, offering us a drink. "No thank you," I said, glancing around. "Where do we go to see Miss Cleary?"

"In the waiting area." He led us to the waiting room, where a gigantic wraparound aquarium lived. Tropical fish I had only heard of in fairy tales swam around the tank, but nothing was more mind-blowing than the actual shark that swam with them.

"There's a friggin' shark," Jessa beamed, racing up to the aquarium. "He's incredible." She placed her hands on the glass.

"No hands on the glass, miss," the man said with a sneer.

"Sorry!" Jessa took her hands off the glass but pushed her nose right up to the surface, admiring the marine life.

Eli joined Jessa, entranced by the shark as well. "Wonder how much a shark costs," he said to no one in particular.

I sat down in a leather chair, admiring the architecture of the building, only to stand right up, as our names were called. Single file, we made our way into President Odette Cleary's office.

Incredibly, the aquarium made its way into Odette's office as well, and the shark had followed us. Jessa watched mouth agape, and I figured I couldn't rely on her help while we were here—the shark had bewitched her. Odette's office overlooked Florence's town square, and art from who knows where crowded her walls. One painting in particular caught my attention: a fair-skinned, redheaded woman standing on a large shell that floated in the ocean.

I braced myself for meeting the devil herself, praying to God that Eli would remain cool and collected and not say something offensive. I wasn't sure if seeing Odette would trigger anything, either. All we had to do was follow the plan. Just follow the plan.

"Come in," the president called, rising from her chair. "My name is Odette." She wore a white-as-snow mid-length dress. Spider veins crept up her bony legs, and her fire-red hair stood atop her head in a tight bun. Crow's feet graced what I assumed used to be beautiful eyes, but all I saw was evil in them.

She reached out her hand, and we each shook it.

Please, Eli, don't act like a freak. Don't act like a freak. Don't act like a freak.

"Pretty choice office, Miss Cleary. I take it that's . . . *Miss* and not *Missus?*" Eli collapsed into the cushy chair and crossed his leg over the other one.

Oh, kill me now. Sweet angel of death, take me away.

"*Miss* is correct. What can I do for you today?" Odette took her seat and placed her hands on the desk, but not before squirting antibacterial gel into her palms.

I cleared my throat, hoping to stay calm. "Miss Cleary, I'm Julian Taylor and we're here today to talk to you about a donation."

Her smile widened, and I could see her snow-white teeth behind her cherry-red lipstick. "A donation? You could've emailed me about that or talked to my secretary."

"Yes, I know. But it's such a personal matter to all of us that we wanted to meet you and discuss it in person."

A quizzical look crossed her face. "I see. What kind of donation?"

I had to make this woman think we wanted a donation, so I kept the lie simple. All she had to do was say yes or no, and then when we left her office for a tour, I could do my thing. Of course, I'd have to convince her to give us a tour too.

"We represent First Aid for Every Child, a nonprofit organization striving to help children in Europe who need immunizations, medicine, and medical attention. We're looking for someone to donate to the company so we can continue our endeavor to help each child get what they need for a healthy and disease-free life."

She perked up. I had her attention. "I love this. I really do. But I haven't heard of you before. Why is that?"

"We're quite new," I answered. "As you can see, we're both quite young. We believe our generation, Generation Z, needs to be responsible for the health of those who come after us. However, we've enlisted the help of Robert here"—I gestured to Eli—"to help us with the financial and business side of things while we handle the online spectrum."

She titled her head to the side. "Do you have a packet of information I can study?"

I hesitated for a moment. Thankfully, Jessa came to my rescue. "Of course. It's a digital file to avoid wasting paper. Should we email it to you or to your secretary?"

"My assistant, actually. Here's his email." She slid us a business card and Jessa stuffed it in her purse. "I'm very interested in donating and would love to discuss this further. The health of humanity, children especially, is quite a soft spot for me."

For someone who threatened to slice up little Norah until she was un-recognizable, this woman sure acted kind and generous.

"Oh?" I said. "If I may ask, why is it a soft spot for you?"

Her posture stiffened now and she looked away for a brief moment, as if deciding whether or not to share this information. "Some people find fulfill-ment in becoming a doctor, a lawyer, a police officer. Others find it through creative outlets like art, writing, and design. I, however, find fulfillment in ridding our world of infectious diseases. It is a longtime dream that will continue decades after I die. It is my legacy: to heal people and to keep them healthy forever."

"Wow," Eli said. "That's amazing, Miss Cleary. Sounds like you've got a good heart."

I resisted giving Eli the stink eye. "Yes, Miss Cleary, that's beautiful. Thank you for sharing that with us. We want to be a part of that legacy as well."

"I'm glad to hear it. In fact, do you see that bottle of champagne behind you?" We each turned in our chairs. A corked bottle of Dom Pérignon sat on a marble table. "I've been saving it for decades. I'll drink it when I win the Nobel Peace Prize for my work."

"Wow," Jessa said. "That's pretty cool."

She nodded. "Pretty cool indeed." Odette arched her eyebrow. "Due diligence will be required, of course, but if everything looks clean and to my standards, you have yourself a donation."

I perked up. "Wow! Thank you, Miss Cleary. Thank you. We greatly appreciate that."

"Yes," Jessa said. "We can't thank you enough."

"Well, it's not official yet." She offered us a kind smile. "But you're very welcome."

"Would you be willing to give us a tour of your facility?" I asked. "We'd love to do a write-up on it for our blog."

Odette stood up and grabbed her cup of coffee, but not before pushing down on the antibacterial gel dispenser, rubbing her hands together like a fly before a feast. "That sounds just fine. I need to stretch my legs anyway. Plus, you can tell me more about your organization and the legacy you wish to leave behind."

"That sounds just—" But I stopped. Something had caught my attention that I hadn't seen before. In her office, behind her desk, a medium-size oil painting of an ocean rested against the wall. In the middle swirled a vortex, sucking in boats and airplanes and people. Even the sky itself escaped into the mouth of the whirlwind.

The Bermuda Triangle.

I started coughing, spit flying out, my eyes watering. I reached for my inhaler and inserted it into my mouth.

"Are you okay?" Jessa patted my back and I put up my hand.

"I'm okay." I kept coughing until my face turned red.

"There are bottles of water downstairs," Odette said, walking away from me as quickly as she could, guarding her mouth with her hand. "I'll have my assistant get one for you."

I nodded and motioned for them to go on without me.

"We'll be over here." Jessa followed them out, and when I was sure they were out of sight, I booked it to Odette's laptop, inserted my Linux USB (the same one my parents had given to me), and began downloading all of her files.

Come on, come on. I kept my eyes on the door, praying to God that Odette wouldn't peek back in here to check on me. I could still hear them talking in the hall.

Ninety percent done. Please hurry.

"You comin', man?" Eli called out.

"Yeah, I'm coming!" I shouted back, swallowing my spittle. The USB dinged, indicating the files were completed, and I pulled it out, racing out of Odette's office with contents that I knew would give us a huge win.

Except for one snag: I knew this woman.

CHAPTER 24

Don't Test Her

Odette gave us a tour of the facility, and although I was drooling all over the sweet tech, I was itching to plug in the USB and see what we had to work with. I was ready to finish this once and for all.

We toured labs where Odette's team worked on disease control. Access to every room required a key code and a badge. She showed us what her team was currently working on: a cure for leukemia. "We're almost ready to test it," she said, and I caught a tear pooling in her eye. "One day," she continued, "no one will have to endure the hardships of this disease."

We saw a hallway of awards and photos and even a research library that I had to pull Jessa away from.

"And that concludes our tour," Odette said, leading us back to the atrium. "Feel free to stick around. We have a coffee bar in the west wing. Give them these little coupons, and the coffee will be free." She dug into her pants pocket and pulled out three coupons for us. Then she pulled out a tiny hand sanitizer bottle. She squirted a generous amount into her palms and rubbed away.

"That's very generous of you, Miss Cleary," I said. "You've been amazing. Thank you for taking the time to give us a tour. And we look forward to getting started with your donation."

"Of course." She gestured back to the main desk. "Please see my secretary to get my assistant's information."

"We will." We each waved goodbye as she entered the elevator.

But we didn't see her secretary. In fact, we hightailed it out of there as soon as the elevator doors closed.

"You guys," I said, looking at Jessa and Eli as we passed the atrium's water fountain. "We need an internet café and—I can't believe I'm saying this—some espresso."

"You got her info?" Jessa asked, keeping the pace.

"Yes, but that's not all."

"What else?" Eli asked, lagging behind.

As quietly as I could muster, I replied, "I used to work for Odette."

We found a coffee bar and parked our butts in a corner, hidden away from everyone else.

"Start talking," Jessa said, sipping from her frothy mug. When she licked her lips, she left a small puff of foam there.

Blinking in bewilderment, I said, "You . . . uh . . . have some . . ."

"Oh!" She wiped it off her lips, and I tried not to fall over.

"So here's the deal. Back when I was a hacker, I used to protect websites on the darknet that sold some super illegal stuff."

"Like what?"

"Like . . . anything you could ever dream of. Guns, forged documents, credit cards—"

"Knox!" A look of disappointment crossed Jessa's face. "You really did that?"

I winced. "Yes, but I never bought anything, really. My job was to put up firewalls so these websites could do what they wanted without getting in trouble by the feds. So anyway, there was one in particular called the Bermuda Triangle. It was my highest paying job."

"Why?" she asked.

"Why was it so well paid? To be honest, because the Bermuda Triangle sells every drug you can think of, including ones that are brand new, ones that haven't been FDA approved yet. It's not just 'make you feel good' drugs, either. You can even get my parents' cure for the common cold on there."

"Why not just get it from a doctor?"

I gave her a funny look. "Because not everyone can afford health insurance, so it's way cheaper to just buy it on the dark web. So anyway, the owner of this website is named Miss Disappear."

"Because when you go to the Bermuda Triangle, you disappear?" she asked.

"Right. I think that's the joke. Well, did you notice the oil painting Odette had of the Bermuda Triangle behind her desk?"

Jessa thought for a moment, setting her mug down as her eyes bulged. "Oh, wow. You're right. You think she's . . . Miss Disappear? The owner of the Bermuda Triangle?"

"Yeah, I do. Think about it. It makes perfect sense. The drugs that are sold on there that most people have never even heard of? And she owns a research facility that creates medications for diseases. Why not sell them on the dark web?"

"Well, yeah, I mean, it makes sense."

I held the espresso in my hand, bracing myself for impact. "What if the one person the feds have been trying to take down for years on the Bermuda Triangle just happens to own a cozy research facility right in the heart of Florence?" I downed the espresso in one rapid gulp.

"Let's say you're right. Then what? We find out Odette is Miss Disappear as well as the one responsible for what happened to Arlo. Then what?"

"Then we use it as leverage. If she did this to Arlo, which we know she did, then she probably has a cure for it. If she has a cure, then we tell her to hand it over, or we go to the feds with her name and let them handle the rest."

"You want to threaten this woman?" Jessa asked, her voice low.

"I don't know what else we can do. I found the woman, which was what Arlo hired me to do, and now we have her. But things are more complicated now. My parents worked for her, she owns the Bermuda Triangle, and she deserves justice for what she did to Arlo and God knows who else."

"Pull up the USB," Jessa said, motioning toward Josie. "Let's see what we've got on her first, and then we can start making decisions on how to take her down for good."

I plugged in the USB and waited for Josie to wake up. "Okay, so we're looking at her computer, basically."

"That was easy. You didn't even have to hack anything. You just literally took the files and walked out."

"Yeah, it's not so much called hacking as it is theft." I brought up the files and started searching through them. I looked up to check on Eli, who was at the bar buttering something that looked like a biscuit. He sure was switching over a lot recently, I noticed.

"Hey, gorgeous," Eli said to a barista. "Do you have any honey here?"

Now able to see Odette's little projects, my shoulder slumped. "It's going to take me forever to go through all of this. I don't know where to start or what to look for."

"Then, we need to narrow it down. We need to figure out what she's working on *now* or what she's working on all the time."

"You're right. Let me do a search for the files she visited most recently." I pulled up some contracts and banking statements, but I stopped when I saw something entitled NovaVita.

"What's that?" Jessa asked, setting down her mug of coffee.

"What the—?" I clicked on it. It was page after page after page of lab reports on NovaVita. Each and every one had the same stamp at the top: Unsuccessful.

"What's Odette doing with NovaVita?" Jessa asked, fear in her voice. "I thought it didn't exist anymore."

Eli plopped down with honey in hand. As he poured it onto his bread, he looked up at us. "What's wrong with you two? You look all freaked out."

A heavy, exhausted sigh left my lips. "Odette has been doing her own little experiments on NovaVita, the cure for the Raven Virus that my parents created."

"But I thought the cure didn't exist anymore."

"It doesn't," I said. "And that's clear in these lab reports. They're trying to recreate it somehow. But . . . how?" I leaned back in my chair, now full of more questions than I ever thought possible.

"So Odette is using her research team to recreate the cure for the Raven

Virus. Okay, so far, this isn't that bad. We want a cure for the Raven Virus. We *need* a cure."

"Yes, but my parents didn't," I countered. "They sacrificed their lives to stop people from getting that cure. They would never tell me why they wanted it destroyed, though."

Jessa contemplated for a moment. "Then we have to figure out why your parents didn't want it released to the public. If Odette is recreating the cure and that cure is bad news, then we've got to stop her."

"It looks like we've got a lot of leverage on her," I said, sipping my water. "Let's hope she complies."

———————

To take our minds off everything, we all agreed to see Michelangelo's *David* since we were in Florence anyway. Paying money to see a statue of a naked man was the least weird thing I had done in the last week. Entering into the museum, we observed unfinished statues of the great artist, until, at the end of the long hall, was a nine-foot marble statue of David himself.

"He has muscles," Eli observed. "Would ya look at that? Michelangelo sculpted actual muscles throughout his body. I'm not impressed by much, but that's wicked cool."

"I've seen him a few times now, and every single time I'm so caught off guard by how real he looks," Jessa said, resisting the urge to touch the statue—which would result in, like, four grown men tackling her. People crowded around *David*, marveling at something that truly stole the room.

"That's funny," I remarked. "This statue shows David as a young adult holding the slingshot, but he killed Goliath when he was a young boy."

"Nice catch," Jessa said, smiling. "You're absolutely right. You should be a tour guide," she teased.

"I'd love to," I said, raising my eyebrows, "but I'm too busy saving the world."

We left the museum feeling refreshed and inspired—and to be honest, a little hungry. So we stopped at *Vecchio Carlino* like Norah said and ordered *arrabiata.*

The waiter told us, "*Arrabiata* means angry—it's a'spicy!" He set a large plate of spaghetti in front of me topped with red sauce and grape tomatoes sprinkled with red peppers.

I considered licking my plate clean, but I figured that would warrant some funny looks.

I made a mental note to hug Norah for the recommendation.

———

We were back in Sorrento by midnight with more questions than answers, and all of us were physically and mentally exhausted. I went through my to-do list, trying to categorize by priority. The first thing on my list was to get some real sleep. It had been a taxing day, and I was ready to snore it all away.

Jessa slid her key into the lock and opened the front door. Her bag suddenly fell to the floor, its contents spilling out.

"Jessa, what are you doing?" I said, stepping around her. But once inside, I saw Norah waiting for us in a chair in the living room—but I stopped when I saw her wrists duct-taped to the chair and a kerchief wrapped around her mouth. All the lights in the house were off except for a lamp next to Norah. Jessa shouted for her mom, but I firmly placed my hand on her shoulder. "Stay here," I whispered. I motioned for Eli to keep Jessa in the entryway.

Cautiously, I walked toward Norah, bringing my finger to my mouth. She was brave—not a single tear slid down her cheek—but I could see the terror in her eyes. The television was on, a muted game show in Italian.

I walked into the living room, just a few feet away from Norah. I knew we weren't alone; I could feel it. The way your hair sticks up on the back of your neck. She shook her head, telling me no, and right as I reached for the duct tape that was stuck so tightly to her wrists, someone interrupted.

"It's about time you all made it back. I was beginning to think my theatrics were all for naught." Odette waltzed into the room, almost merrily, holding a drink and plopping down on the couch. "I mean, what were you guys doing? Sightseeing while I tortured Norah here? Shameful." She let out a bellowing laugh that made my stomach turn.

I tried to think through every possibility of why she would be here. "What have you done to her?" My nostrils flared and I clenched my fists. I silently prayed Eli was keeping Jessa safe.

Odette brought a hand to her cheek, feigning surprise. "Uh-oh. Is Knox getting angry?" Then another sinister laugh took over the room. "How cute. Go ahead. Try to do something. Let's see what you're made of."

I easily had a good seventy pounds on her. All I had to was tackle her skinny butt to the ground and hold her down until Eli came.

"Oh, but before you think you're going to detain me . . ." Odette walked to Norah's chair and ran her bony finger down the armrest. She reached her finger out and put it right under my nose. I jerked away.

"Smell that? That's gasoline. If you do anything stupid, I'll light a match."

I pushed her finger away from me. "Why are you here?"

"I don't know, let's see. Why did you come to my office today? Because you know exactly who I am, don't you? *Knox Kevel.*"

The blood drained from my face upon hearing my name. How did she know who I was?

"I'm not a fan of nosy little brats." She picked at her polished red nails and took another sip of her drink. "But it's a good thing you visited me today after all. You see, if you weren't so nosy, I wouldn't have met the son of Benjamin and Athena Kevel. I didn't even realize they had a son."

"They had me later in life," I muttered. I kept my eyes on Norah, afraid to leave her side. I reached out toward her hands, for the first time noticing blood on them. *Where are her fingernails?*

"Oh, I wouldn't do that," Odette cautioned. "I mean, you can touch her if you want. But see, if you do that before I tell you to, then I'll walk over to your little girlfriend who's standing at the door and slit her throat." She stood up, still holding her drink, and brought her nose to mine. "You know what's funny about slitting someone's throat? Hollywood always makes it look like they die instantly, but that's not true." She took another swig of her drink, pointing her hand to me as if signaling for me to wait while she finished. "You don't die in a second. You have to bleed out. Death takes time."

I felt my knees buckle and tried to hide it, but I know she saw.

"Let's get something straight right now. You can free her after you tell me what you know about NovaVita. And I wouldn't mind hearing some stories about your parents." She lifted her hands to the ceiling. "Besides! We've got all the time in the world. I've been so bored here, waiting on you all. In fact, when I sat here pulling off Norah's fingernails, it only took forty minutes, and then I had to come up with something else to do." She pouted her lips, and I realized that this wasn't the woman we spoke to earlier today. This wasn't a woman at all; she was an animal.

I glanced at the floor to see fingernails on the ground. I winced and prayed Jessa wouldn't see that. "Okay, I'm going to sit down and tell you whatever you want to know."

She leaned in, her lips inches away from my face. "Good." And then she downed the rest of her drink and set it on the coffee table. On the coaster, of all things.

I sat down on the chair across from her, keeping my eyes on Norah. She was conscious, but she looked like she was fading.

"Let's start at the beginning." Odette crossed her skinny legs and rested her arms on the couch. "What do you know about me?"

"I know that my parents worked for you and that they created NovaVita while working for your research facility. I know that you created a drug to cure William Jenson of epilepsy, and then as a favor, he allowed you to experiment on his son, Arlo Jenson."

"You seem to have done a little bit of research. That's good." She bent forward, resting her elbows on her knees. "But you see, I don't give a crap about the epilepsy drug. Or the mental disorder drug. Think of those creations as little hobbies of mine. A side hustle, if you will. What I want to know is where the cure to the Raven Virus is hiding. Where is NovaVita?"

No, no, no—not this again. This is it—this is what's going to get me killed: not knowing the location of a cure that no longer exists because it was burned to ashes.

"I know you don't believe me," I began, "but I'm telling you: it doesn't exist anymore. My parents' lab went up in flames, and there was not one thing left. Nothing. You can put me on a lie detector test if you want—it's the truth."

She rolled her eyes, annoyed by my lack of knowledge. "Is that what you think, sweetie?"

Heat rushed to my cheeks, and I wanted to just risk it and tackle her to the ground. "I don't know what you're talking about."

"Tsk, tsk. You shouldn't lie. When you lie"—she stood up, walking toward Norah—"people get hurt." Odette pulled a match from her pocket, and my stomach dropped.

"Do you want to be the cause of that?"

"No," I breathed.

"Good. Then play my reindeer games, or I will strike it and kill her."

My lungs tightened and I tried to calm my breathing, but I wasn't sure how long I could make it.

"Do you know where the cure is?" I shouted. "Because I don't. I don't have it, I swear on my parents' graves."

She struck the match. "Uh-oh! You shouldn't swear. That's not very nice." The match got closer and closer to Norah's dress.

"Stop!" I yelled. "What do you want from me? Huh? Just tell me, and I'll do it, but please don't hurt her."

She stopped moving the match and walked toward me. "I want you to come back to my facility in Florence, and I want you to open a file from your parents' lab and get me the formula for NovaVita. Pretty simple. If you say no, I will kill everyone you love—which, I'm guessing you don't have too many left—and leave you alive, so you can be tortured by what you have done." She blew out the match, the smoke lingering in the air.

"W-wait. You have my parents' formula for NovaVita? Like . . . their *original* formula?"

She nodded. "I have the hard drive they kept it on, but guess what? Someone encrypted it for them, and it's impossible to open. Know anyone who could open it?" She got right into my face and stared me down.

"Why did you ask me if I had it then—if you had it all along?"

She shrugged. "Just wanted to see what it would take to get you to play along. Seems like you get the picture now. So! I'll see you tomorrow at my facility, say, six in the evening? You'll decrypt the hard drive, give me the NovaVita formula your parents created, and I won't kill everyone you love."

She patted me on the shoulder, and before she exited, she said with artificial sympathy, "It really was a tragedy what happened to your parents."

CHAPTER 25

Cheat Code

A first-aid kit wasn't going to be enough for Norah's nails. We rushed her to the emergency room of Sorrento Hospital, keeping the blood at bay with two old T-shirts Jessa had found in a bottom drawer. But no one got out of the car. We just sat there.

Eli had switched back to Arlo on our drive to the hospital, which I was thankful for. I think seeing Norah hurt must have triggered him to come back, to be her big brother and help her. "We can't take her in here," he said, staring at Norah's bloody hands.

"Why not?" Jessa asked, keeping her mother calm and awake with a damp towel on her forehead.

"Because they will call the police immediately, and we can't let anyone know it was Odette."

"Why not?" Jessa asked. "Why on earth does it even matter? She's in pain."

"Odette has every single person in this country paid off, like Knox said. Think about it. They're going to ask what kind of monster would do this, and if we tell them, they won't help her."

"They can't . . . *not* help her!"

"You wanna bet?" I said.

We had to come up with a better plan, a smarter plan.

"We need a private doctor," I finally said. "Someone who can be easily persuaded to take care of Norah and not call the police."

"We'll need money for that," Arlo said, nodding. "Which, fortunately, I have. But we need to stop at the ATM first."

"But how are we going to find a private doctor?" I asked, grimacing at Norah's hands.

Jessa spoke up. "I know a retired doctor who lives here in Sorrento. But you can't hurt him or threaten him. He's a good man. He delivered me, actually. He was Mom's doctor."

Arlo and I both looked at each other. "That'll work," we said in unison.

"Do you know where he lives?" Arlo asked, putting the car in drive.

"No, but I'm sure Knox can find his house. His name is Dr. Antonio Rossi."

I pulled out my phone and checked Google. It didn't take long before Dr. Rossi popped up on my screen. "He lives off Via Parsano. Arlo, start driving to the ATM. I think this might actually work."

After Arlo got some cash, we turned onto Via Parsano, where a modest stone home sat on the corner of the street. Arlo helped Norah out of the car. She didn't speak a word. She was semiconscious, so we mostly carried her to the front door.

Jessa knocked, and when no one came, she rang the doorbell. We all held our breaths, praying this doctor would be home.

Sure enough, the front door opened and a short, hunched-over man with balding hair greeted us, but not before glancing at his watch. "Jessa? Is that you?"

"Dr. Rossi, my mother is hurt—badly. Can you help her? We can pay you."

He looked to Norah, and a gasp left his lips. "*Mi Dio!* What has happened to sweet Norah?" He approached her and held her hands in his, delicately pulling off the T-shirts to reveal her wounds. He covered his mouth with his hand and shook his head. "Who did this to her?"

"A very evil person, and we can't take her to the hospital. If we do . . ." I trailed off, not wanting to finish my sentence.

"We need your help—your silence too." Arlo waited for the doctor to respond.

Finally, Dr. Rossi opened the door wider and ushered us in, checking behind us to ensure no neighbors had witnessed the bloodied woman on his porch.

"Rest her there on the couch while I get some disinfectant and fentanyl. And I don't want any money. Keep it."

We did as we were told, gently laying Norah on the couch, only to be met with a groan when her left hand dragged across the cushion. The three of us sat adjacent to her on another couch, waiting for Dr. Rossi to return. We were in an office, full of medical books and portraits of what I assumed were family members from decades past. After a few moments, Dr. Rossi came back into the room and shut the door.

"Now, gentlemen, Jessa, I have to disinfect her wounds. You might need to turn away if you're a bit queasy."

"B-but," I stammered. "She's not out yet. You have to dull the pain."

"I'm giving her the fentanyl now, but there's no time to wait for it to kick in."

"Wait," I said. "How do you have fentanyl? I mean, it's a narcotic, right?"

He nodded and gave me a playful smirk. "Just because I retired from being a doctor doesn't mean I didn't sneak a few things before I left." Dr. Rossi quickly placed the lozenge under Norah's tongue. "By the way, her wounds do not look fresh. How long ago did this happen?"

I tried to think back. How long ago *had* it been?

"Roughly five hours, we believe." Arlo stood up from the couch toward the shelves, probably to avoid watching Dr. Rossi clean Norah's wounds.

The doctor nodded and began his work. He poured the disinfectant onto her fingers, which hovered over a tin pan. Immediately, Norah woke from her semiconscious trance and yelped in pain. I winced, wishing I didn't have to hear what Odette had done to her. I reached for Jessa's hand and held it tight as she cried for her mother. As she cried for the unknown.

"W-will her fingernails grow back?" Jessa asked through sniffles.

"The bed of the nail is meaty and that's what it adheres to when it grows. It appears whoever did this to her didn't pull it to the root, which is good. She has a chance for them to grow back." He stopped for a moment, smelling something. "Is that gasoline I smell on her?"

I nodded. "Yes, it is."

"I see."

After he finished, Dr. Rossi wrapped her fingers in gauze and taped them off. The pain medicine had set in, and she was resting now. He left to wash his hands and dispose of the bloodied T-shirts. When he returned, he pulled up a chair and sat in front of us.

"Now, I do not want your money, as I've stated, but I will give you your silence. Norah is a dear, dear friend of mine, who fed me and kept me company after my wife passed. Even brought me groceries from her store. I owe this to her, and so much more. But with my silence comes a word of caution."

We leaned in closer to hear him, for his words grew softer.

"Whoever did this to Norah—and not just ripping her fingernails off one by one, but pouring gasoline on her—is a vile monster. This wasn't an assault in an alleyway by a drunk man, now was it? This wasn't something she did to herself—no. This was cruel torture. And I know you all know who did it. But for some reason, you cannot tell me."

He stopped talking for a minute, and we wondered if he wanted us to tell him who it was. But instead, we waited, fearful of uttering her name aloud.

"And because you know who did this to Norah, you must stop at nothing to find her. Find her and stop her."

"Her?" I breathed. "How did you know a woman did this?"

Dr. Rossi abruptly got up from his chair and stood over Norah, looking at her limp sleeping body. Her chest raised up and down. He faced us, more serious now than ever. "Let's just say I'm familiar with Odette's work."

We all looked at one other. "How could you possibly know that?" I asked, my voice hushed.

"Son," he said, "this is not the first time I have treated a person whose fingernails have been pulled off one by one. And if that vile woman stays alive, it will not be my last time. Now why on earth Odette would want anything to do with Norah, I'm not sure that I'd want to know. The less I know, the better. One last thing."

He opened the door to his office, suggesting we gather our things and help Norah up. "What is it?" Jessa asked.

"Be grateful she didn't light the match. She must need something from you, because she lit the match on the last one I tended to."

———————

"So what's the plan?" Jessa asked, sipping on her coffee. She made this smacking noise after swallowing. Kind of reminded me of a squirrel or something. We had all grabbed coffee to go from a nearby café and were drinking it in the car in a parking lot. We had the heater on to keep Norah warm. She shivered anyway. "We're supposed to be at her lab by six p.m."

"*I'm* supposed to be at her lab by six," I corrected. "No one else is going."

"What?!" Jessa slammed her coffee cup down a little too hard, and milky coffee poured over the cup like a tidal wave. I reached for a napkin from the console. "You can't do that. We're all in this together."

"She said she wanted *me* to come, not anyone else." I motioned to Norah and her bandaged fingers. "Norah clearly can't go, we can't risk Arlo turning into Dean with something triggering him, and I'm certainly not letting you anywhere near that psycho."

She pouted the way only a girl can do, and if I weren't so certain that I was falling for her, I would've given in. But I couldn't risk losing her.

"Aren't you worried about what she's going to do to you?" Jessa asked, sopping up the coffee with the napkin I handed her. "Look at what she did to Mom. You think she won't do something like that to you?"

"Or worse," Norah said sleepily. "I forgot to tell you the oddest thing. Before she . . . did this to me . . . she put on a pair of latex gloves. At first, I thought it was so she wouldn't leave any fingerprints. But then . . . she stayed there so that you all would know it was her."

"Weird," I said. "She kept rubbing her hands with antibacterial gel while we were there." I shrugged. "Anyway, I don't know anything, but I do know that if I don't open up that file for her, she'll kill us all. So I'd rather take the risk and do what she wants. But you are right about having a plan. I need to be prepared in case she tries to, ya know, murder me."

"What about my gun?" Norah asked, shuddering. I remember her thrusting it into my palm one night, the same night I hurled it through the air and knocked out Dean.

"You seriously think it won't trip off in her security system? Or that one of her goons won't pat me down?"

"Good point," Arlo remarked. He sipped his coffee, which oddly enough seemed to calm him more so than excite him. "You have to think like a fox this time around."

"Cheat," Jessa said, turning her eyes to mine. "You have to cheat."

She was right. If I was going to get out of this thing alive, I needed to be worse than a fox: I needed to be a dirty, double-dealing weasel.

We spent the rest of our time in the car scheming and plotting, hoping that our strategy would not only keep me alive but also give Odette Cleary what she wanted so we could get away.

"Ibisco," I said with finality. "That's our cheat code."

––––––––––

I was back in Florence, this time without my faithful companions. Josie was tucked safe and sound in my messenger bag as I left the taxi. Noticing a nearby café and with hours to scheme before I had to be at Odette's research facility for whatever torture she had in mind for me, I decided to swing in and grab some espresso.

The bell dinged as I opened the shop door, and an attractive tall Italian woman greeted me. "We have samples!" she proclaimed.

"*Grazie.*" I reached over and picked up a piece of chocolate. While glancing at the menu, I heard the bell ding once more. But this time, it wasn't a customer like myself.

"On the ground—now!"

The woman's frightened face met my own as I slowly put my hands in the air, wishing I had had enough sense to hide Josie anywhere else.

"I said get on the ground!" the man yelled.

I did as I was told, and my hands touched the sticky, cold tile while the man approached me, his gun drawn. He ripped the messenger bag, including Josie, from my clutches. I winced, wishing so badly I hadn't come here alone. I didn't have to ask the man what I did wrong or why he was here. I knew. And I was screwed.

While he cuffed me, he said, "Get up. I'm Agent Hannigan, and we're going to have a little talk, man to man."

I grunted as he pulled me up by my shirt and shoved me out the door, but not before I called out, "Thanks for the sample, ma'am!"

The man in black pushed me into an unmarked vehicle, and off we went. After about twenty minutes of driving, we pulled into a modern building, reminding me of what Jessa had said. The nameless man pulled me out of the car and led me up the steps, into the building. Once through security, he took me to a small room, an interrogation room, I surmised.

I would probably be shipped back to the US and thrown into jail. *Hooray.*

Interestingly, that didn't bother me as much as leaving this job unfinished. Leaving Norah and Arlo to deal with Odette. They'd think I abandoned them. And then there's Jessa.

I really, really screwed up.

"Sit down," the man barked. "Now I want to know what you're doing all the way over here in Florence. Just because your charges were dropped doesn't mean you get to fly overseas. We made that pretty clear. Yet here you are! Did you get lost, little boy?"

I rolled my eyes. "No."

"No?" He looked at me incredulously. "Did you think that just because you're off the hook we wouldn't be checking up on you? I had to leave the cozy US just to fly my butt over here to track you down, which wasn't too hard."

Crap. Aunt Jane.

"Yeah, see, we dropped in to check on you in Pensacola, but the surfer dude living in your condo said you were in Italy."

Double crap. Dax.

"What are you doing here, Kevel?" he finally asked. "Or should I call you Julian Taylor?" He threw my fake passport onto the table, but I didn't reach for it.

"I just . . . came here with a friend for a vacation, which you're interrupting."

He feigned laughter. "Oh no! Is little hacker boy stressed?"

"I'm not hacking," I said. Okay, that was kind of a lie, but it wasn't any of his business.

"That's funny," he said, pulling out Josie from behind him and slamming her a little too hard onto the table. "Because a little birdy told me you were."

"It's not like that."

"It's not? Well, I think that's exactly what—"

His radio interrupted us. "Hannigan! You there?" He responded with an affirmative. "You've got a woman here who wants to see you. ASAP."

"Well, tell her I'm busy," he snapped.

"Already did. She is uh . . . quite insistent that you come *immediately*. Said it has to do with the . . . Suicide Tree."

His eyes met mine, and I knew who was here to see me. My saviors wouldn't have used my handle like that. Rather, my demon was here to meet me in person. Why? Why would she come here? How did she find me?

"The Suicide Tree, huh?" he said to the radio. "Be down in two minutes." He looked me up and down. "What kind of crap are you trying to pull? Is this part of whatever scheme you're plotting?"

I vehemently shook my head. "I'm not. I swear to God. I have no idea who that is." But I did know.

He left me alone, and while he did so, I tried to wriggle my way out of the cuffs, but it was of no use. Finally, I laid my head on the cool table and waited.

The door opened, and Hannigan pulled out the keys to the cuffs. As he uncuffed me, he said, "There's a woman here who apparently has more power than me and wants us to let you go." He leaned into my ear and whispered, "For now. This isn't over, Kevel. Just consider this a little break while I think up new ways to bring you down for good."

Ah, she paid him off. Wonderful.

I withheld a thank-you and left the interrogation room, where I met Odette Cleary, the woman who had ripped off Norah's fingernails and attempted to set her on fire. The woman who had ruined Arlo's life.

The woman who had just set me free.

She stood before me wearing black leather pants, a cherry-red blouse, and stilettos. "Knox, dear. I didn't want you to be late for our meeting, so I came here to bail you out. My, your bail was set awfully high. They must really want to keep you, hm?"

"What are you doing here?" I asked. "How did you even know I was here?"

She opened the door that led to the parking lot. "Oh, I didn't. At first, at least. But thankfully, my boys kept a very close watch on you and notified me when the mean man brought you here. You see, *I'm* the one who gets to interrogate and torture you, not anyone else. I don't have time for other people, especially the authorities, to get in the way of my business. Speaking of which, we have some business to attend to, don't we?"

We stopped at her Audi, and some goon of hers opened the door. She stood by it and looked at me. "Let's not waste any more time, Knox."

"Odette," I said, my voice suddenly dry. "I know you."

She gave me an incredulous look. "What is that supposed to mean?"

"I worked for you once on the Bermuda Triangle. You're Miss Disappear."

A Grinch-like smile formed on her face, and she tilted her head, eyeing me, as if seeing me for the first time. "Very good, Suicide Tree. Glad you put that together."

"I want you to know that if you screw me over, I will get you thrown in prison for life. I can prove you're the owner of that website."

She threw her head back and left. Then she got into the car and slammed the door. I stood there, staring at the car and the parking lot and the building. I stood just long enough to wonder what would happen if I ran. If I ran as fast as I could and never looked back at any of this.

Until Odette rolled down her window and said, "Tick, tock."

The Cleary Research Facility smelled the same way it had last time: sterile. I think even the employees bathed in bleach. I guess if you're working in the world of infectious diseases, your being paranoid is understandable.

Up the elevator we went—Odette and me. I noted a tiny camera in the corner watching my every move. As the doors opened, she led the way to her office, the one with the shark tank.

I took a seat in the same chair I had sat in hours before. I reached into my back pocket and pulled out my inhaler, only to suck in the precious medication before she came in.

"Knox, we've got a lot to do, so let's get to work." She sauntered past me and headed straight for the Germ-X, rubbing it into her chapped skin. Today her red hair was brushed perfectly straight, where it lay over her shoulders. Odette sat down in her chair and crossed her legs. "I did a favor for you, and now it's time for you to do a favor for me."

"Cut the crap," I said. "I'm here to do what you said so you'll leave me and everyone else alone. So can we stop pretending like we're helping each other? A deal is a deal."

She smirked. "A deal *is* a deal. But before we start, I don't want you getting the feeling that I'm growing soft, so I want to go over a few ground rules." She turned around, still seated in her chair, and pushed a button on her remote, which brought down a large flatscreen TV. "You understand, right?"

I nodded.

"Did you know that over ten million people have been infected by the Raven Virus?"

I shrugged. "Okay. So what?"

"It's disgusting. I wanted a cure for it. I didn't want people to suffer anymore."

I stifled a laugh. "Sure, okay. Tell that to Norah, the woman suffering right now because of your antics."

"Don't make me the villain here. I'm trying to cure the world of one of its deadliest diseases. That's why I brought in your parents. They were brilliant.

And I knew that if anyone were dedicated enough to finding a cure, it was those two."

The television turned on, and there on the screen were two different earths: one that looked dirty and one that looked clean.

"You see, with all of these diseases—the Raven Virus being one of them— our world is filthy and disgusting and riddled with germs. We can't all live with infectious diseases, or the whole world will kill itself. So that's why the cure was created. And why more cures will be created in the future to halt all other diseases."

"What? Like a . . . germ-free Utopia?"

"Precisely."

I rolled my eyes and chuckled. "All right, so you wanted to have a clean world. Got it. What does this have to do with the ground rules you mentioned?"

She shook her index finger at me. "Don't be so hasty. I'm not done with the show."

The next picture popped up. It was a bar graph depicting statistics on mental behavior.

"Now, the only problem with the cure your parents created, NovaVita, is that it caused mental instability, if you will."

"What kind of instability?" I asked, my attention more focused.

"They were just going a little . . . mad. But not all of them. Just some. They were . . ." She sighed loudly. "How do I say this—trying to eat other people."

My mouth nearly hit the floor. "Y-you mean the cure for the Raven Virus caused people to become . . . are you kidding me? Are you saying they were cannibalistic?" So *that's* why, after all this time, my parents wanted nothing to with NovaVita. That's why they wouldn't let anyone have it. Because if they did, then anyone with NovaVita in their system would . . . *oh, God.*

"Yes, but not all of them. Just a few hundred."

"*Hundred?* How many people did you test this on? Are they still cannibals?"

"What does it matter?" she asked.

"I just . . . did the desire to want to eat people ever go away?"

"Oh, that." She waved it off like it was nothing. "I'm sure they've found ways to cope with the side effects."

"You don't even know what happened to them? You just let them back into society?"

"Let's stay on topic, hm? So your parents"—she turned back around to face me, still holding the remote—"wanted to keep testing for another six months. Can you believe that? Six months with millions of people walking around and coughing up black blood."

I wasn't sure if I should answer, so I just held still.

"But we didn't have another six months. I didn't want to wait. So I told them to skip the testing and let's get it out in the field. And do you know what they did?"

I did. I knew exactly now, after she painted a picture, what my parents did. And so does the whole world.

"They holed up in that little Florida lab of theirs and wouldn't let me have it." Her lips feigned a pout, and I felt the anger rising up in my chest. I knew what she was going to say next, but I had to hear it. I had to hear it come from her own mouth.

The next picture on the TV was of the burning lab.

"You remember this, don't you?" She laughed. "Of course you do. That was a dumb question. So since they wouldn't give me what was rightfully mine, I decided to take it. But accidents happen, Knox, and you see, there was an explosion. I couldn't save them, but I did save *this*." She opened a drawer in her desk and placed a hard drive upon it. "The cure's formula is there, but I can't open it. For three years, we have tried. And do you know why?"

I did know why.

"Because their son, the Suicide Tree, encrypted it."

My parents came to me on a Sunday afternoon, before they holed up in their lab, and asked me to encrypt it. They told me that they wanted it to be impossible for any person, including myself, to open it once it was locked up. Dad had said, "I want it locked down better than Alcatraz."

So I did what they asked. And now here I sit, being asked to decrypt my own creation.

Odette slid the hard drive closer to me, but I didn't reach for it. I only stared at the woman responsible for letting my mother and father burn alive in a brick building on a Thursday afternoon so she could save her precious cure.

"Now for the ground rules." She stood up from her desk and clicked a button on the remote, and a monitor showed Arlo sitting in a room on the floor by himself, his hands tied behind his back. I watched as a man I didn't recognize entered the room and grabbed Arlo's arm, only to inject him with a needle.

"No!" I shouted, standing up from my seat. "You can't do that! Please, don't! Please!"

"Uh-huh-uh. It's not polite to shout." She turned off the TV, and all that remained was a black screen. "He'll be just fine. I have the antidote right here." She patted her pocket. "You are to pick up the hard drive, and—why are you not picking it up? Aren't you going to do as I say?"

I willed my hand to move and grabbed the hard drive, holding it in my palm.

"That'a boy. You will decrypt the hard drive for me. You have until dawn. That means that tonight, you will decrypt it. And if it's not all done by to-morrow morning, the fun little liquid Joe just injected Arlo with will become permanent. If you get my drift."

I gripped the drive tighter, wishing I could just break it and then break her neck. "What does it do?"

She left her desk, walking past me, and I assumed that meant I was to follow. "It will give him a heart attack and he will die. I took your beloved suicide tree plant, made some enhancements to it, and now it will very, very slowly stop his heart. Unless, of course, you fulfill your favor to me."

CHAPTER 26

Cat and Mouse

Odette led me down a long hallway. I shivered and wondered how she would kill me when I couldn't decrypt the hard drive. She didn't seem like the get-it-over-with-quick kind of killer. More like the sit-down-and-stay-a-while kind of psycho.

We reached a large steel door. Odette tapped her fingers on the keypad's buttons, and the door slid open.

"Right this way," she said.

So cordial, this one.

If I weren't about to die an excruciating death, I would be fanboying all over the place. Whatever this room was had to be worth millions. Gigantic computer screens surrounded the walls. Buttons and keyboards and wires and gadgets commanded the room. And there was a single swivel chair in the middle. Just for me.

"Take a seat."

Cautiously, I walked to the chair and sat down. Odette placed the hard drive on the desk, a few inches away from me.

"Are you ready to begin?"

I cleared my throat. "Listen, I will do everything I can to get the cure, but there's one tiny problem."

She neatly placed her hands in her lap, as if she were talking to a child. "Oh?"

"I need my computer. My own computer."

She laughed. "You need your flimsy computer when you have all this?"

She swept her hand across the room, her eyes shining bright at the illustrious electronics at our disposal.

"Look, I've got my computer at the secretary's desk in my messenger bag. They made me check it at the door. Can't you just get one of your goons to grab her? I can still use this other stuff, but I need her for some other things. Josie's got all my codes and programs that I created, and I don't have them all memorized."

She pushed a button on a remote, clicking on the intercom. "Joe! Go to the lobby and get the little brat's computer. He has work to finish, so do hurry."

The intercom went off, and she leaned against a desk adjacent from my own. She tapped her nails on the desk and stared at me. I stared back but didn't feel any braver. In fact, I thought I might wet myself with the spawn of Satan so casually standing in front of me.

How long is Joe gonna take?

"I suppose there's no sense in hiding it from you anymore," she began. "About your parents. Of course, you're a smart boy. I'm sure you've figured it out by now, yes?"

I didn't speak. I waited for her to continue.

"It was just over three years ago that I trapped them in their own lab and let them burn alive." She clapped her hands together. "Can you believe it? Crazy, huh?"

I shut my eyes, willing myself to forget their deaths. I wanted to pretend she wasn't here, pretend I couldn't hear her. Pretend she was lying to me to mess with my brain.

"Did you know that the security cameras in their lab were fire-resistant? So the whole shebang was recorded. In fact . . ." Her finger caressed the desk and inched its way toward a remote control. "I could play it for you if you'd like."

"No," I whispered. "Please don't." You know how when something terrible is happening, your heart starts pounding? For me, it was my lungs. Except lungs don't pound. They constrict, and it felt like a boa had wrapped its scaly body around my lungs.

"Oh, but why not?" She walked toward me and suddenly her cold hand was wrapped around my chin. "You see, sweet Knox, I don't think you fully understand the gravity of your situation. You don't get me what I want, and I will take away everything you love." She pushed my chin back and walked to the remote. "So it only makes sense for you to see just how far I will go to accomplish my goals."

With the push of a button, on the gigantic screens, there were my parents in their lab. Everything looked as normal as could be, except they both looked like they were in distress. And why wouldn't they be? With scores of civilians outside protesting them, they must have been experiencing chaos in their minds as well, I'm sure. It sounds crazy, but for a split second, I was so happy to see them. So happy to see their faces. In this moment, they were alive.

"Funny thing about explosions," Odette said, the remote still in her hand. "You can die in more ways than one. You can die from the shock wave, of course. It rapidly compresses your body and everything inside. Your organs will rupture, veins will explode, and Knox, even the eyes in your head can explode."

I winced, wishing she'd just kill me now. But she couldn't. She needed me. Like a cat with a mouse, she loved to play sadistic games with her prey.

"And if that doesn't get you, rapid heating of the air can sear your airways and cook you from the inside out. Then if you somehow missed all of that, there's always debris. Shrapnel. It could be rock, metal, anything slamming Athena and Benjamin, tearing through their bodies. How do you suppose they died?"

I shook my head, tearing my eyes away from the screen, knowing what was going to happen next.

"I asked you a question, Knox." She pressed pause on the video. "It's rude to ignore me."

I looked up at her. "Shock wave," I murmured.

"Oh, excellent answer, but a wrong one. Let's see, shall we?" She pressed play and the video continued. I kept my head low so I wouldn't have to see them die. I remember that day when I watched the outside of their lab explode. I had watched them die from the outside, and now Odette wanted me to see them die from the inside.

"Open your eyes, Knox, or I'll have Joe staple your eyelids open."

So I did as she said. And I watched the screen. I watched Mom hold Dad's hand, their bodies leaning against the table, their beakers and other things occupying the table. I watched as Dad rubbed Mom's hand and smiled at her, as if to say, "Everything will be okay. This will all be over soon."

And that's when it all went away.

The entire room filled with dark smoke and reddish-orange flames as the building shook. Now I was glued to the screen, begging for them to be okay, when I knew how it ended. How it always ended in my dreams. The smoke took an eternity to clear before I knew if they were still okay.

And there they were, my parents, on the tile floor of their lab, still alive. But I could tell not for long.

Tears streamed down my cheeks as I watched my mom will herself to move—to get to Dad. The lab was more blood than room. She rolled over to Dad, where she shook him, trying to wake him up. He was breathing, miraculously. She held him in her arms, and his arm, barely able to move, made its way around her waist. They lay like that for several seconds until a shadow approached them.

Odette spoke up. "I didn't mention every single way one can die from an explosion, did I? Bit of a plot twist, you might say."

"No! No more! Please! I can't do this. You have to stop." I tried to suck in a breath, but nothing would come. I didn't reach for my inhaler, because I hoped the asthma attack would kick in and just kill me. Just stop me from watching my family die before my eyes.

"Not yet. The good part's coming."

And there she was, Odette Cleary, with smoke and flames around her, and she truly, absolutely did look like the devil. I had never felt so helpless.

She stood over my parents, looking at their bloodied bodies as they held one another. It was my mom who first looked up and saw Odette. And I could see it in her eyes that she knew why Odette was there.

And that's when Odette pulled out a Glock and shot them both in the head.

Bang.

Bang.

Just like that.

I wasn't sure how long I had been wailing before Odette stopped the tape.

"Such a pain in my butt. An explosion should've killed them dead, but not your parents. No, they're too resilient. Fortunately, I was there to ensure everything went according to plan."

I was sobbing now, snot and tears covering my face. After all this time, I finally knew for absolute certain how they died. I had always wondered if the smoke got them first or if they had to suffer the flames, licking at their skin. But now I knew the truth.

I felt the vomit come up and cover the floor.

"Disgusting!" She stepped several feet back, and I noticed how pale her face was. This lady did not want me puking anywhere near her. Frantic, she dove for the antibacterial hand wash and furiously rubbed her hands together. "Clean it up!" she screamed. And I wondered, *With what?*

Joe walked in with Josie, set her on the table, and left, but not before revolting at the sight of my vomit. Odette put her hand on my shoulder and whispered in my ear: "I suggest you suck it up and get to work. You don't have much time left before you lose another person you love. And this time, there won't be a video. I'll make you watch it in real time."

With that, she left me there in a heaping mess, my shirt stained with tears, my blood boiling.

I rested my head on Josie.

I lost them all over again.

———

I remember the first day Mom and Dad moved into the lab in downtown Pensacola. Cardboard boxes full of beakers and flasks and test tubes had clanked as we carried them up the steps into the lab. The lab was sterile, yet my mom still scrubbed the counters with bleach before setting up everything.

"That box goes on that table," she had said, directing Dad and me as we unloaded the moving truck. "And be careful not to break anything."

"Mom," I said, "everything in these boxes is breakable. I promise we'll be careful."

She stopped bleaching for a moment to give me a quick kiss on the forehead. "I know, sweetie. I just don't want any other messes to clean up."

"Was there really a mess to clean up to begin with? This place was clean before we got here."

She shrugged. "I know, Knox. But you know how I am. I'm a bit of a clean freak."

I snapped out of my daydream and wiped my tear-stained cheeks. *A clean freak.* That's what Odette was, but somehow a million times worse. It's like it was *her* disease: to be obsessed with cleanliness. If I could somehow use that against her, I might actually be able to beat her.

But how?

And then it hit me. The entire plan was to use Ibisco to defeat her, to distract her. But I had better intentions. A better idea than just hypnotizing her for a few moments.

———————

The clock was ticking, and Odette checked up on me by popping up on the screens every now and then. "How's it going, Knox?" she asked. "Staying busy?"

I told her I was, but I didn't tell her what I was busy doing. While she thought I was decrypting the code on my parents' hard drive, I was really coding Ibisco to do something I wasn't proud of. At least, I hadn't ever intend to use Ibisco this way. But we all agreed I'd have to cheat to win a battle against Odette Cleary.

"There's just one thing, though," I said to the screen. "I'm starving and my blood sugar is dropping. Is there any way you could bring me something to eat? Or maybe bring me some juice? Anything to help me stay awake?"

Odette leaned into the camera, where I could see her pores and every wrinkle and blemish. "Does this look like a resort to you? Do you think you're on vacation, that I'm your maid?"

I didn't answer; I only stared.

"You can eat when you've decrypted the hard drive." With that, she signed off. A dark screen reflected my face, and I looked worn and tired and just plain awful. Yet it didn't compare to whatever they were doing to Arlo. I willed him out of my mind so I could focus on the task at hand.

CHAPTER 27

Ibisco 2.0

I knew Odette was watching my every move, but lucky for me, there was no way that woman spoke code. Norah, Arlo, and Jessa were told to be at the computer at all times back in Sorrento–yet Arlo had somehow managed to get to Florence. I began sending them messages in binary.

"Arlo is here," I typed to Norah and Jessa. "How did he get here?"

"He insisted we not stay in Sorrento," the message read. "He left to come here to be nearby, and we couldn't leave him alone."

"Well, now Odette has him. Stay safe."

For all Odette knew, I was working on a code to decrypt the hard drive.

But I had something else in mind.

After watching her use enough antibacterial gel to properly sanitize an army, I realized she would be the perfect guinea pig for Ibisco 2.0. I'll admit: before this trip, I would've never thought of doing something like this to another human being.

But after everything she'd done and everything she was planning to do, I wasn't left with much of a choice.

Sure, I could probably have gotten smart and just beaten her over the head with something and called it a day. But I didn't want to physically kill anyone.

It had been a good twenty minutes since I last heard from them. I wondered why Jessa wasn't answering any of my messages. Maybe it was the binary code she was having difficulty translating. I'd given her a website to translate it through, though.

I had mere hours to finish the code for Ibisco 2.0. No pressure at all.

Suddenly, a voice came on the intercom. It was Odette.

"Guess what, Knox? You probably don't know this, but Joe is such a caffeine addict, and you'll never guess who he found at the café!"

I jumped out of my chair, looking around the room for Odette. But I didn't have to look for her. Norah and Jessa came on the screens. Sitting next to Arlo. Their hands were tied to chairs, and they were blindfolded. They must've followed me out to Florence. I was angry and scared at the same time. Now everyone was endangered because of me.

"I didn't put tape across their mouths, because I thought you'd like to hear their screams."

And I could hear them. They were begging for me not to listen to anything she said. Begging me to do what I had to do.

"I would hate to have to kill your friends here, Knox. Do you know why? Because your spirit would be so broken that I wouldn't be able to get you to decrypt the hard drive. What would be the point without these people in your life? So you know what I decided to do? To torture them instead. I won't kill them, because that won't benefit me. But I thought it would be fun to . . . rub salt in their wounds, so to speak. Now, you get back to work, and later, when I feel like you're slacking again, I'll pull up this screen and show you what new, fun torture method I've used on them. Bye-bye!"

I shook it off. I had to. I had to block out what Odette was claiming to do and focus on taking her down once and for all.

Two hours had passed, and I felt like I had a million lines of code. Of course, I couldn't test this program at all, because I'd be testing it on myself. I had to hope and pray it was actually going to work.

But the tricky part was transferring over the code to the hard drive. Odette would have to connect the hard drive to her computer to get the cure. However, what she'd see on her screen would be my greatest and latest creation. Before, Ibisco made the viewer tell someone something they had hidden deep in their brain. But now? It would make their worst nightmare seem real. Ibisco 2.0 would hypnotize Odette into seeing her worst nightmare, which should give me enough time to hit her over the head with something and rescue everyone.

If it worked, then I could save Norah, Jessa, and Arlo.

And if it didn't?

Well, then I guess I'd be seeing my parents again really soon.

CHAPTER 28

Bugs

"Ummm. Odette?" I said to the empty room. "I don't know how to page you, but I'm guessing you can hear—"

"All done, Knox?" Odette's voice came over the intercom.

"Y-yes. I'm done."

"I'll be there shortly."

Odette came in through the same door I entered hours ago. I couldn't help but notice she moved a little more quickly than normal.

"It's all yours." I gently set the hard drive into Odette's palm and moved out of her way so she could sit in my chair.

"What do you know? Turns out you *are* good for something after all." She sat down in the swivel chair and tucked her legs underneath it. I thought about just grabbing her hair and slamming her head into the computer, but I knew her goons would see it and kill Norah, Jessa, and Arlo in an instant.

Plus, I kind of wanted to watch the grand finale.

Odette connected the hard drive to the computer as I stood a few feet behind her, watching her . . . watching the screens.

"Knox," she said, turning to face me, "is there any reason why my screens are still black? I connected the hard drive, and nothing is happening. I'm starting to lose faith in you, and the clock is still ticking."

"Give it just a minute to boot up. It's a *huge* file." I carefully grabbed Josie and stuffed her in my bag. I swung the bag around over my shoulder.

She arched her eyebrow and slowly turned the swivel chair back to the center of the screens.

Sweat glistened my forehead, and I was coming up with a plan B when suddenly, the screens all began blinking.

Just like they were supposed to.

Immediately, I shielded my eyes, praying Odette wouldn't take hers off the screens.

"Why is it blinking? I don't understand what's—"

When she stopped talking, I peeked her way to see if she was charging toward me. But she wasn't. She was mesmerized by the hypnotic images blinking on the gigantic screens. I didn't dare look at them. As she watched them, entranced, I slowly backed up to the main door. Right as I was ready to bolt out of there, she began screaming.

"Get them off of me! They're on me! They're everywhere!" Her screams rang in my ears, and she started scratching at her own skin. Scratching so hard and furiously that bloody streaks popped up on her arms. Then her legs. Then her stomach.

And the face was the worst part.

"What have you done to me?" she screamed. "Get them off! Bugs are on me!"

There wasn't a single bug in sight, but that didn't matter to Odette. Ibisco 2.0 had worked. She thought bugs were crawling all over her skin.

And she was literally trying to scratch them off.

I couldn't watch another second of Odette bludgeoning herself. I turned my attention to the keypad to get out of here. Earlier, Odette had typed in six numbers. I had to (quickly) figure out what they could be. I racked my brain, which was impossible to do with her screaming in the background.

Right as my fingers touched the keypad, the door slid open.

And you'll never guess who was standing there with a gun pointed at my face.

"What's going on in here?" Joe said.

Oh, you know, just hanging out, having a picnic, shooting the breeze.

He kept his aim at my face, and my hands went in the air. Odette was on the floor now, her once-snow-white skin now a dark crimson. It looked like a beast had come upon her, scratching and clawing its way into her body.

"Help me!" Odette screamed.

"What did you do to her?" I heard the bullet load into the barrel.

"I swear, I have no idea. I was working, and she started screaming bloody murder. She's been clawing at herself, and I have been banging on this door for help. What took you so long?"

He bought it, and lowered the gun. "Stay put. Don't even breathe."

Well, that part shouldn't be difficult.

Joe cautiously approached Odette to calm her, but she only worsened.

"Get away from me!" she screamed. "They're on you too! They're everywhere!"

She was now in the fetal position, like a baby. I wanted to feel sorry for her, but she deserved this. Right as Joe tried to help her, I heard nails make contact with skin. She had scratched him.

He withdrew, looking helpless, and Odette began to bang her skull onto the metal floor.

"Don't move!" Joe yelled, coming toward me. "I'm going to get backup, and I swear to God, if you're not here when I get back, I'll slit their throats."

He didn't have to clarify. I knew who he meant.

I turned my attention to Odette. The woman had nearly beaten herself to death trying to fight off insects that didn't even exist.

"You did this to me," she screamed. "I don't know how you did it, but you did this to me." Tears streamed down her face, and she began to rip the hair right out of her head. "And do you want to know the best part?" she said through gritted teeth. Her eyes were crazy now.

I kept my distance as she pulled her bloodied body up off the floor. She could barely stand she was shaking so hard. My feet stayed glued to the floor.

"You're just like me. You think you're the hero, but you're not. No real hero does this to another human being." Then she let out a bloodcurdling scream like I've never heard from any human or animal. It pierced my ears, and she wouldn't stop. It just kept going. When she'd run out of air, she'd inhale again and scream once more.

Until she stopped screaming to reach into her pocket and pull out the antidote.

"Stop!" I yelled. "What are you doing?"

Odette crushed the vial in her hands and opened her palm to reveal shards of glass protruding from her skin. "Now you have only *two* to save. Choose wisely."

This was my chance. I had to run out of this room as fast I could and free Jessa, Arlo, and Norah. Odette wasn't going anywhere; she was freaking out too much to even know what room she was in. Not to mention, I didn't know how long this lasted. Did it last until someone poured water in her face?

I decided not to wait around to find out. Before I left, I crouched down next to Odette, who lay on the floor screaming in the fetal position, and took her keycard off her blouse. "Thanks," I muttered. For a fleeting moment, I felt bad for her, until I thought about Norah's fingernails and Arlo's disorder and my murdered parents.

I rushed out of the computer lab and into the hall, where a hundred possibilities lay before me. Where could they be stowing them?

CHAPTER 29

Arrivederci

I wasn't going to wait around for Joe any longer. All I wanted to do was find the people I prayed were still alive.

Not that it really mattered anymore. I was going to lose one of them despite my best efforts. After everything, one of them would die.

The entire facility was like a maze. No matter which way I went, I felt like I was still going in circles. And I didn't even know where they were being held.

I knew there had to be a control room with security camera footage. If I could find that room, I could spot Norah, Jessa, and Arlo.

I went to a dozen rooms, slamming them shut one at a time until I finally came to the end of a hall where a door was left wide open. This must've been where Joe was watching us when he came down there, which immediately reminded me that he could be back at any minute. I shut the door behind me and pulled the monitors closer to me. I scanned as fast as I could until I saw the three people whose lives I had endangered. They were in Odette's office, of all places. Why would she put them there?

I bolted out of the door, sprinting up the stairwell until I got to the top floor. I peered around the door, looking for the assistant who had greeted us a few days ago. No assistant in sight and no Joe or any other goons. I approached Odette's office door, put the key card to the code, and opened it.

"Knox . . . we're in . . . here." It was Jessa. She was still alive!

"Hang on! I'm coming!" I rushed into the room, and Norah, Jessa, and Arlo were still alive. They looked awful. Their faces, grim and pallid, barely lifted when I entered the room.

"How did you find us?" Norah whispered as I untied her wrists and took off the blindfold. She didn't even move. It was like she had given up.

"It's a long story."

"What about Odette?" she asked. Her eyes were vacant. "Is she . . . is she still alive?"

I nodded. "Barely. I don't know how she could possibly still be alive after . . ." I trailed off. I didn't want to tell them what I had done to her.

There was a thick silence in the room. I untied Jessa and took off her blindfold. Her tear-streaked cheeks showed off those dimples. I bent down to kiss her, but she jerked away. "The poison! Don't kiss me . . . yet."

I nodded. "Sorry. I was so worried about you," I whispered. I held on to her and tried to stay strong, but it was no use.

I untied Arlo and took off his blindfold. "Are you okay?"

Arlo nodded, but I knew he wasn't okay. He was dying. All of them were dying right before my eyes.

"Where's the third vial?" she asked, her eyes following my hands.

I grabbed the two vials from off the table and stood before Norah, Jessa, and Arlo. Yes, Odette had put the antidotes within a few feet of them, knowing they'd never be able to reach them.

"Knox, there's no time. You have to give us the antidotes. We're not going to—" Suddenly, Jessa was throwing up, and I raced toward her to hold her hair out of her face. In the confined space, the bile stunk up the entire room.

"I don't have the third vial," I announced. Their eyes all stared up at mine, and I felt like the worst human being in the world. "She destroyed the other vial right in front of me. There are only two antidotes."

The realization hit them. One of them was about to die in Odette's office.

"Give them the vials," Arlo said, his voice gruff. "And don't argue with me."

"*Fratello*, no!" Norah said. "Please, no. There has to be another way." Her pleading eyes scanned my face, but I could offer her nothing.

"Arlo, I don't want you to die," I said, walking toward him.

"Death is always inevitable, son. You can't beat it. You can't win." I knelt down beside him and felt his hand on my shoulder. "My dear boy, you have given me something no one else could. You gave me the truth. You took me on an adventure. You let me live my last few days on earth the way I could only dream of. You are good, Knox. You are a good man." He stopped for a moment to cough, his shoulders quaking. "A good man with a compassionate heart. You are, in more ways than one, just like your parents. They see you now, and they are proud." He stopped for a moment to wheeze, and I reached into my back pocket for my inhaler. He shook his head and told me to put it back. "This is where Fate, the beautiful, mysterious Fate, has brought us, and I have never argued with her. Hand the vials to Jessa and Norah."

I stood up and gave the vial to Jessa, where she drank it down in an instant. Then I handed the second one to Norah, and she did the same, although hesitant at first. Their eyes turned to Arlo, and we waited.

Suddenly, the door flew open, slamming so hard into the wall that it rattled the room and startled the fish. I didn't have to turn around to know who it was. "Norah, Jessa, Arlo," I whispered. "I'll handle her. Just run away when you have the opportunity. Do you understand me? When I say run, you run like your life depends on it."

"Knox Kevel." Blood peeked out of Odette's tattered clothes, where she had ripped and clawed at them. Her eyes were crazed with fury, and fresh meat was under her nails from where she had tried to scratch the invisible bugs off her body. She stumbled into the room until she was mere inches away from me. I stood my ground, protecting my family. And that's what they were to me: family. She glanced at her desk, noting the empty vials. "I see you've saved two of three while you left me to die. I should slit your throat right now, but instead, I'm going to let you watch them all die."

"You can't kill them, Odette." I puffed out my chest, daring her to come closer. "Look at yourself. You're a wreck. You're filthy and disgusting. You can't hurt them and you can't win anymore."

Odette let out a laugh unlike any I've ever heard. She was manic. "Is that what you think? That this is over? That you've won?" Her hand made hard contact with my cheek, burning through my whole face.

Before I even knew what was happening, I bulldozed her legs, pushing her to the ground. Her head slammed onto the floor and I punched her as hard as I could, until her teeth, like vampire fangs, bit into my flesh and I screeched in pain. She threw me off her and made a beeline for Norah. I latched onto Odette's ankle and dragged her into the middle of the floor.

As I wrestled with the devil, her blood smeared all over my clothes, and the rusty smell nauseated me. She straddled me and socked me in the jaw so hard I heard something pop—whether it was my own bone or hers, I couldn't tell. Odette wrapped her hands around my throat, but I slammed my fists into the crease of her elbows and head-butted her. Her head flung back so I took the opportunity to push her off. I could almost see the stars floating around her head. She stood up but stumbled.

I screamed to the others, "Run! Run! Go!"

Jessa, Arlo, and Norah, despite their weakness, began running out of the room.

"They're all over you!" I yelled at Odette. "Just look at those nasty bugs crawling all over your skin."

She twitched and looked at her legs. Her broken, bloody nails dug into her gory skin. Odette screamed out in pain but continued to scratch, trying helplessly to get rid of the bugs.

"You'll never get rid of them," I said, taunting her.

Her body backed up against the desk, and she reached for a letter opener and pointed it at me. With some quick thinking, I seized the famous champagne bottle by its neck and broke it against the wall.

She snickered a pathetic laugh. "You're not man enough," she mumbled, motioning to the broken bottle with the letter opener. "You won't kill me."

"I have no other choice but to kill you."

"Just like you're letting the millions die of the Raven Virus?" She used her free hand to paw at her open wounds.

I caught my breath. "What are you talking about?"

"You never finished your project," she said through gritted teeth. "You never decrypted the formula for NovaVita."

I kept my hand steady. "You know why I can't do that."

Before my very eyes, she rotated her wrist and pointed the letter opener toward her chest. "Yes, you can. Somebody out there can fix the cure. Don't let your parents' deaths be in vain."

My arm dropped, the bottle still tight in my hand. My eyes narrowed. "You're the one who killed them!"

She took a deep breath. "I killed some to save millions. All of it, all those diseases . . . cured. The Raven Virus is technically cured, isn't it? Think about it. All because I made the hard decisions. Decrypt the hard drive, Knox. Finish what I couldn't do."

Odette closed her eyes, a strange peace coming over her face. Her trembling hand gripped the letter opener harder. Without a sound, she plunged it into her chest and her eyes shot open. Not a tear graced her cheeks as her knees buckled and she collapsed to the ground. The champagne bottle left my hand as I raced out of the office.

———

We were down in the lobby now, where all was vacant. The attendants and other goons had barely missed us as they hopped onto the elevator. My hope was that they'd stay there long enough to retrieve Odette's body. Our faces were all over those security cameras, and I'm sure Joe wouldn't let us escape that easily. But I could take care of all that later.

With all of us itching to get out of the lobby, we made our way outside past the enormous fountain and found a shade tree with a bench under it. We helped Arlo to the bench and then sat next to him. I, however, knelt down on the ground to give the girls room.

"*Sorella*," Arlo began, coughing much harder than he had before. He was the weakest out of the three. "You are just like Mama. You are strange and beautiful and strong. You are everything she'd want you to be. And I'm sorry I wasted decades of my life not getting to see you grow into her."

The tears were flowing down Norah's cheeks, and she couldn't muster anything else except, "I love you, *fratello*. You are my hero."

"Jessa," he said. "Listen to your mother. She has intuition unlike any I've ever seen. She knows what's best for you. Keep running. Keep telling your stories. And don't ever let go of your eccentricities. They make you lovable."

She nodded and wiped a tear from her eye. Jessa squeezed his hand and told Arlo she loved him.

Arlo's eyes were nearly vacant now. His skin was no longer clammy, but ice cold. I knew as his breaths grew farther apart that I didn't have much longer to say what I wanted to say. "Arlo," I began, "you are everything I want to be. You took *me* on an adventure. You showed *me* the truth. You made me a better person. If it weren't for you, I'd still be a recluse, stuck in my condo with Cheetos dust all over me." At this, we both chuckled. "It's because of you that I want to be a better man."

He took one big breath and said, "But you always were, my boy. You always were." And with that, the man who was too special to be confined to one personality slipped away from me and into Fate's hands.

"No." I gently shook him. "No, Arlo. Please don't. Please!" I wrapped my arms around him and pulled his limp body into mine. "You're going to be okay. It's not real. It's not real. Please, God. Please."

I wept into his chest.

––––––––––

We buried Arlo Jenson the next day. The sun had just peeked over the horizon, and the three of us trekked up the hill behind Ibisco carrying Arlo's body. Jessa suggested the tree in the middle. We all agreed because he liked that tree the most. Jessa and I dug and dug while Norah sat under the tree, staring at her bandaged fingers and wishing she could help. We couldn't do a normal funeral, since that would bring attention to us. We couldn't be in the spotlight, and this intimate funeral with just the three of us was what we needed.

Once his grave was ready, we stopped and stared at one another. I wiped my brow and reached for a glass of water from Norah.

"What should we say?" Jessa asked.

And what *should* we say? How would we have the time to describe how this man had changed our lives?

"I think we should tell a story," Norah said. "Tell a story about Arlo. Any story."

And so we did. We spent an hour trading stories—some funny, some somber—about Arlo Jenson, the quirky, wise, and sometimes calamitous man who made a big impact on our lives and hearts.

After a prayer and setting Arlo in his new home, we got back to work shoveling the dirt over his body. When the ground was patted down, we stared at the mound and felt emptiness wash over us. How could we sleep now? What nightmares would awaken us as soon as our heads hit the pillow?

"*Mi amore*," Norah said, her hand on my shoulder. "Would you like some breakfast and coffee?"

I smiled at her. "Yes. Just no eggs."

This brought a smile to her face, and she wrapped her arms around me as she cried. Jessa joined us, and we stood near Arlo's grave mourning his loss. The wind picked up, and I shivered.

Norah pulled out of my embrace. "My sweet Knox. It will take a long time to get over this, if we ever will. Won't you stay with us?"

I looked at Norah and then to Jessa, who nodded in agreement. "Please, Knox. Don't go yet. We need you here."

I stepped away for a moment and went to the tree, where underneath Norah's chair was a basket full of daisies. I picked up a few of the fresh flowers and brought them to Arlo's grave. I smoothed over the dirt and patted it. While kneeling at his grave, I said, "I'll stay."

CHAPTER 30

Venice

"**D**id you pack enough for a weekend trip, Jessa?" I said, heaving her third suitcase into the trunk. "Geez, what did you *pack*? An actual person?"

A few days after Arlo's death and Odette's just desserts, Norah, Jessa, and I thought it would be smart to get out of town for a while, what with the ongoing police investigation. Jessa had driven by Cleary Research Center, and she said there was enough caution tape to wrap around the whole country. Sticking around for the investigation would've been idiotic.

I had written over the video camera files, making it impossible for anyone to actually prove we were in Odette's facility that day. But I didn't want to take any chances. Plus, some downtime would be good for all of us.

Jessa stood before me with her hands on her hips. "No, I did not pack an actual person, Knox. But if you want your tip, little bellhop, then I'd load my stuff with a better attitude."

I shut the trunk and leaned over it. "Tip? What tip?"

Jessa smirked before kissing me on the lips, a long-lasting, make-you-forget-your-name kind of kiss. "That tip," she whispered.

"Wow. I've never . . . uh." I cleared my throat. "That was a good tip."

She winked at me as she headed to the front seat. "Good. Because I've got more."

Norah closed the front door and locked it, hesitating for a moment too long. I strode up the walkway to the front porch, where Eli and I had stood not too long ago, waiting on Norah to answer the door. Waiting to meet her for the first time. "You okay?" I asked.

"Yes, yes." She stuffed her keys into her purse. "I'm fine, just . . . wishing he were here. I didn't get to spend enough time with him."

"I know," I said, the image of Arlo flashing in my mind. "Me neither. But he's still here. He's here with us."

She gently kissed me on the cheek, a tear welling in her eye, and we walked to the car arm in arm. I opened the door for her and then got into the back seat.

"So how far away is Venice?" I asked, buckling my seatbelt.

"About eight hours," Norah said, adjusting her mirrors and wiping at her eyes. "Hope you brought something to do, like a book."

I pulled out my laptop from my messenger bag and powered her on. "Oh, I think I'll be just fine."

Jessa perked up. "Mom, he brought Josie."

"Knox!" Norah screeched. "We don't need to be working while we're gone or give anyone the ability to track us. You need to get rid of it immediately. Throw it in the ocean or something."

I waved my hand. "No fear, ladies. This isn't Josie. Meet Cindy."

Norah scrunched her eyebrows. "What happened to Josie?" she asked as we headed onto the main road.

"I destroyed her last night. After I deleted all the files, I set her on fire and then dunked her in water."

"Is that what that smell was?" Jessa asked, scrunching her nose.

"Yeah, sorry about that. But it was the right thing to do." I shrugged. "Time to start over."

"So if Josie is gone and Cindy took over her, then what about all those other files and Ibisco 2.0?"

"Ibisco 2.0 is gone. It has the capability to do some really evil things, so I didn't want anyone else to have the opportunity to use it the way I did." I thought about Odette scratching at her skin, the imaginary bugs tormenting her as I stood before her, doing nothing to help.

Jessa reached back and grabbed my hand. I squeezed it and we sat that way for a very long time.

———

We arrived in Venice in the evening. Our hotel was a few steps away from a piazza and a bridge in the middle of the canal. Norah decided to stay in for the night and rest while Jessa and I toured the city.

"Be safe, kids," she called out.

"We will."

I grabbed Jessa's hand as we headed out onto the old streets, the smell of chocolate and coffee in the air. The bridge beckoned to me, so I led her to it and found a cozy spot in the middle. Tourists walked by, chatting about God knows what. The moon shone brighter than it ever had in Pensacola. I could reach out and touch it.

"Knox?" Jessa said, her head resting on my shoulder as we took in the moon.

"Yeah?"

"If you got rid of Josie, then what about the hard drive that Odette wanted you to decrypt? For NovaVita? What happened to it?"

"I still have it."

She looked up at me. "You do?"

"Yes, I kept it. It needs to go to scientists who will take care of it, who will do what my parents did: withhold it from anyone until the kinks are worked out."

"Will you be able to find someone who can do that?"

"I think so," I answered. "Especially for the right price."

"Knox!" she said with a swat to my arm. "You're going to make money off it?"

"Why not? Besides, I have to lay low for a while, and I might as well enjoy my new life in Italy with some extra cash on hand." I winked at her.

"Wait—you're staying *staying*? I thought you were just staying for a few weeks. How long are you staying?"

I took a deep breath and pulled her into me. "As long as you'll have me."

"Stop looking at me that way." Her chin rested on my chest, and her cheeks glowed a crimson red, and maybe it was the heat or maybe it was my racing heart, but I couldn't help but blush all the same.

"Stop looking at you like what?" I asked, wrapping my arms around her just a little tighter.

"Like ya love me or somethin'."

I thought about her strange stories and the way she told them, as if they were more beautiful than the events themselves. I thought about the freckles that peppered her shoulders. I thought about the first time I saw her, which felt like an eternity ago, standing there in the villa's study among all those books. And I thought about spending the rest of my life with this woman who embraced my own messy life.

So I brought my fingertips to her chin and raised her head to mine. I said, "I do love ya or somethin'. Do you love me?"

The cool air swept her hair over her eyes, so I tucked the loose strands behind her ear. Her violet eyes stared into my own, deep into my soul, as I waited for her response.

She brought her lips to mine, and it was so slow that I thought I might be delirious. She pressed them to my lips and, when she let go, said, "I do love you. Or somethin'."

ACKNOWLEDGMENTS

Thank you isn't enough, but I'll give it a shot. A million pounds of gratitude to:

JAMES MCDONALD, my creative writing professor, who was kind enough to point out how melodramatic my characters were. Knox does cry in this novel, but hopefully not too much. Also, thank you for teaching me to "kill the puppies and set the meadows on fire."

THE YUKON WRITERS' SOCIETY members for critiquing specific chapters, holding me accountable, and encouraging me when I wanted to slam my forehead onto my keyboard.

JANEY MERRY, GARY MEDINA, AND OREN PATTERSON, also YWS members, for cheering me on and helping me with specific scenes in my novel.

STEVE GAGNE AND DROWSY POET in Pensacola Beach, Florida, for providing a safe haven for this writer and for creating the Jimi Hendrix that Knox (and I) loved so much.

INKA NISINBAUM for calling me after reading the first chapter and proclaiming, "You have to pitch this!" It instilled in me the confidence I needed to continue on with my many-to-come drafts. I didn't pitch it, but I much prefer this method, don't you?

MINDY SCHOENEMAN for her listening ear when I had no idea if I could ever finish this wretched novel.

MY BETA READERS: Stephen Peoples, Eric Wrightson, Jessica Jobes, Angela J. Ford, Michelle Rascon, Marian McCarthy, Tianna Doyle, Stephanie BwaBwa, Inka Nisinbaum, Susan Lutz, Shannon Veurink, Andrea Stunz, Melanie Glinsmann, Kristina Brune, Mindy Schoeneman, Judy Heaney-McKee, Nichole Brewer, and Sandra Samoska. If it weren't for your honest feedback, this novel wouldn't have been publishable. I'm eternally grateful to each of you. And please forgive me for sending you that awful draft that was pure dribble.

MONICA HAYNES of The Thatchery for going back and forth (and back and forth) with the mockups of my cover until we finally found *the one*. You are a gem. Oh, and up your prices. You deserve more moola.

SARAH GRACE LIU of Three Fates Editing for taking this atrocious draft and making it remarkable. Seriously, you will always have a job with me as my content editor for all future projects. You outdid yourself.

ANDREA AND ASHLEY HULTMAN of the Polished Opal for proofreading my manuscript. I knew months in advance that I would hire you both to handle the last step in the editing process. I'm so glad I did.

MELINDA MARTIN of Martin Publishing Services for handling the interior formatting of this book and for being such a fantastic friend to me. Not to mention, you once helped me clean out my mother's office and sing to my family, so you're basically everything I want to be.

DERICK STRAWN, my brother, for constantly annoying me with the following questions every few days: "When will your book be out?" and "Will I get a copy?" and "Is it, like, a real book, though?" and my personal favorite, "But will it have your name on the cover?"

JOSHUA AND JUSTIN, my nephews, for asking me all about Knox and my story. Also, I'm so glad you enjoy reading as much as I do.

JESSALYN, my niece, for letting me borrow her name.

BREANNE, my sister, for . . . well, I know you might not read my novel because you don't read fiction, so let's just go eat guacamole and queso and I'll give you the CliffsNotes.

MOM AND DAD for kindly nodding their heads and feigning comprehension when I rattled off about yet another plot hole in this book that made zero sense. Thank you also for instilling in me the love for the written word and for sending me to college a year early because I just couldn't wait any longer to start in the writing world.

Finally, to **THE WRITER WHO CAN'T GET UNSTUCK**: keep trying. Don't give up. It took me from May 2015 until October 2018 to finish this poor thing. There were months when I wouldn't go near it; funny enough, that's when I was at my lowest. Cling to writing, and never let go.

AUTHOR Q&A

The Suicide Tree **has a few remarkable settings like Sorrento, Capri, Pompeii, and more. Have you visited these places?**

Yes, in 2011. I have been to Sorrento, Capri, Pompeii, Amalfi (Ravello, which is in Amalfi), Rome, Florence, and Venice. Each place has a special memory for me, but I fell deeply in love with Sorrento and the people. My three friends and I rented a boat in Capri and took it halfway around the island just as Arlo and Knox did. And yes, there is a place where stairs lead up the mountain.

How long did it take to write *The Suicide Tree?*

From May 2015 to September 2018 with many breaks in between called *writer's procrastination.* This was honestly the most difficult thing I have ever written. Most of it was because of my insecurities as a novelist. I love fiction and wanted to give it the attention it deserved. It would've taken less time had I followed a stronger outline—er . . . an outline at all.

What was the biggest issue you had in writing your first novel?

Besides crippling insecurity? Plot holes. They multiplied like rabbits straight out of prison. I could not contain them.

Your protagonist is a twenty-year-old male. Did you ever find it difficult to write in the voice of the opposite sex?

As someone who climbed trees, beat up boys, and cried when she had to wear a bra for the first time, I can tell you that I found it easier to write in the male voice than the female. In fact, Jessa was more difficult for me to write because romance was in the background with her and Knox, and I thought, *I'm not sure I know how to make this believable.* Thank God for beta readers.

What was the most difficult scene to write?

Emotionally? Probably when [SPOILER] Arlo leaves the world for good. I will admit: I teared up. But I always knew he would die in the end. That was always the plan. As far as mentally, basically any scene with Ibisco (the program, not the villa). Too much brainpower needed.

What's next after *The Suicide Tree*?

I don't have a title, an outline, or even a plot, but I have an idea and that is all I need. I'll tell you at least one thing about that idea: it involves blood.

ABOUT THE AUTHOR
SHAYLA RAQUEL

An expert editor, seasoned writer, and author-centric marketer, Shayla Raquel works one-on-one with authors and business owners every day. A lifelong lover of books, she has edited over 300 books and has launched several Amazon bestsellers for her clients. Her award-winning blog teaches new and established authors how to write, publish, and market their books. She is the author of the *Pre-Publishing Checklist*, *The Rotting* (in *Shivers in the Night*), and *The Suicide Tree*. She is the organizer for the Yukon Writers' Society and lives in Oklahoma with her two dogs, Chanel and Wednesday.

CONNECT WITH THE AUTHOR

shaylaraquel.com
Facebook.com/shaylaraquel
Twitter.com/shaylaleeraquel
Instagram.com/shaylaleeraquel
Goodreads.com/ShaylaRaquel

LEAVE A REVIEW

If you enjoyed this book, will you please consider writing a review on Amazon and Goodreads? Reviews help self-published authors make their books more visible to new readers.

Amazon:
amzn.to/2xzc4jm

Goodreads:
goodreads.com/book/show/41914928-the-suicide-tree

Made in the USA
Columbia, SC
25 May 2019